A SOLDIER'S PLACE

THE WAR STORIES *of* WILL R. BIRD

EDITED BY THOMAS HODD

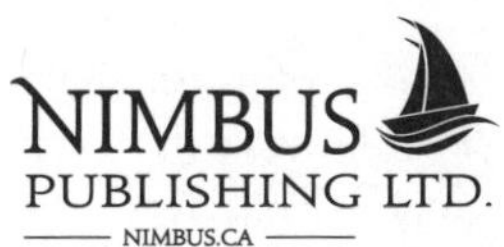

Nimbus Publishing Limited
PO Box 9166
Halifax, NS B3K 5M8
(902) 455-4286
nimbus.ca

Interior and cover design: Heather Bryan
NB1352

Library and Archives Canada Cataloguing in Publication

Bird, Will R. (Will Richard), 1891-1984
[Short stories. Selections]
A soldier's place : the war stories of Will R. Bird / edited by Thomas Hodd.
Includes index.
Issued in print and electronic formats.
ISBN 978-1-77108-630-1 (softcover).--ISBN 978-1-77108-631-8 (HTML)

I. Hodd, Thomas Patrick, 1972-, editor II. Title.

PS8503.I67A6 2018 C813'.52 C2018-902858-0
C2018-902859-9

Nimbus Publishing acknowledges the financial support for its publishing activities from the Government of Canada, the Canada Council for the Arts, and from the Province of Nova Scotia. We are pleased to work in partnership with the Province of Nova Scotia to develop and promote our creative industries for the benefit of all Nova Scotians.

Printed in Canada

To Master Warrant Officer Daniel Joseph Hodd,
and to all the soldiers who struggle
to tell their stories

Table of Contents

Will R. Bird

Introduction

Trench-fighter, military medallist, and the "unofficial Bard of the Canadian Expeditionary Force," according to historian Jonathan Vance, Will R. Bird (1891–1984) dedicated much of his life to storytelling. Over a writing career that spanned more than five decades, the Nova Scotia-born author amassed a store of travel pieces, short stories, novels, edited books, and other works of non-fiction that number in the hundreds. He published more than a dozen novels, as well as a history of Nova Scotia. He also wrote two memoirs, a handful of poems, and several dramatic pieces. But what many Canadians don't know is that a large portion of these publications were inspired by Bird's experience as a combat soldier during the First World War. What's more, had it not been for a belief in the supernatural he might never have seen action at all, let alone wrote about it.

Born in East Mapleton, near Amherst, Nova Scotia, Bird's early years were marred by emotional and financial hardship: his father died when Bird was four years old; he was also forced to leave school in grade eight to help support his family, before moving out west a few years later. To make matters worse, while his friends and even his youngest brother, Stephen, had been able to join the war effort, Bird had been rejected twice due to medical reasons. Then, in 1915, while working in a field in Saskatchewan he saw an apparition of his brother:

> I was [...] pitching sheaves on a wagon, when Steve walked around the cart and confronted me. He said not a word but I knew all as if he had spoken, for he had on his equipment and was carrying his rifle. I let the fork fall to the ground and the nearest man came running to me, thinking I had taken ill. I did not tell him what I had seen, but I left the field, and never pitched another sheaf of grain. All that day, and the next, and the next, I wandered by myself around the prairie, and then the

> message came, a wire, 'Steve has been killed. Come home.'" (*And We Go On*, 8–9.)

Bird returned to Nova Scotia and tried again to enlist. This time he was successful, and was assigned to the 193rd Battalion, the Nova Scotia Highlanders, although he was eventually transferred to the 42nd Battalion to serve out the remainder of the war with the Black Watch. He first saw action in the fall of 1916, and spent a short time as a sniper before turning patrolman. He also took part in some of the most important battles of the First World War, fighting at Passchendaele and Amiens, as well as at Arras and Cambrai. Remarkably, he survived the war with no lasting physical injuries, an impressive feat for an infantryman. He was even awarded a Military Medal for Bravery at Mons, Belgium, on the final day of the war.

After being demobilized, Bird moved back to Nova Scotia and, for a brief time, ran a general store before having to close shop and take a job at the local post office. Then in the early 1920s, he entered his first writing contest and won, which inspired him to begin sending out his stories for publication. Success soon followed. He decided to try his hand at writing full time, but in order to do so he needed to find a subject that would interest readers. Luckily for Bird, very few veterans wanted to write down—or even talk about—their experiences in the trenches, so he made it his mission to tell their stories.

The result? No Canadian author who served overseas has published more on the First World War than Will R. Bird. Although a handful of his contemporaries, such as Prince Edward Island native Basil King and Ontario writer Ralph Connor, each published maybe a handful of novels on the subject, during the early 1930s the Great War became almost an obsession for Bird: he penned no fewer than five books on the subject as well as numerous short stories and other non-fiction pieces. His main non-fiction works include *Thirteen Years After: The Story of the Old Front Revisited* (1932) and *The Communication Trench* (1933). He also wrote a novel, *Private Timothy Fergus Clancy* (1930). His most lasting book from this period, however, is his soldier memoir, *And We Go On* (1930), recently republished with McGill-Queen's

University Press. It has become a staple for Canadian military historians and to those interested in reading about the soldier experience during the First World War.

But a memoir about the soldier experience does not capture the imagination in the same way that a novel or short story might. Equally curious, the majority of Canadian fictional responses to the First World War published during and after the conflict tended to be novels, not short stories. So once again Bird chose the road less travelled: beginning in the late 1920s and continuing for the next two decades, he published more than fifty war stories. His tales of courage, survival, and self-doubt eventually appeared in a variety of publications and trade magazines, including *Maclean's, Colliers,* the *Toronto Star Weekly,* and the *Maritime Advocate* and *Busy East.* Most of Bird's war stories, however, first found a home in one of three literary outlets: the *Legionary,* a magazine launched in May 1926 and meant almost exclusively for military veterans; the short-lived New York "pulp" magazine *War Stories;* and the Canadian pulp periodical, *Canadian War Stories,* published out of Chatham, Ontario, but which lasted less than a year. The majority of these publications are no longer in print, nor are they digitized. So for the last several decades Will Bird's extraordinary tales of war have fallen ever deeper into Canadian literary obscurity.

Until now.

This selected edition of Will Bird's war stories represents less than a third of his combat tales. In making the selections I have tried not only to choose the best stories in terms of detail and depth, but also to demonstrate how diverse they were in terms of perspective and outcome. For instance, although Bird served with the Nova Scotia Highlanders and the Black Watch, he did not limit his stories to personal battalion experience. The tale "White Collars," for example, is about the Princess Patricia's Canadian Light Infantry, while "Sunrise for Peter" is about the Newfoundlanders. Nor did Bird confine himself to stories about Canadian soldiers: the last piece in this collection, "A Soldier's Place," is about an American veteran, whereas Australians take centre stage in "The Creeping Phantom." Even more extraordinary are those moments when Bird pushes his imaginative powers to new heights, as when he describes the emotional roller coaster of a young woman named Priscilla who goes searching for the soldier she fell in love with at Union Station in Toronto, or when he reveals the inner fears of a Canadian flying ace in the RAF, or when he articulates the despair of a German soldier named Otto in "The Russian Coat."

In addition to the stories is a short bibliography as well as a selected glossary to help readers with military terms, references, and slang sayings common during the First World War period. I hope that after reading these tales you will have a better appreciation for Bird's craft as a short-story writer, and for his ability to capture the emotional trials of the soldier experience, the horrors of trench warfare, and the camaraderie that can emerge in times of war. This collection may also go some way to help kindle (or rekindle) your interest in Will Bird's other writings, which have likewise fallen into obscurity. Above all, it must be said that this book is more than a recovery project: it is a celebration of one of Canada's great writers, who was both a combat veteran and a proud Maritimer.

His Deputy

It was an inky black night at Aldershot Camp, one of those soft, suffocating kinds of night that make a person unaccountably irritable. Private "Red" McLean of the Second Battalion, Nova Scotia Highlanders, was coming into camp by way of the brigade road, trusting to find his way by the feel of the ground under his heavy army boots. A glimmer of light to his left told the location of the brigade guard tent. It was an hour after Last Post had blown, but Red was noted for his indifference to army regulations. He neither swerved towards the guard tent to report nor stole cat-footed by way of the rear, but bumped solidly into a sentry who stood leaning on his rifle.

"Halt; who goes there?" It was the recruit's first turn on guard and he was excited.

"If you p-punch me again with that f-fool bayonet I'll knock you b-back to the barnyard," came Red's answer. "Q-quit your yellin'. I'm McLean of B Company, Second Battalion."

"Where's your pass?"

"In my p-pocket. Why?"

"You come to the light and show it," ordered the sentry.

There had been a mild commotion in the guard tent and a sergeant came outside holding a flickering candle.

"Y-you first battalion guys are n-nuts on this guard stuff," growled Red, but he followed the sentry.

There came a shouted command. Two individuals, one bearing a flashlight, had appeared and the guard turned out with the awkward haste of new soldiers. The officer of the night was making his "rounds."

Red shuffled by his attendant, who had halted in a bewildered manner, and unfolded his pass in the candlelight. "Here's your p-pass," he called roughly. "C-come and have a p-peek at it."

The officer ordered the guard to "stand at ease," and, accompanied by his sergeant, went to the tent.

"Who are you and what are you doing here?" he demanded of Red.

Red let his eyes travel over the lieutenant, from the polished brown boots to trim balmoral. Identical in build, with the same cut of chin and broad independent nose, blue eyes and red hair—here was his twin if ever there were twins!

"This g-guy wanted to see my p-pass." He indicated the perspiring sentry.

"I asked who you were." There was nothing sarcastic in the remark, only mild insistence. "No. 8778 P-private Murdock Malcolm M-McLean, B Company, Second Battalion."

"What platoon?"

"S-six."

"Say 'sir' when you're speakin' to an officer," snapped the sergeant.

"Six, s-sir."

The "sir" was drawled with just a touch of insolence and the NCO's eyes gleamed angrily.

The officer scanned Red curiously.

"Ye gods!" he murmured, as if to himself. Then he smiled. "Some coincidence," he remarked. "My name is Murdock Malcolm McLean, and today I've been given command of number six platoon. Are you from Cape Breton?"

"No," said Red shortly, then added, "Sir-r."

The lieutenant's smile faded. "Carry on," he said to the sergeant, and left the tent. Red lurched out into the dark and disappeared.

On his blankets in a tent noisy with varied snoring Red twisted about in a vain effort to sleep. Every time he shut his eyes he could see that replica of himself in carefully tailored tunic and glistening Sam Browne; could hear that soft, cultured voice say, "Ye gods!"

"Some blankety-blank three weeks' wonder p-playin' at solderin'," he swore to himself a dozen times.

The next morning the wag of six platoon bowed gravely to Red and stuck out his hand. "Never knew your twin was in the army," he said gravely. "When do you get stripes?"

"W-what do you mean?" asked Red in ominous tones.

"If that new 'looey' isn't your brother, Nature's done a lot for nothin'," came the reply amid shouts of laughter. "You must be his deputy, anyhow."

Red's reply was drowned in the raillery that followed, but his fist caught the wag on the chin and that gentleman went down heavily.

"Any more want to have fun?"

No one replied. They were astounded by Red's fury, and helping the wag to his feet, they filed down to the mess tables murmuring among themselves.

Red had signed up in '14, but after a hectic week at Valcartier with the First Contingent, had been discharged on account of a missing third finger on his left hand. Fierce arguments had availed him nothing. Men were aplenty, and over plenty, and so he went back to the logging camps with a grouch that did not leave him. Early in '16 he learned that men were needed badly for the Highland Brigade of Nova Scotia, and found that two years had made a vast difference in physical requirements. He was passed without a question, and the smouldering fire he nursed was fanned to a flame. If he were fit in '16, he had been fit in '14, he complained to all who would listen. Soon he was more or less shunned, not comprehending that many of his listeners had borne the same disappointments, and the appearance of Lieutenant McLean gave him a subject on whom to vent his spleen.

"The dude has dodged the war till the women have run him out of their parlours," he declared, and found no listeners.

The officer with red hair and blue eyes was popular with his men, from the hour of his arrival.

The Second Battalion was proud of its athletes. There were many sprinters in the ranks, a nifty baseball nine, good wrestlers, and last but not least, promising boxers. Red chose the mitts as his form of recreation, but unfortunately for him, carried into the ring a soured temper that made his boxing not what the instructors desired. Men he met would be roused, and a hammer-and-tongs contest generally resulted.

One evening, as he lingered by the ropes awaiting a suitable opponent, he was amazed to see his platoon officer leap into the ring, arrayed in boxing togs. Without waiting to see whether the officer was to meet another or not, Red hopped the rope barrier and saluted mockingly.

"Any objections to swappin' a few?" he asked in a strained voice.

"Why, no, McLean. Not the slightest," said the lieutenant good-humouredly. "Get someone for timer."

Stripped for action, it was seen that the officer was the lighter of the two by several pounds, and he had not the bulky muscles that Red had acquired in many lumber camps, yet his reach was as long and his greater speed was undeniable. In addition, he was a cool and experienced boxer. Red soon found this out, but his determination to "down" his man over-ruled his better judgment. He tore in like a mad bull, and by chance one of his battering rights rocked the lieutenant. A fierce joy fired Red to greater efforts, but the round ended before he could follow up his advantage. When the second round finished Red felt that he had encountered a boxing octopus. Hard-driven mitts had met him from all directions; he had been jabbed to dizziness; one eye was completely closed, and a vast weariness had seized his knees.

Dimly Red realized that Lieutenant McLean must be a far harder-boiled gent than he seemed. The private had no idea of quitting, however, though he was forced to clinch desperately throughout the third round. To his surprise he found this easy to do, and did not comprehend its meaning until the timer leaned over and whispered, "That guy let you go the round, but you better pull the mitts off. You'd be pie for him if he wanted to finish it."

A gory mist blinded Red. "Let me go, did he?" he snarled. "Tell him he's lyin'. I'll show you this time!"

He launched an attack more like the onslaught of a wild beast than that of a boxer, but his swinging fists never landed. In turn, padded pile-drivers drove him back relentlessly. In vain he tried to rally, to break down the barrage by sheer strength. His opponent seemed made of spring steel. Bright lights danced across his vision. As he staggered back he released all his reserve in one wild swing. That swing was unexpected by his conqueror, and it landed flush on the "button." The lieutenant went down like wet paper!

Red was too groggy to appreciate his victory for some time, and then he read enough contempt in the eyes of onlookers to understand that the officer had lost nothing by the bout.

From that evening Red never went in the ring again, but his fires of hate still simmered unceasingly and his prejudiced imagination tried hard to find wrongs aimed his way. He failed in this, however, for Lieutenant McLean joked off their match and was ever just in his rule of the platoon.

The battalion went to England, and there Red welcomed an opportunity to escape the Nova Scotia Highlanders and all they meant to him. He volunteered for a draft to the famous Canadian Black Watch, and was in France for his Christmas dinner of bully and lumps of soggy plum duff. It was muddy wherever he went; he was always hungry, lousy, and was worked long shifts in the trenches, but among his new mates was pronounced a "full" private—meaning that he would take his share of bone labour and dirty weather without squealing. They judged he was anxious to acquit himself in new company, but Red was a changed man, because he had at last reached his goal and was among comrades he did not despise.

The Black Watch were on the Vimy sector and Red was assigned to a dangerous post known as "Vernon Crater." With him was Bob Young, a canny veteran of sixteen months' service.

"Them Heinie snipers know every tear in these sandbags," said Bob, pointing to their protection. "Don't ever shove your bean up unless you're tired of war."

All night Red watched the Hun flares soaring and falling along the front, ducked instinctively at the crackling of Hun machine guns, shivered and stamped his feet. At the first break of dawn old Bob stepped down from the fire step and arranged a bayonet periscope.

"Don't pay to chance lookin' over any longer," he explained. "Them Heinies has eyes like hawks."

Up the sap from the main trench came two blurred figures. The one ahead proved to be the sergeant with the rum issue. The second person came slowly, picking his way and scrutinizing everything. He stepped in close and stared at Red.

"Ye gods," said a low, well-modulated voice, "If we haven't met again!" It was Lieutenant Murdock Malcolm McLean.

"I came to the base two weeks ago," he confided to Red as if to an old friend, "and I've managed to get in this battalion in charge of fourteen platoon. How's things?"

"Rotten," snarled Red, and he did not add "sir."

He was chilled outwardly, but inwardly a seething fire had rekindled. Was he to be haunted by this "dude soldier"?

The lieutenant inspected the post and asked old Bob many questions. Then he placed a foot on the fire step.

"It's dark yet," he whispered, "and I want to see what it looks like." "Stop!" hissed Bob. "Get down!"

But the officer would have heard him too late had not Red thrown himself in football style in a tackle that brought the lieutenant to earth with a grunt.

"There's a sniper g-got this place m-marked," Red rasped into the ear of his superior. "He couldn't m-miss."

The sergeant looked back toward the line they had left. He could barely trace the sap in the grey light.

"It's safe enough if you're quick, sir," he said in a low tone. "Just take a glance, like this."

His foot was on the fire step and as he spoke he straightened. The others felt, rather than heard a snap-like report as if it was alongside them. The sergeant's steel hat was carried back over the trench and what had been a warm, animated human slithered down to the padded clay at their feet, leaving a ghastly trail as it slid.

For an instant no one spoke, and then the officer thrust out a hand to "Red." "Thank you, McLean," he said quietly.

That was all, but in his grip was something that stirred Red oddly, and though he tried to forget the experience, he always remembered the hand-clasp.

In the dugout he had to answer countless queries. Was the new lieutenant his brother? Were they any relation? Did they spell their names the same? His emotions developed a dual personality—a determined self that hated the sight of his platoon commander and a weaker part that he could not wholly subdue which was proud of that handshake, of his quick action in a crisis. So he lived until a sleety morning in April when the Black Watch assisted in the capture of Vimy Ridge.

The battalion leapfrogged one another and fought doggedly until its objective was gained. Rain, blinding snow, and mud churned to a quagmire made the advance extremely difficult, and in places the Hun stuck to his trench and died fighting. Into one such place tumbled Red and three others. Rifles were clubbed and bayonets were used in ways not prescribed by bayonet instructors. In a few terrific seconds the actors were reduced to Red and two opponents, one on each side of him. A quick look revealed to him the helplessness of his position. He could only fight one at a time in that cramped space—the other would get him in the back. Red charged the nearest Hun with a frenzy that hurled them both into the corner of the bay. Too entangled to regain his feet on the instant, he glanced up to see the second German plunging in with ready bayonet. In that split second a catapult in khaki dove from somewhere above, driving the onrushing killer for yards down the trench. The catapult resolved into man-size and clambered upright. Clothing and flesh were torn in many places, the uniform was unrecognizable under mud and slime, but hair and chin could not be mistaken. Red's life had been saved by Lieutenant Murdock Malcolm McLean!

No one else knew of that incident. The officer had hurried on with the consolidating of the line and Red had rejoined his platoon. After controlling a first impulse to proclaim the lieutenant's deed, he had settled back into his rut of venomous brooding.

Out again for rest Red began to sense a slight leniency towards him. It was subtle enough; he was missed from obnoxious fatigues, he was never checked for a dirty rifle or shortage of equipment. Such happenings galled him. He wished no favours and he purposely went unshaven until Lieutenant McLean "put him up" for an interview with the Major.

In July the Black Watch were on the Mericourt Front. There, No Man's Land was six hundred yards in width and while this rare occurrence afforded less danger from snipers and machine guns, it provided constant excitement at night. Patrols roamed about in force and savage combats in the dark became regular events. Fourteen platoon furnished a patrol one night and Red was thrilled by the tense moments out between the wires. Suddenly word was given to "halt" and "down" followed instantly.

Red, crouched in a shell-hole, saw the lieutenant crawl close. "There's a bunch of Heinies coming," the officer whispered. "We can pocket them if you'll take charge of one side."

"Sure," Red grunted, pleased in spite of himself by being thus recognized.

He took five men over to the right, so as to leave a lane for the enemy. Soon he could see a file of shadowy figures coming in their direction. The German patrol paused a moment as if listening, and then walked directly into the "pocket." Like magic, kilted men rose on each side of them and harsh orders of "Hands up!" carried a threat that did not have to be repeated. Eight soldiers of the Kaiser dropped their weapons and reached for the stars.

When the patrol escorted their "bag" into the trench, they created unusual excitement, but when Lieutenant McLean learned from a prisoner who could speak English that a second patrol was to follow in a few minutes, he had a deluge of volunteers. The officer refused them all. He was still on duty and all honours were for his men.

"That's an officer worth havin'," breathed a voice in Red's ear. "He's a prince."

"You bet!" came the response before Red could catch back the words. For an instant he hated himself.

The second Hun party was not so easily handled. They were using a fan formation that prevented them from walking into a trap, and they were also full of fight. As the Black Watch men arose, the Hun officer shot down the machine-gun carrier and shouted commands. Lieutenant's revolver barked twice and there were no more orders. Red snatched up the fallen machine gun and its fierce spitting settled matters. Three of the Black Watch patrol were casualties, but there were ten Huns with more or less lead in them, and two sound ones who held their arms aloft. For days the dugouts and billets knew no other topic, and then battalion orders were posted stating that Lieutenant M.M. McLean had been awarded the Military Cross, and Private M.M. McLean the Military Medal for "conspicuous work on July 11th, when they were responsible for the capture of two enemy patrols in one hour."

Thereafter, Red knew no peace. "McLean and McLean, the Hun catchers," "the Ruddy Raiders," and such quips passed along cookhouse queue and the transport lines. From the descriptions that circulated the other battalions in the brigade were able to pick them out as they marched by. "Look more alike than twins do," was the usual expression. "Red hair an' guts to the backbone—oh, mamma!"

Then came a day when a bomber was needed for headquarters company, for the staff that took care of bomb stores and taught newcomers the trick of explosives. Red was an artist at bomb throwing, and here was a chance to leave the lieutenant. He hurried to the sergeant and requested the transfer. It was reluctantly given. Red, as a decorated man, was entitled to the change, but it meant a loss to the platoon.

For five weeks the red-haired private led a happier life, then inexorable fate pushed the officer after him. The old commander of fourteen platoon returned from "Blighty" and Lieutenant M.M. McLean was appointed Bombing Officer.

It was a bleak morning in October. Rations were short and the billets were abominable. Red was nursing an aching tooth.

"Cherrio, old timer," said the bombing corporal as he came in, wet and chilled from a tramp to brigade bomb stores. "Great news for you! Your twin is to take the bombers."

"Who?"

"Lieutenant McLean, MC, your better half, Red."

"Don't try kiddin'," said Red slowly, "and don't mention that guy to me." A vitriolic note had crept into his voice.

The corporal was a trifle thick headed. "One of the chaps called you his deputy," he chuckled.

It was the first time that Red had heard that title since leaving Aldershot, and, as then, his heavy fist sped true. When the corporal revived, Red was bending over him, his face livid with passion. "I'll k-kill you if you s-say that again," he croaked, as if strangling.

"I won't, Red, I won't," was the hasty answer.

The NCO felt that he was dealing with a maniac. He said nothing of the penalty awarded those who strike a superior in the army.

"'That dude has hoodooed me since I enlisted," Red explained after a few minutes of heavy breathing. "He's a smart Alec and f-four-flusher. I come to France to g-get rid of him and he c-chased me. I joined the b-bombers and now he's coming to them. I tell you, Jim,"—all the long-pent rage, the festering brooding of the man was released, and his countenance grew almost inhuman—"either his bones or mine'll be rotting soon!"

Thoroughly alarmed, the corporal marshalled his slender stock of diplomacy and tried to reason with Red. All he accomplished was a promise that the lieutenant should not be tricked by foul methods.

"But I'll show him up for what he is," Red reiterated again and again. "Why didn't he enlist in '14?"

Ten days later the battalion left for Passchendaele.

The war affected men in different ways. Some endured trench life and its attendant horrors in a mechanical fashion. They moved as if in a state of intelligent automation. Others lived each hour a hundred times and were mere wrecks in short order. Again there were those like Red, who lived intensely every day in the line, and yet retained, apparently, the individuality with which they left England. Unlimited natural courage bore them through until they gained a control that men differently endowed could not understand. Red was not aware of the need of this control until he found himself at the Ypres Salient.

There was something unspeakable about the Salient, something that gripped men's souls, that brought to them as nothing else could the awfulness of Death. The wreckage, the stench, the rats, the slime, the never-ceasing shell-fire and carnage, the invisible presence of five hundred thousand dead, undermined those who had left Vimy unshaken.

Four long miles of narrow "duck walks" led to Passchendaele ridge, and all that long route in the clammy dark was intersected with varying frightfulness. Flares and gun flashes revealed gaping black holes, with arms and legs protruding. There were broken trench mats, tangled bits of equipment, foul concrete emplacements, crumpled by high explosives, ends of stretchers upthrust from the mud, human debris beyond description. Near Grafenstrafel Road the battalion passed a party that had just encountered a few minutes "strafing." Wounded men lay everywhere. Some were being trodden underfoot by frantic comrades, and cries for succor were heard above the drumming of the guns. The Black Watch hurried by, but Red was conscious of pictures painted indelibly on his mind. He began to understand why men in that region attempted almost impossible things, laughed at danger. Their surroundings had overmastered them. And to him came suddenly a tremendous longing for Life; for the first time he sensed a flinching of his flesh, a growing fear.

They relieved the remnants of a Welsh regiment and after much confusion Red found the bombing corporal established by the end of a brick wall that stood shoulder high, and was all that remained of a Belgian village.

"The lieutenant isn't up yet, and this place looks as good as any," said the corporal. "We'll stay here for orders."

"Where's McLean?" demanded Red. He was keyed mentally to a pitch that strove with his control.

"He had sore feet, or something, and couldn't keep up. He'll be along some time."

"Sore feet—bah! Cold feet, you mean. I knew it! This place 'll get his goat all right."

To beat back his uneasiness, Red summoned all his vindictiveness. He reviled his superior in countless ways and as the hours wore on recalled every grievance he had nurtured. A little past midnight someone dragged wearily into their post.

"All right, Corporal?" came a hoarse whisper. It was Lieutenant McLean.

"I was six hours making the grade," he explained. "My 'mules' have gone back on me."

"Peeled heels, sir?" queried the corporal.

"No, fallen arches," came the answer. Red grunted oddly in the gloom.

"They put me out of the 'Princess Pats' on account of them in '14," the tired voice went on, "just a week before we were to leave Valcartier."

There was a quick movement as though Red had slipped in the

mud, and an incoherent exclamation.

"Did you fall asleep, Red?" asked the corporal. "I have—twice." There was no answer.

"They say the company's got to take a pill-box that's ahead of us before we're relieved," said the officer. "I wish it were over."

At dawn he left them and went down the trench to find headquarters. Red watched his going and then turned to the NCO. "Jim," he said calmly, "I'm going to show him up this trip, the q-quitter."

"Steady, Red, remember—"

The rest of the corporal's speech was drowned by the arrival of a salvo of shells just behind their trench. They were deluged with sloppy mud. The men cowered low in their cover, their faces grey with strain.

For an hour the fusillade lasted. Shrapnel and high explosives traversed the entire front. Parapets were blown in and fresh craters pock-marked the slopes. Reeking shell fumes stifled and sickened them. Then, gradually, the firing slackened until only an occasional big one rumbled overhead.

A sergeant came clambering over the broken-down places.

"Sit tight today," he wheezed, "we're goin' to go after the pill-box when it's dark."

Red straightened his cramped muscles and deliberately looked over the wall. Every fibre of his being cried for action.

About one hundred and fifty yards in front a dirty grey monster reared itself like the head of a one-eyed ogre. Its ponderous cement formation had withstood a terrific pounding, but low hits in the boggy terrain had rocked it to a lurching position.

Red attributed the lack of sniping to the misty haze that obscured details, and to the tilt of the pill-box which must hamper its occupants' observations. He felt that he could crawl out to a new-made crater without drawing fire. As he gazed, the lieutenant returned.

"Keep down," he ordered crisply, "we'll have risks enough tonight."

Red looked at the corporal, turned and looked the officer full in the eyes. "I'm going out n-now," he announced thickly. "Y-you can do what you like."

He was over the bricks before they could reach him, and he never looked back. From the new-made shell hole he could see three shell craters, almost linked, ahead of him. A scramble put him in the first, but a whip-like snap in his ears and a spitting thud in the mud told that he had been spotted. Keeping low, he broke down the partition he faced, and lying flat, pulled himself into the second cavity. The procedure was repeated and he was in the third hole. From there he risked a glance and saw that a short distance in front of him the surface was so upheaved and torn that a man might squirm in almost any direction without being seen. To reach it he must cross an open space.

His brain cleared suddenly, the crazed impulse that had driven him weakened, and he realized his situation. He had only his revolver and one Mills bomb, was alone, in daylight, part way to the pill-box, and had no definite plan of action or hope but to lie there until night. The desire to make a desperate plunge back to Jim left him sweating. He peered back. Something rose into view on the lip of the first shell hole—a steel hat and then the set features of Lieutenant M. M. McLean!

A madness seized Red. The officer had followed him and was going to out-do him in courage. The corporal and others would be watching. Gathering his strength like a sprinter facing the starter, he leaped up and raced for the torn ground. It was a matter of seconds, and he dove head-long the last bit. But a perfect hail of machine gun fire had greeted him, and a stinging blow on his left shoulder made him dizzy. He thrust his right hand to the spot and it came away sticky. He was wounded!

His helmet had been slipping about and with an angry gesture he hurled it from him. Working on his knees and elbows he wriggled on among the distorted mounds and at length risked a look. He had advanced beyond range of the front vent of the pill-box, and the sniper's slit in the side of it had been obscured by continuous upheavals from well-aimed shells. Staggering to his feet, he stumbled straight towards the stronghold.

Dimly, as though in a memory, he heard a cheering, but knew that it did not come from the pill-box. In the roof of these concrete "forts" the Huns always left an opening from which to shoot signal flares, and Red's ambition was to toss his bomb so that it would descend inside. He was strangely weak, but as unhurried as when on training grounds, when he braced himself and made the throw. The bomb looped high—and disappeared. Immediately a dull report reached him, mingled with yells and groans, while smoke eddied from the vent in front. Red reached the rear as a gasping Hun emerged, and he shot the man with great glee. Others crowded the narrow doorway, some shooting. Once-twice-Red fired before something struck him sharply above the knee, crumpling him to earth, still shooting.

Over him swept a tortuous despair. His revolver was empty and the Germans were thrusting forth a machine gun. In one heartbeat the absurd futility of his enterprise struck like an agony and drove him, without sensing his incongruity, to a formless prayer for—Lieutenant McLean.

Pin-n-ng! Whining shrapnel ricocheted from cement and smoke flurries blotted the doorway of the Huns, lifting to reveal a shambles indescribable. Another Mills bomb had landed with deadly accuracy. Two quick shots sounded just behind him and every German outside the pill-box lay still.

"Kamerad—Kamerad!" The cry came distinctly, shaken with animal fear.

With an effort Red raised himself and looked back. Swaying towards him, his face a chalky pallor, one side of it torn and bleeding, his left arm dangling useless while more blood dripped from his fingertips, came Lieutenant Murdock Malcolm McLean. The officer's eyes met Red's, and his features distorted in the semblance of a smile. The quavering pleas of surrender were redoubled, but the man on the ground – as soon as he had essayed an answering smile – allowed himself to sink into delicious oblivion, knowing that the arrival of his "twin" had assured all else. The last thing that registered on his mind was that kilted men were swarming about the battered pill-box.

When Red became conscious, strong odours of iodine reached his nostrils. Other wounded men lay near him, and attendants hurried about speaking in a quick, jerky fashion. He lay awhile, too weak to ask questions, wondering how the lieutenant had fared, and thus wondering fell asleep. In spasmodic dreams he lived again those vivid moments at the pill-box, each time experiencing the feelings of a frightened child, until he envisioned eyes that smiled through torture.

In the night he was moved to a field hospital and the jogging of the ambulance set his wounds raging like demons, but dominant in his mind were thoughts of the white-faced, wounded man who had arrived in the nick of time.

Late the next afternoon he was feeling much easier in body, his rugged vitality having asserted itself, but was anxious to learn something about his rescuer. When, therefore, he turned his head and saw his colonel standing by, his eyes and fever-hardened lips asked the same question: "How's the lieutenant, sir?"

"He's resting fine, McLean." The grim old Scotsman's voice was none too steady. "And he's wanting to know about you. He can't talk for a day or so, for a machine gun bullet creased his jaw, and he's got about seven other wounds. What's that? Sure, he'll live. You can't kill a McLean!"

The old veteran's laugh was noisy, but it relieved emotion. His leathery countenance sobered again. "Now, I've just a few minutes, the Doc says, and I want some facts, McLean. That stunt at the pill-box is worth a Victoria Cross, but no one seems to know which of you led the way." The Colonel's hand shook as he tugged at his pocket and withdrew a notebook.

"It was a fool thing, understand," he growled fiercely, "and against discipline. If it were anyone else, I'd court-martial 'em."

He sat down on the edge of the cot. "The bombing corporal is worse than a child," —he was still bear-like—"for he told me ten different stories in half an hour. Now—the truth, my man."

A doctor had come over and stood listening.

"It was the officer d-did it all." Red's voice was eager, if weak. "He thought we c-could manage and s-sent me under cover. H-he let them s-see him s-so they didn't spot m-me, and I just heaved a b-bomb inside; then he r-rushed up with another and d-drove them inside. He was the whole w- works."

The doctor turned and walked away, and the Colonel blew his nose violently. "I know the both of you should have the Cross," he rumbled, "and the lieutenant'll get it if I have to tip hell over. But I'll put you down for the Distinguished Conduct Medal, McLean, for I've heard of you two before. Are you twins?"

"N-no sir," stammered Red. "I'd be proud if I were, but—but," he hesitated, and then his chin set with its characteristic resolution, "I'm just his deputy, as it were."

"His deputy,"—the Colonel's features wrinkled with humour—"That's a good one, McLean! His deputy—I'll say you are!"

The Creeping Phantom

There was a clank of equipment in the deep front trench that cut across the outer fringe of Mustard Wood, a "flat iron" of stubs and thickets on the left of the Ypres salient. The thick, warm darkness was like that of a dark tropical night, and the Australians moved with caution as they relieved a battalion of the London Rifles.

"Have you called in your covering patrol?" asked the officer commanding the company that was taking over the Wood Front.

"We haven't any out, sir," answered a nervous voice in the murk.

"What—no patrol out while a relief is on?" asked the captain, peering to see who had spoken. "Where's your officer?"

It was a sergeant who had answered him, and the man spoke again. "He was killed last night, sir. He was out on patrol in that Wood, sir. They were all killed."

"In that Wood? Was it machine guns or bombs?"

"It weren't neither, sir," came the husky answer. "There weren't a sound, sir, and it were the third night a patrol went out and didn't come back."

The sergeant tried to push past and follow his men, who had fairly scuttled from their posts as they were relieved.

"Wait you," commanded the officer. "Come here, Sergeant Rader, and hear this fellow."

"We haven't any patrol out yet, sir." There was mild protest in the words, then a tall figure loomed alongside the sergeant of the Rifles.

"Perhaps you won't want to put one out, after you hear all this man tells you," said the captain grimly. "Tell him, Sergeant."

"That Wood isn't safe, sir." The Londoner's teeth almost chattered. "There's a creepin' death in there. We've lost ten men in three nights. Not a bomb, not a shot, nothin' you could hear. You can see one of the chaps when it's light. He's back of a bush, like as if he were froze when he stopped to listen, but his throat's cut, sir. The outfit we relieved lost two patrols, four men each time, then they didn't send any more out. They said their chaps were caught the same—throats cut, sir. It's a creepin' death gets you in there."

"But you chaps sent out patrols, eh?"

"Yes, our officer he were bound to," replied the sergeant, shivering. "Last night he went out hisself, sir, and he never come back. I'd stay out of it, sir."

"Why did your officer go?" The Australian captain asked his question sharply. He sounded as though the information had tautened his own nerves.

"He heard things, sir. The Germans were in there, talkin' and whisperin' like. And there were noises like a bush crackin', sir. He were sure he could find them."

"I see. You may go, Sergeant." Captain Hazlett let the man squeeze past. Then he turned to the tall form beside him.

"Rader," he said quietly, "tell your patrol all the sergeant said, then let them go outside our wire, not much farther. Don't you go out at all. You're too valuable to lose before we know what we're up against. We'll look the Wood over tomorrow, and we'll put up flares as soon as weget our posts established."

"But, sir, you know these Londoners. There can't be anything out there but Germans. I'll be careful."

"Not tonight, Sergeant. That chap was scared stiff and he seemed to be an old soldier. There must be something out of the ordinary."

A runner found them in the dark. "Message from the CO," he said. "No patrols to go out till you've seen him, sir."

"All right, runner. You heard that, Rader? I'll be back as soon as I can."

Sergeant Rader stood on the fire step and peered into the thick gloom beyond the wire entanglements, listening to every sound. There was not much shelling, and the machine guns were fairly quiet. Now and then a startled sentry shot into the dark, but on the whole the night was unusually still.

To the right and left, flares were going up regularly. But in Mustard Wood no light flickered. It was as if the Germans knew perfectly well that no patrol dared venture into its death-ridden tangles. The sergeant started. A slight sound had come to his ears, a muffled crackling, as if a stick had been snapped under a heavy body.

Sergeant Rader was the champion scout of the battalion. Tall, lean, lithe as a jaguar, without making a sound, and he could sense his direction with a sureness uncanny to his fellows. His record of trapping enemy patrols was not equalled in the entire brigade; and as he stood and watched and listened, he tingled with a desire to match his craft with whatever phantom was stalking the Wood before him.

There were hurried steps along the trench and Captain Hazlett returned. "Rader," he said anxiously, "that sergeant wasn't stretching things any. There's a big Bavarian officer here they call the 'Creeping Death,' and he's been here for two weeks. They say he can find his way like a cat in the dark, and he's killed over thirty of our best men who've tried to beat him at his game."

"Did anyone ever see him, sir?"

"Yes, the Manchesters' scout officer was allowed to come back to his company—after the Bavarian had captured him. The officer had three men with him and was in the left part of the Wood. He said he never heard one of his men speak. They were crawling in an open patrol, and the German killed every one of them with his knife without the officer hearing him. Then he stunned the lieutenant with a sort of blackjack and picked him up like a child and carried him into the German tent."

Rader grunted as if he were incredulous. "How could that German crawl around without making any noise?" he demanded.

"That," said Captain Hazlett, "is the mystery. He said he never heard a thing at all. From all accounts this Bavarian is as big a man as you are, too, but he must be very tricky in the dark. One of the Manchester patrols stumbled over him near their wire the first night he came, but he fought like a tiger and killed two of them before he got away."

The sergeant looked at the dark wood. "I'd like to meet him, sir," he drawled calmly. "Did the colonel give any orders?"

"Yes, you are to send out the two-man patrol, just outside our wire. You tell them what has happened along here, and tomorrow we'll get all the observation we can. I'm having plenty of flares put up tonight and we'll keep a sharp watch. Did you hear anything while I was away?"

"Yes, sir. There was a queer noise, as if someone had crawled on a dry stick."

"Ah, that's him. They say he's so bold now that he doesn't mind you knowing when he's in the Wood. He's their watchdog, that big Bavarian, and I don't mind telling you that I wouldn't like to go in there tonight. When he let that Manchester officer go, he told him that he was doing it in order to let the Manchesters know how little he feared them, and that he would cut the throat of any man who dared go into the Wood. 'You don't use bombs or shoot, and I won't,' he said. The officer was allowed to come back in broad daylight, and he saw his three men lying not ten feet from each other—with their throats cut. He was so furious that he got six volunteers to go out with him that night for revenge. Every man of them was a six-footer, and had a knife and club. Not one of them got back, and when it was daylight the Manchesters could see the six of them, with their officer, piled in a heap in an open space—all with their throats cut."

Sergeant Rader never got excited. Long years in the never-never lands of Australia, with only his horse and his dog, had rendered him impervious to emotion. "Some chap has been telling a heap of lies," he said coolly. "There isn't any German like that."

"It was their own major." Captain Hazlett stopped speaking. Another dry stick had snapped in the dark of the Wood. Whoever prowled there was careless of who heard him. Rader stared in the blurred gloom. "That Heine's out there now, askin' for trouble," he drawled softly. "I'd like to go meet him."

The captain shook his head. "You wouldn't have half a chance, now," he said. "Wait till you've had a look in daylight. Say, that damned place makes me creepy. Did you notice how queer things sound in there?" He stirred himself. "Send your men out," he ordered. "I'll have flares going up right away."

The two scouts went out, crawling through the patrol gap in the wire, and going to the left. Then flares soared over the array of broken stubs in front. Their eerie, wavering light revealed a jungle of snarled and ragged stumps, spaced by little clumps of trees that had escaped the spasmodic shelling of that sector. When the flares fell with a sizzle into the brush tangles they vanished, as if they had fallen into a pit. A hundred men could lie hidden among the stumps and thickets.

The captain rejoined Rader. "I never saw a worse mess between the wires," he said gravely. "No wonder that Bavarian can creep up on a man."

The scout sergeant nodded. "But every man has the same chance in there," he drawled, "and there's other men as good as he is."

The flares were shooting over the right, but the tangles there seemed as bad, or worse. After a long period of watching and listening the captain went back to report. "Soon as your scouts come in, have the Lewis gunners shoot off a few pans," he ordered. "A chance bullet might do us a lot of good, and we'll let that German know we're here. I think the best idea would be to let the artillery shoot that bunch of stumps and brush off the map."

Rader made no response. He gazed into the darkness. When the officer had gone, he moved quickly. He went along the trench and softly called signals to his scouts. There was no response. He waited a time and tried again. There was no answer. Then a sentry came to him. "Are you callin' to your scouts?" he asked. "They came to my post about an hour ago and got two of my mates to go out with them. They said they could hear a Heine patrol close by in the Wood."

The sergeant grunted. He left the sentry without speaking to him, and hurried along the trench, peering, listening. The darkness seemed more intense, like moist black velvet. There were no sounds at all from the Wood. Its stubs showed at times the glimmer of the flares like the fangs of some great monster, waiting, noiseless, sinister, for unwary intruders.

At that moment, Captain Hazlett returned. "Where're your men, Rader?" he asked. "Didn't they come in?"

"No, sir," said the sergeant. "And they didn't answer any of my signals."

The captain started. He peered at the tall man. "What—they couldn't have—" He did not say it.

"Brogan and Woolard are my two best men," drawled the sergeant, "and I told them not to go far from the wire."

"But it's over four hours since they went out. How long did you tell them?"

"An hour, sir." The officer looked worried. "They came in to one of the posts on the left and got two of the sentries to go out with them. They said they could hear a German patrol quite near."

"Two more—four of them. Good heavens! Let's get busy. You go one way in the trench, and I'll go the other. Signal to them, and let me know as soon as you get an answer."

They went back and forth many times, listening, straining their eyes in the darkness, giving low signals that were not answered—and at dawn the four men had not returned.

Rader arranged a number of loopholes before it was light. He removed sandbags from the parapet and replaced them with others, special contrivances, hollowed to admit his head and field glasses. From a dozen different angles he peered into the Wood, and then he saw them!

Brogan was drooped over an upheaved tree root, his tunic pulled and twisted as if he had fought. Woolard was quite a distance from him, sprawled on his back. Beside him were the two sentries, contorted, grotesque. All had had their throats cut.

All the morning, Rader went up and down the trench, visiting each peephole in turn until he had a fair idea of the Wood. It was not over two hundred yards through it to the German lines, and in many places he could see their wire barricade and the tops of sandbagged machine-gun emplacements. There were several wide gaps in different places, and so cunningly had they been cleared that they afforded the enemy a chance to cross-fire with their Maxims, so as to sweep all the Australian trench. The Wood formed a salient in the line, and from either flank German sentries could watch all the Australian Front.

The sergeant made his last trip carefully, checking up at every point, then stopped and pondered. He saw that the enemy could watch all the front, and he cautiously raised his steep helmet at one of the lower parts of the trench. Ping! A bullet struck it from his hands. Snipers were watching to see that no one entered the Wood in the daytime.

Rader went to a loophole and looked long and carefully. Shell-fire had stripped the trees of their upper branches, had left but stumps of many, and here and there had gouged great holes in the moss and black earth beneath the brush. On the left the Wood was more open. A wide roadway had angled through it, and it was now strewn with a tangle of wires, shell cases, and the charred remnants of a lorry that had evidently received a direct hit while laden with ammunition. He saw marks in ferns, where his scouts had gone from the post they had visited. What had they met in that sinister darkness? How had the Bavarian been able to strike without making a sound? Why had his men not used their automatic pistols?

It was a mystery he could not solve, and he spoke to no one as he studied the problem. When the captain came at noon he accosted him. "I want to get out there in daylight, sir," he said. "I think I can do it."

"But my officers tell me his snipers have a clear view of all our trench," protested the captain. "How could you do it?"

"I can tunnel under the parapet and outside there's very soft soil, sir—mostly old leaves and moss. There's two or three stubs lying out a distance, then an old stump. I can make it, and I'd like to get out there when they're never suspecting it. I might find something, sir."

"All right, Rader. Go ahead. But be careful, and come in before dark."

Under the sergeant's directions, sandbags were removed from the lower part of the trench wall. Improvised props held the upper bags in place and then three experts worked with their entrenching tools, tunneling. They filled pails and passed them back, making rapid progress through the loose soil. In two hours they had cut a narrow ditch out to the first brush beyond the wire, and so well had they worked that a watcher a hundred yards on either flank could not detect the little trench.

Rader had donned special clothing for his venture. He was armed with a bomb, a knife and his pistol. He worked through the hole in the trench wall and into the ditch. For a few yards it was comparatively easy to wriggle along the trough-like cutting, then came the matter of getting into the brush. He had proved the enemy snipers were alert, and to draw their attention was ruin to his plans of surprise. Very slowly he raised his head, then drew himself forward a few feet. A long wait and he repeated his advance. Yard by yard, he ventured, and after an hour's time he had wormed himself into a bushy tangle.

To his right he could see a maze of fallen trees and dried underbrush, and he knew that it would be practically impossible for anyone to crawl there after dark and not make a noise. No human being could do so. Therefore the Bavarian must work on the left of the Wood.

Ahead of him ran a wide roadway that angled, the one he had seen from the trench. Several trees had fallen across it near where he lay, and the wreckage of the charred lorry extended for yards on either side. Under it, over it, and tangled everywhere were twisted, broken wires. Beyond, the Wood was more open. It was floored with moss and rotting beech leaves, and an experienced man could move there with little noise. Here it must be that the Bavarian came.

Rader saw that he could cross the road without being seen. He crawled slowly, watching and listening. Not a shot came his way. There was the usual amount of shelling and rifle fire, but in the Wood all was dark and still. No living thing save himself moved in it.

Where he crossed, two or three trunks lay, bridging the wires on the road. They were close together and gave him excellent cover. On the other side he found tracks of heavy boots, deep markings in the soft soil. Men had used the road quite frequently and the imprints told of burdens carried. He puzzled a time, then understood. The killer's victims had been carried to the German trench via the wide roadway. Then he was puzzled again. There were marks on the bark of the fallen trees, as if someone had occasionally crossed the road on them. Why had they done so?

Once over the road, he kept on until he could peer through a last bushy covert and see plainly the German trench. His trained eye had no difficulty in detecting the exit the killer used in leaving the trench. It was a narrow lane in the wire. Then he looked long at the ground about him, scanning every exposed tree root, every stick and log, every foot of soil. Years with the blacks of the "out-back" regions of Australia had taught him many things. He could read a trail as if it were inscribed with information. Even a crushed twig could give him facts. Backing inches at a time, he maintained his scrutiny of the Wood, and was rewarded. He found the killer's path.

In the dark it would furnish an excellent guide. It ran in zig-zag style among the fallen trees, but all protruding branches had been carefully broken off, and there was nothing to hinder the prowler who was acquainted with its turnings. No stinging branches would sweep his face.

After finding the path, Rader moved more quickly. He explored farther to his left, but the brush was not so plentiful, and the ground was bare in many places. Successive salvos of heavy shells had torn and plowed the earth, uprooting trees and scattering them like matchwood. He turned and worked back toward the road, then halted.

Two soldiers and an officer were standing on the fire step of the German trench, exposed to their belts, gazing at the district back of their lines. It was a splendid chance. He could not miss the officer at such close range, but he did not shoot. There might be an opportunity later, and it would not do to let the enemy know that he had observed them. Such careless exposure drove home to him, however, the confidence the enemy had in his daylight domination of the Wood.

He had almost reached the path again when he saw a length of tree trunk that had been neatly severed by a shell. It was six feet long and quite heavy. The ordinary scout would not have given it a second glance, but Rader was not an ordinary scout. He had seen the blacks construct deadfalls with just such lengths of tree trunks.

He went on to the road, and there salvaged a loose wire, and then waited until it was dusk. As soon as he was sure he would not be seen by sentries or snipers, he carried the short log to the path. If anyone was to pass underneath and strike the trip with his foot, the log would strike him with a swinging blow as it fell on his head and shoulders.

When he had it ranged to his satisfaction, he hurried toward the road, then crouched quickly. He was too late. There were guttural voices speaking in the dark, and he could distinguish the forms of two husky German soldiers coming along the roadway. They reached the tree trunks and scrambled over them, the last man slipping and stumbling, so that he almost trod on the crouching Australian.

Rader, sure of discovery, struck like a rattler. His victim's stifled cry disturbed the quiet. The knife had plunged deep, and the man slumped back on the road. His mate, some distance ahead, turned, and stared. He asked something in a hoarse whisper. Rader rose from where he crouched and hurried toward him. The German, partly satisfied, turned off the road, leading toward the four dead Australians. He asked some question over his shoulder as he went.

The sergeant sprang like a panther. He struck, but his blade sank in the German's shoulder. The fellow screamed with pain, and seized Rader's arms. The sergeant tore loose from his grasp, tried to strike again, and they went to earth in a frenzied tangle, Rader keeping the man from yelling again. A moment later and it was over. The knife was driven home.

The sergeant was not a second too soon with his victory. Machine guns suddenly crackled and spat, and Very lights soared over the Wood. Bullets hissed and snapped among the branches and for several minutes he was forced to hug the protection of a huge stump. Then there came a lull, and in a short time he was in his trench again.

So nervous were the sentries and their non-coms that Rader was obliged to explain the cry in the dark before he could get back to report. The captain had been anxiously awaiting him, and they both went to the colonel's dugout.

"What did you find out?" asked the CO. He had been a keen scout himself.

Rader explained all that he had seen, in his terse fashion. "The Heinies think they own that Wood," he added at the finish. "I'll bet that creeper will have an awful surprise tonight. He'll have a couple of his own men to carry in. Can I take out a patrol, sir?"

The officers looked at each other. "I think, sir, that he can risk it," said Captain Hazlett. "Rader has been over the ground, and he knows where our chaps were killed last night. He can avoid that area."

"I just want to go out near that road and listen," the sergeant explained. "We can look out for ourselves. There's some game played here that's different from anything we've been up against, or they'd never have caught men like Brogan and Woolard."

"All right, you may go," said the colonel. "This part of the line has been held too long. The Germans have been there so long they've had time to fix up anything they fancied. There's a French village just back of their lines, and it's rumoured that the Germans have taken half the furniture of the French to fit up their dugouts. They've got stoves to heat them, and they've actually got them lighted with electricity. They use the power house in the village."

Another still, warm night, pregnant with mystery. It was so dark that Rader could not see the man beside him. He had installed himself under a heap of tree wreckage and had four men with him, spread in a little circle. They were husky lads, picked for their fighting qualities, not their scouting abilities. They knew the fate of the four adventurers of the previous night, and were determined to avenge them.

They were in a black mud and utter darkness, and only slight sounds from their own trench came to them clearly. For an hour they waited, then there was a sudden shout, a cry in the darkness, and the thud of something falling. The deadfall had been sprung.

Rader tingled from head to foot. He longed to glide under the brush and investigate, but this was a game of no mistakes. He heard shuffling noises, dragging sounds. Someone was trying to move another. There was a groaning muffled sound as though a hand was thrust over the sufferer's mouth.

Shortly afterward there were grunting comments in the dark of the road, then the snapping of a twig. Heavy feet trod on a dead branch. Some party of men were coming toward them. Rader grew uneasy. If they were discovered, if by some mysterious means, the killer had guessed the presence of the Australians, then they would be taken at a disadvantage in the brush heap. He whispered with his men, and they crept forth to a cleared space. Then it happened.

There were two short gasps in the dark, as if a throat had been throttled suddenly by a giant hand, then the threshing of bodies. There were guttural grunts, the thud of blows, sounds of wrestling, struggling men—the groan and gasp of death. The thick silence had been torn to shreds. There was a crashing of brush as men fell into it.

Rader had leaped back and crouched at the first sounds of fighting. He sensed, rather than heard, an enemy near him, and suddenly thought of capturing him. If a prisoner could be taken, one of the prowlers, surely valuable information could be obtained. An arm brushed his, and his grasp was desperate. He was fortunate. A sharp blade merely grazed his wrist; then he had twisted its wielder's arm so that the weapon was dropped, and they locked in a tremendous struggle.

His man twisted and wrenched to clear himself, and the fellow was very strong. Rader was surged back and forth, but he maintained his grip, and gradually shifted his hold. Another moment and he could throw his captive. There was a panting of hot breath near his face and the grinding of teeth; then the German swung himself with all his weight and at the same time drove his shoulder into the sergeant's chest. Despite this sudden move, Rader did not lose his hold. He was thrown partly off balance, but he wrenched an arm so that the man shouted out in pain. In another moment, Rader would have conquered him. But an eager figure blundered into them.

"That you, Sarge?" came a whisper.

A hand caught his arm. There was a great surge, an upheaval of arms and legs, and before Rader could free himself his man had escaped.

"What—who are you?" came a hiss in the sergeant's ear.

"I'm Rader. What the devil did you bump into us for?"

The sergeant was angry, but Crump, the blunderer, was one of his best fighters.

"Sorry I upset you, Sarge," he whispered. "I got the chap who pitched against me at first. Hell, he didn't amount to nothin'. Where's your chap?"

"You knocked him out of my hands," said Rader. "He may be within ten feet of you, with his knife ready. Watch yourself." They listened.

"Who's there?" The whisper was as sibilant as a snake's challenge. "It's Timmins. That you, Joe?"

It was another of the Australians. "You chaps hurt?" he wheezed. "I just got a scratch. My man was awkward as a cow, but he hung on. Where's Harvey? He smashed into the brush first shot."

They began to look for him, and found him entwined with a burly German, both dead. Then there were more worrying, snarling sounds in the dark, and the fall of a body. A crackling of branches. Quick feet. A low call. "Where you chaps at?"

It was the fourth man of Rader's patrol. He gulped for breath. "I got three of them," he panted. "Two right off the bat, easy. They'd grabbed each other by mistake. Then I heard a guy sneakin' by me and I jumped him."

There had not been any shooting. It was as dangerous for friends as foe, but the sergeant could not understand the reason of their easy victory. Six Germans for Harvey. Then he remembered.

They had been a carrying party, going to bring in the dead. And the killer had come by his own path, and got hurt by the deadfall!

Two hours went by and nothing happened, then Rader led his men in and reported. The moment he reached the trench he asked the Lewis gunners to spray the Wood with bullets, and to keep shooting regularly. Flares were sent up on both flanks. They were not taking any chance of the enemy coming on a reprisal raid. And at stand-to there had not been any of the mysterious noises of the previous night. The Bavarian must know that he had a different foe to deal with.

At daylight Rader was back to his peep holes, peering into the grey gloom of the Wood. The first sun rays revealed field-grey uniforms under the trees. The victims of the night's fighting lay as they had fallen—proof that no other prowlers had reached them. The Germans had had an unlucky night.

The sergeant went to his dugout and slept till noon. Then he returned to the trench and wormed through the hole under the parapet. Captain Hazlett had given him permission.

"Go it your own way," he said. "But remember that the Bavarian knows now that you've been around the Wood. He'll spring his best tricks."

The sergeant crawled as carefully as he had done the previous day and reached the brush without being spotted. He did not venture near the dead Germans, as he knew they could be seen from the enemy trench. He crossed the road and wormed over to see where his deadfall had sprung.

The log was beside the path. Then he was startled. Three quick shots came from the German trench—signal shots.

He looked through a thicket. A soldier climbed out of the enemy trench on the right of the Wood. He bore a white flag, and he walked half way across No Man's Land. An Australian went to meet him, and was given a note. The pair returned to their respective trenches. Rader was eager to know the contents of the message. He spent a tedious hour making a safe return trip to his lines. Captain Hazlett met him with a note. It was written in English.

"According to a letter in the pocket of one of your scouts, you have a Sergeant Rader who excels in patrols. I also excel in patrol work. I challenge him to come into the Wood alone, armed only with a knife, at ten o'clock tonight. The best man will win. Captain Fritz Hempel."

Rader read the note a second time, then discarded his pistol and bombs. "I'm going out now, while it's light. I don't believe he knows I was out there yesterday. It's all the surprise I have for him."

Captain Hazlett was nervous. "There'll be a trick somewheres," he said. "This Bavarian is wild because you killed his men last night, and he has figured if he can get you out of the way, he can do as he likes."

"But he's not planning on me being over there now, or being near his own trench to meet him. I'll like it better, too, not having anyone else to look out for."

Rader went back and got a long rope from his dugout, a signal cord he and his men used at listening posts.

"I'll tie the end of this to a loose stick," he said. "You'll pull on it at about a quarter past ten, just enough to make a noise in the brush, then pull it again every ten minutes or so."

The captain was still shaking his head as Rader crawled from view.

It was as dark as pitch. Along both trenches that enclosed Mustard Wood there was little or no movement. Both sides were tense, waiting. The Australians knew that their champion was out in the dark, awaiting his challenger, and they guessed that the Germans were watching their famous Captain Hempel make his preparations.

An hour dragged by like an eternity. Artillery on the left had burst into an uproar of hate, then subsided. Wheeled traffic, far back on some cobbled road, had rumbled out of hearing. Then he heard it—the slight twang of taut wire. Someone was passing through the lane in the German wire.

He stared into the darkness, listening intently, so that his ears seemed to throb. His fingers were moist as he gripped the handle of his trench knife. At last he was meeting the creeper at his own game. The darkness was as thick as black syrup, and every flickering reflection of flares that rose and fell on either flank slid weird, wavering light fingers among the stubs. Every muscle seemed cramped and in an agony. Then he heard something.

It was the sharp snapping of a twig, as if someone had stepped on it suddenly, a step off balance. Silence, a pulsing, sinister stillness, followed. The sergeant knew what the sound had been. It was far over the road, and had been the moving of the stick to which he had tied the rope. His mates in the trench were doing their part. Then he tensed anew. A voice had spoken, so low that he could hardly hear it. "I am ready," it mocked. "Hurry, Rader."

Rader took the blade of his knife in his teeth and set to clearing the dry twigs from his path. He would make his way toward the mocker. Then he marvelled that the killer had called out. Ah, just so had he called and baited the other patrols who had been caught.

But the Bavarian was in a hurry. He had not waited long. Captain Hazlett and the colonel had suggested that the man must be partly insane, and Rader realized that it was more than possible. A man with a fevered mind would be impatient.

With painstaking care, Rader removed all the dry sticks from his way, then crawled forth. Every foot of ground, every step into the plush-like darkness was a new venture. He had chosen the same path as his challenger had taken, and he meant to meet him on it.

The sergeant was not far along the path when he heard another cracking sound. The rope had been tugged again. There was a long moment of listening, then the mocking voice spoke again, louder. "This way, Rader," it said. "Are you afraid?"

A Very light that had shot up at the end of the Wood seemed to hang in the air before it wavered downward. Rader rose silently and stared, and could barely make out three dark stubs on his right, then a break. He recognized his position as darkness engulfed him. He was at the little clearing before the roadway. His enemy must be awaiting him on the bank.

A few dragging seconds and he was sure. He heard a long-drawn breath. "Are you a coward?" The mocking voice was right beside him.

The sergeant took one long step, then paused. Two flares went up at once on the right, and as he squatted quickly, he could see, the head and shoulders of the killer. The German was not six feet from him—and had his back to him.

Sergeant Rader did not have the killer instinct. He did not spring like a great cat and drive his blade in the man's back—he hated to do such a thing. He took another step, settling his feet with infinite caution, and pushed his knife in its sheath. Then he leaped.

His hands caught his enemy's wrists, as they hung by his side, and he swung them backward and upward with a terrific jerk. Both men staggered ahead with the shock of contact, and the German grunted in pain as he writhed. His knife fell, striking Rader as it dropped. "I came," the sergeant grated. "Are you ready?"

The answer was a wild struggle. The German threw himself backward, lashing a vicious kick as he did so. He was as big a man as Rader, and he was infuriated.

Rader matched him, grip for grip. Twice he brought the German to his knees, and twice they went to earth together. They surged and twisted, gasping for breath, locking arms and legs, then Rader slipped. The German instantly caught him around the neck with an arm lock that was terrific. "You—your log got me," he gritted.

He tried to drive his knee into the sergeant's throat, and if he had been cooler-headed, might have succeeded. As it was, the Australian caught him off balance. He heaved his man from the earth, forced him backward over his thigh, crushed his arms to his body, conquering him by sheer muscular power. It had been one surging red-hot drive. Hempel wilted, and Rader relaxed.

His enemy dropped, an arm slid down. Just in time the sergeant struck it away. He had stepped on a knife the moment before. In a burst of fury at such treachery he picked his man up bodily. "I surrender," gasped the German.

Rader heaved him forward. The German just caught the bank with his feet. "Not—the—road," he panted. "Nein—no—Gott—*no*." Fear rode in every gasp. The man was quivering.

Rader caught him in an iron grip as he flung back. He collared him and exerted all his strength. There was a terrible sigh of anguish, terror, cut off queerly. A twinging of wires, then all was still again. Rader had hurled the German down the bank onto the road.

In an instant he had cupped a match and peered. The German lay as he had struck the earth—dead!

That scream of mortal terror seemed still in the air when the Australians heard someone approaching their trench. It was Sergeant Rader, and he had half-dragged, half-carried the body of his opponent to the wire.

"How—what—that yell?" Captain Hazlett could hardly speak coherently.

"Was Captain Hempel's last one," answered the sergeant. "I found his trick. He had live wires running through that wreckage on the road, the juice brought from the powerhouse in the village. I got wise to it when I found the logs he crossed the road on when the current was on. He'd switch it on, then come by his path to the side of the road and make noises in the dark till our lads crawled in the live wires. Then he'd get the current off, and drag them away and cut their throats, to make it look as if he had killed them."

"Of all the devilish—" The captain could not express his loathing. "And you surprised him on his side of the road?"

"I did," admitted the sergeant. "I got close to him before he knew I was there. I could have knifed him in the back, but I didn't. I handled him, then threw him down on the wires."

"That was the yell, then." The captain shuddered. "I never heard such a scream before. The man sounded crazy with fear. But, say, how did you get the body?"

"Just pulled it off the road, sir."

"How—won't electricity kill you?"

"Sure, but I cut the wires when I crawled out today. The Heinies never have the power on in the daytime."

"Cut them? Then what killed the—the captain?"

Rader yawned. "Nothin'. Bad heart, I reckon." He yawned again. "He sounded mighty scared, anyhow."

Captain Hazlett gulped. "You—you did it on purpose. Poor Brogan and—the terror he had, the German I mean—" He broke off, then turned and hurried toward his dugout. He had left his flask there, and he wanted a drink very much. There were times when Sergeant Rader made him shudder.

Wire Overhead

They used to say, in the 25th Battalion, that "Nervous" Johnson had the greatest imagination on the Western Front. Given a dark night and a slight wind he could make the noise of rustling dead grass the whispers of a Heinie patrol, put up a flare and could build whole platoons out of weed tops and shape old stakes into German officers. Most any new man, and plenty of old hands, could do this, but none so vividly as Johnson, for he would tell the colour of the officer's eyes or how many of the platoon were bow-legged. One misty morning he looked over the top and actually saw a German scuttling to cover. The platoon was in the Lens area, where old wire and trenches and wrecked buildings made the landscape fit for any war picture, and straightway he made out a Hun working party busy with the construction of a Minniewefer emplacement.

The sergeant hopped up a minute later and stared himself cross-eyed and couldn't see anything but a small, broken-topped bush and a wrecked French cart. Johnson stuck to his story, however, and described things so vividly that the officer heard of it and had him go down to company headquarters and tell his story.

It didn't take the company commander long to find flaws in his fiction, but Johnson's command of detail made a lasting impression on Sergeant Buck. Buck did most of the scouting for his company and led all patrols. He loved the work and could crawl over and among old craters and brick heaps without losing his sense of direction in a way that made his fellows declare he must be a full-blooded Indian. He had courage galore, was a good shot, enjoyed his work, but had one failing—he could not make good reports!

When he came in from a patrol that had simply thrilled with adventure he would get his pad and scribble: "Patrol of four men and Sergeant Buck from Piccadilly Post at Cow Trench into No Man's Land at 11 p.m. Advanced forty yards. Saw enemy sap. Heard Germans working.

Was out two hours. No enemy patrols."

Major Squibbs, the company commander, would read this epistle to the Romans and shout for the sergeant. "Why the hell don't you use your lead pencil more?" he would snort. "How did you advance forty yards? Walk? Crawl? Run? Swim? Where was this sap you found? Were the Huns in it? Was it a new one? What—where—blast it, man, wake up. Go write out a report of everything, something I can understand."

And Sergeant Buck would spend the rest of the time till stand-to, sucking a stubby lead pencil and sighing, now and then making a jumbled disjointed statement.

"Johnson," said Buck, after the interview at headquarters, "from now on you're a company scout. You don't do any gas guard or day sentry, and tonight you'll go out with me to a big shell hole on the right. We're going to try and locate a Heinie machine gun post and..."

"But Sergeant," pleaded Johnson. "I'm—I'm not a scout, I—I—"

"Who said you was?" Buck demanded. "You're just to be a reporter. I can't make these blasted reports to suit the major, and you're just the kid for that stuff. Now go pound your ear till I come for you."

That night the sergeant and Johnson established themselves in the mentioned shell hole. It was about ten yards from the German wire and the sector was fairly quiet, but Buck had such difficulty in leading, driving and pushing his recruit to the hole that he was tempted to boot him back to trench duties. They lay in their hiding till two o'clock in the morning and then crawled in. Buck showed Johnson a report blank as soon as the fellow had stopped shaking and got control of himself.

"Now fill this in. Put in everything," Buck said, "and bring it to me when you're finished."

The sergeant had hardly reached his own bunk and pitched his steel hat in a corner before Johnson was with him. Buck swore, then checked his language. The report was filled with fine writing. Getting close to the candle he read:

"Patrol consisting of Sergeant Buck and Private Oliver Wendell Johnson proceeded from Birmingham Post on Cow Trench to shell crater six yards from the enemy trench. The patrol passed through barricade wire, moved along trench frontage for seven yards, then twelve yards towards enemy, after which proceeded on south-easterly direction until crater was reached. The crater was nine feet in circumference and only a few inches in depth. It was in a foul condition.

"Enemy Trench. Hostile parties seemed continually on the move in the enemy trench. At least two companies of soldiers were there on sentry duty. Flare-light firers established at ten-yard intervals. Germans are of a large stature and believed to be special unit of Prussian Guards.

"Condition of Enemy Trench. Strongly wired, strongly constructed, strongly manned.

"Work on Enemy Trench. Several working parties at different points. Sounds of shovelling, of hammering, and sawing. Would estimate that a battery emplacement is being constructed for use in a surprise attack. Several noises like the installing of gas projectors. Would suggest that a special alertness for gas be maintained.

"Hostile Patrols. No hostile patrols were encountered, though several were heard passing in the rear of the shell crater occupied. Owing to shortage of men and ammunition your patrol did not take the offensive.

"Flares. Twenty-seven flares were shot up; four of these failed. Highest reached an elevation estimated at two hundred feet.

"Remarks. As the enemy has wired himself in great strength and is strongly entrenched as well as having superior numbers in forward positions, would suggest that any movement against him in this area would only meet with disaster. Would point out that patrols run great risks in advancing near the enemy wire, as cover is very slight. Maxim machine guns seem placed at every ten feet along trench and men were heard bringing minnenwefer shell to gun position."

The sergeant reread the entire report and then, with his stubby pencil, did some crude editing. His corrections made sad work of the neatly written report, but Johnson did not seem to mind. He was back twenty minutes later with the revised edition. Buck passed it in to the sergeant-major and went to his blankets with a happy heart and dreamt through rat-haunted hours of his assistant, publishing an eight-page "Trench Daily" with flaring, four-inch headlines.

All went well for several tours. Sergeant Buck became the most successful patrol leader in the battalion. The reports he sent in were simply marvels. They were waited for as priceless treats and were passed along reverently from company to company. Other sergeants with like responsibilities tore their jerkins and swore that all was not according to Hoyle, that a dark-skinned gentleman was somewhere in the lumber dump. And then Buck was wounded. It happened during an evening strafe, just as he was to push out, with Johnson, toward an old cellar that had been reported as being used as a night post by the enemy.

Major Squibbs had bet C Company's captain that it was not occupied, placing his francs on the strength of information Buck had brought in that the old cellar was entirely surrounded—on the Hun side—by an impassable barrier of wire. When he heard that his sergeant was wounded he was dumbfounded for the moment and then recalled that Private O.W. Johnson always accompanied Buck on his nightly expeditions. Forthwith he summoned the victim. "Johnson," he said curtly, "you know the cellar you were to watch tonight. Take another man and carry on with this patrol the same as the sergeant would have done."

"But—but, sir," protested Johnson. "I—I'm—"

"That is all," said Major Squibbs.

Johnson knew enough to go, and he chose Tommy Lark to go with him. Tommy was far from a husky fighter, but that was why Johnson chose him. Tommy was the only man he felt he could command during a crisis, and the only member of the platoon not imbued with foolhardy notions of what to do when close to the enemy.

They crawled through tangled grass and weeds, skirted old craters, crossed a slimy garden patch and circled a brick heap. Directly to their right a dark blur showed the position of the cellar. It was not far out from the Canadian Trench and had once been used as an outpost until Fritz developed an ugly trick of dropping fishtails into it. Wire, well tangled and massed, protected the front and both flanks. Johnson was puzzled as to the best position for him to take. He decided at last that the safest spot would be under the wire itself. There he would not be seen by any enemy patrol. He beckoned Tommy on.

They found it exceedingly difficult to get under the wire, which was long-barbed and sagged to the sod itself. Johnson led the way, and long practice lent him skill. He managed to wriggle under the thickest portion of the half-moon and lay, breathing deeply, listening. There was no sound of Tommy!

The little fellow had tried to do the worm stunt at three different openings and had retreated with slight wounds after each attempt. Johnson, disgusted, had crawled from view, hoping his disappearance would spur the youngster to a more strenuous attempt. But Tommy had vanished. Had he fled back to the trench? Johnson dare not call; he knew how voices seemed to carry out in that void between the wires.

Then, *tramp, tramp, tramp*; his ear to the ground, he heard the thud of heavy feet. At least three men were coming straight toward him, toward the wire, coming from the enemy side. He tried to shrink into the earth, conscious of chills chasing up and down his spine, and wondered where Tommy was. Then he heard a guttural grunt, hands fumbling at the wire, enemy hands, not ten feet from where he lay. What happened next happened so suddenly and unexpectedly that he could not move or cry out. The wire above him was simply swept back and away, leaving him naked to German eyes.

Johnson was frozen, paralyzed with fright. He lay rigid, unmoving, hardly breathing, and three big Huns tramped past him to jump down into the cellar. Then, with a slight rasping, grating noise, the ten-foot roll of wire was pushed back into place. It pricked Johnson severely, spearing him in a dozen tender places, caught at his tunic collar, hitched his equipment up on his shoulders, pulled his tunic up after it. Yet he did not gasp or cry out. Not until the Huns had their gun in place and were calming sweeping the Canadian parapet with bullets did he essay to move—and found out that he could not.

The Germans, cunning in all tricks of war, had cut the wire so as to have a movable section. This they manipulated by ropes that ran around set iron stakes, the ropes being hidden in the grass. As they approached they pulled the ropes and the wire rolled back over an entrance to the cellar.

Once in they snagged it back into place, and no patrol had discovered the trickery. Johnson wriggled slightly, tried to free himself, worked an arm free from barbs, got his collar tugged loose. Then he became still as if petrified. Perspiration ran down his hide. When coming out he had placed a Mills bomb in each pocket of his tunic, had carried one in his hand, and had thrust another in one of his hip pockets. The wire had dragged his tunic over his back. Then a long barb, with devilish luck, had hooked itself through the ring of the safety pin of the grenade in the hip pocket. If he moved forward or backward, in any way, the pin would be withdrawn and he, unable to make a getaway, would meet a sudden and gory end.

Johnson's brain revolved like a squirrel on a trick bar. He sweat and chilled alternately. For, if he did not move, the wire would be moved when the Germans thought it time to retire, and results would be just as fatal. His only hope seemed to be to call out, but—the Germans could not understand him, and would yank the wire back. Such a position was never devised elsewhere on the Western Front. In his company the old hands all have different ideas of what Johnson thought and did during the three hours he lay imprisoned in his torture chamber. Some assert that he fainted continually and thus passed the time, others claim that he suffered a seizure of some sort—which was true to a barb—and the majority believe that he was conscious every second of the time and lived a lifetime in three hours. They point out the after effects, for Johnson was never the same man.

At any rate, he was very much alive to the situation when Fritz, Otto, and Hans decided to call it a night. They gave a healthy tug on the ropes and the wire rolled back, taking with it the bomb from Johnson's pocket. As the roll turned over the weight of the grenade, or possibly the tug it had as it was loosed, freed the pin. If this was fiction I should write that the Mills packet wiped out the three Huns and Johnson carried in the Maxim as his trophy. The plain truth was that the bomb did not cause any sudden deaths. It probably gave the German trio the surprise of their career, and possibly one of the fragments—how many did instructors state there were in one grenade—embedded itself in Hunnish anatomy. One thing: they did not recover from surprise in time to prevent Johnson from getting to his feet and sprinting homeward, like a phantom of the night. He had one more right on the way. As he passed a crater Tommy shot up out of it and paced him to the Canadian wire. The little chap had heard the Huns coming and suddenly made a move on his own to a deep shell hole, there to await events.

After a stiff "issue" Johnson was led to his dugout to write his report. He commenced:

"Private Oliver Wendell Johnson and Private Lark proceeded on listening patrol at 10 P.M. They left trench at cross section of Bull Trench and Eggshell Sap, going forty yards before turning east. The patrol here separated, Private Lark retreating to safety of a large shell hole in rear.

"Private Oliver Wendell Johnson proceeded alone to within yards of German trench and then concealed himself under wire about old cellar suspected as German post. Shortly a patrol of ten large and determined Berlin Guardsmen advanced...."

They found him collapsed on the bench. He was sent to hospital, suffering from nervous attack. He never came back. A year or so after the war he was cook's helper with a road construction crew, and at nights entertained the boys with the tale of the night he was surrounded by a desperate gang of German raiders, forty or fifty of them, at a cellar—with wire overhead.

Ghost Bayonets

There was a sergeant got lost in there in the dark and he was stepping on graves and dead men. He kicked something like a hard ball and it was a head, and then somebody took hold of his arm, and led him out of there. It was a ghost, a big, tall Frenchman, dressed in a black suit, top hat and all, with his eyes out and his face as white as plaster. He took the sergeant back to the trench and said, 'If you come in here again you're a goner,' or something like that. The other chaps laughed at the sergeant when he told them that, but one night he got mixed again and went in there—and tripped over a wire and broke his neck—"

"Cut that damn tripe." The thin, nervous voice in the dark was cut off by a savage growl. "You got the 'Canary' so scared now that he's shakin'. Cut it out, and no lights or smokin', for we're goin' in to Graveyard Corner right now."

The sergeant of Ten Platoon got up from the bank where they had been resting and stepped down into the black void of the communication trench.

"Where's this we're going?" asked the sixth man in the file behind him. "That chap behind us has been talking about ghosts ever since we started. He's trying to start something."

"Search me, Jimmy," came a soft response from the man in front of him. "This bunch has been lookin' like they're goin' to their own funeral ever since we got word to fall in at billets."

"You bet," said a husky voice in the dark. "You'll wish you was back in the States before we're through this trip. The Corner's a bloody trap of a place, and it's haunted."

"Haunted?" queried Jimmy. "How—"

"Stop that talkin' when I say to." The sergeant's command was as sibilant as a snake's hiss, and the slow-moving file felt its way up the trench without further parleying.

Presently a wan moon peered through the clouds and gave enough light for the in-going platoon to pick out its surroundings as it spread into the front line. They had marched in from Cité Saint Pierre and were taking over a sector between Lens and Hill 70, a frontal area with a reputation that wrung curses from the old hands and blanched the faces of the superstitious.

Jimmy wondered, as he plodded, what sort of a place the Corner was. All day he had heard the old-timers muttering, cursing, and talking among themselves. All the front was bad enough, he gleaned, but the Corner had a category of its own. It was a place where each day was a grim possession, something held precariously. Then he grinned, and tried to get a look at Pete.

Probably these old hands had been trying to bluff them, put their wind up before they saw the front, and so help the sergeant to win his bet.

Jimmy Blake and his pal, Pete Conner, had just joined the "Pig Stickers," one of the best battalions in the Canadian Second Division, an outfit that prided itself on being the best bayonet fighters on the Western Front, and the hardest to frighten. The sergeant of their platoon was an iron-jawed, bull-voiced, thick-skinned giant, who made scornful remarks about all Americans, and especially about Jimmy and Pete, who could not conceal the fact that they were rather young in years.

New men roused little interest, for there were new men after every hard trip, but Jimmy and Pete were Yanks, and that was different.

"What the hell made you kids come and join our mob?" the hard-boiled sergeant had asked. "Don't you know that we're the Pig Stickers?"

"Yeah, but that don't sink so deep," Jimmy had retorted. He was twenty and as big as the average. "Pete and me's always lookin' for excitement and so we thought we'd come over and play tag with Fritz until we got acquainted. Then when Pershing comes with his gang, he'll make us generals on account of us knowin' so much mor'n the rest."

"Is that so?" the hard-boiled one had sneered. "I'll bet fifty francs you ain't got spunk enough to stick a man, and that you'll puke the first time you smell a dead one."

"Take your fifty," said Jimmy. "Put up your money. I never tried my bayonet on a live Fritz and I've never been in the trenches, but my cash says that I can go anywhere you do."

The rest of the platoon had not said anything at the time, but afterward, when they met Jimmy alone, they told him that he had been foolhardy.

"That Sarge is a bearcat," they told him. "He's not afraid of anything on foot, and he's been here so long that he knows all there is to know." Jimmy thought of that now as he moved into the front trench and peered curiously about him.

The platoon they relieved made record time in departing, and their actions spoke louder than words. There was no doubt as to their personal regard of Graveyard Corner.

An enemy machine gun swept the parapet in front of Jimmy and he ducked low as bullets whistled and snapped above him. He was stationed on a fire step beside one of the old hands and had been receiving instructions.

"Don't move when a flare goes up," cautioned the veteran. "And rest your eyes now and then when you're lookin' over. Stumps and things will look like they're movin' if you don't."

A corporal came along the trench. "Keep a sharp lookout," he ordered. "This here's the worst place on this front. You can see by watchin' the flares that we're in a sort of salient, and the ground's so flat ahead that we can't put out patrols. Heinie would just murder them with a cross fire. The only cover there is, and the only chance for patrols, is over on the right, where there's a dry ditch along a French road that runs into his lines. You look over that way and you'll see the stubs of the trees alongside it. Of course Heinie's in as bad a fix about patrols as we are, and he uses that ditch too."

Several machine guns began firing and the Boche began strafing. The sky line was illumined by flickering lights and the air quivered with the passing of shells. They could hear the resulting explosions back near Cité Saint Pierre and Jimmy was conscious of queer tremors as he listened to the strafe. He wished he had not spoken so bombastically to the sergeant.

"Keep lookin' over," ordered the corporal, speaking loud above the din. "There's been three posts cleaned out on this trench inside of a month. Every man was killed or captured, and nobody knew that Fritz was near till afterward."

Jimmy stared into the gloom. He had been able to distinguish the contours of the shell-torn ground in front of him, and to the right he could see the line of stumps that marked the road. The moon was appearing again and as he looked he saw, nearer at hand, other short stumps that he had not noticed the first time.

"Does the road turn this way, Corp?" he asked. "The stumps come right along this wire."

"I told you you'd be seein' things," grunted the veteran sentry. "There's no stumps near the wire." He got up on the firestep. "Where do you see them?" he asked.

Jimmy, crowded over for the moment, got back in his place and pointed, then lowered his hand hastily.

"By gosh, that's got me beat," he said. "I'd have taken my oath I saw stumps out there."

"Just what I thought," rumbled the veteran. "You new guys are all like that."

Jimmy rubbed his eyes and stared again. He was certain that he had seen the stumps, and yet it was an impossibility. Stumps could not move themselves. The corporal brought shovels and told Jimmy and his mate to work at widening the trench as they waited their turn on the firestep! "We want plenty of room at the corners," he said, "so when the alarm's given all the spare men can rush to the spot."

The night seemed endless to Jimmy. The fitful light of the flares cast strange, moving shadows over the flat, shell-scarred area in front and bullets buried themselves with vicious thuds in the tortured sentinel stubs that bordered the old roadway. Behind the front trench a war-shocked cemetery crowned an acre of higher ground and a reflection of the flares was sent back from the shattered tombstones and the debris of a wrecked shrine. Waspy bullets traversed the graveyard continually and the veteran, when he mentioned the place, spoke with awe.

"That there burying ground is haunted," he whispered. "In the daytime you can see dead men sprawled all around it. Fritz had this place once, took it from the Imperials, and they did a lot of killin' among them graves. And it's been shelled so much since then, that the stiffs are pitched around every way and some of the Frenchmen have been knocked out of their coffins. Don't ever go near there, for it's sure bad luck. One outfit had a chap that was scared when it come his turn to do listenin' post. He slipped back there and hid at a grave. A tall Frenchman in a black rig come to him and led him back and warned him not to come there again. Well, the guy got his wind up again and beat it there. He hid in another corner. They found him there, dead, black in the face, just as if he'd been drowned or choked." The veteran shuddered as he spoke.

Jimmy shivered. He hated this talk about haunted places. Despite his assumed indifference he had a dread of anything concerned with the supernatural.

There was a sudden, nerve-shattering report, a lurid tongue of flame. The sentry pitched backward. Then a bomb burst in the trench and the explosion felled Jimmy and left him half-stunned. Dark figures surged on the trench wall. Another needle of flame stabbed the dark and the corporal sank to the trench floor, clutching at his throat with his hands. His heels drummed on the duck walk.

It had all happened in one split second and Jimmy was just jumping to his feet as the first Boche jumped in the trench. Sock! Jimmy lunged desperately with his bayonet, drove it instinctively—in—out—on guard. The instructor at the base had told him how it was done, and, his pulses pounding, he made the thrusts as if on practice, but as he felt live flesh run over the steel, he was filled with an odd exhilaration.

Bombs burst to the left and right. Pistol shots! Bullets snapped about his ears. Dark forms all about him, rushing back and forth in search of opponents who were not there. Jimmy, trapped on both sides, fought like a madman, discarding every caution, insane with one desire—to fight his way clear.

He leaped, dodged, slashed, stabbed, struck and butt-ended, until he slipped as he finally drove his bayonet into a second body, and a blow on the head stretched him senseless. He roused a moment later as men from the next post came rushing in. Four Germans, the corporal, and the veteran sentry lay dead. The rest of the invaders had vanished as mysteriously as they had appeared.

The platoon officer appeared, and he asked countless questions. Jimmy explained that he had been knocked down by the first bomb, and how he had met the first of the raiders while he was still too dizzy to duck back from him.

"You're lucky," said the lieutenant. "That's what saved your life. They expected you were dead when you fell, and you staying right with them and using your bayonet upset their plans so that they beat it. But how in the devil did they get so close without somebody seeing them?"

No one answered him. It seemed impossible, and all knew that the veteran sentry was a good man. A double sentry watch was kept. Jimmy's head ached and he was feverish with excitement. He had had contact with the enemy; he had used his bayonet. How he wished he could see Pete.

At last it lightened and the sun appeared like a gigantic orange ball glinting through the white ground mist. Stand-down was given and Jimmy hurried to the dugout and joined Pete, who had been out most of the night on a carrying party. He told him of the surprise attack and how all the others had been killed, and how he had used his bayonet.

"Gee," said Pete. "I wish they'd put me on a post." He was a tall youth, almost as big as the hard-boiled sergeant. "We've got that nervous guy they call the Canary with us, and he's enough to set a man crazy. He's scared to death of the Graveyard and we have to go by it every trip. He bellyaches about it all the time and that lousy three-striper has threatened to break his neck. I wish I was with you."

They talked a while longer before Pete slept. Jimmy lay awake a long time. He could not help wondering about the stumps he had seen, and how the Germans had appeared so suddenly.

It was stand-to again and the night was very dark. Jimmy hurried to his post, fearing that he was a little late. He had gone with Pete to have a look at the haunted Graveyard. It was a more weird scene of wreckage than he had imagined. Dead bodies were flung in all positions, grotesque, unreal, horribly fantastic. From one shell crater a headless body protruded. Three grinning skulls were rolled together, upside down. A black foot and leg, stripped naked, was thrust through a pile of rotting equipment. "How's that for a nest of ghosts?" asked Pete, who seemed impervious to any spectacle. "Heinie sprays the place all the time with his machine guns so that there's no chance to bury them stiffs, and you can't get any souvenirs without you crawling in there on your knees. I was out there and I heard a noise like whisperin'. My hair went up till my tin hat nearly tipped off, then a bunch of rats run out of a hole. It's a grand feeding place for them and I'll bet they're the ghosts that the Imperials tell about."

Jimmy had drawn back then. He hated the idea of rats among the dead.

"Don't go up there again, Pete," he begged. "I hate the place. It gets me creepy." The sergeant and the platoon officer were at Jimmy's post when he reached it. "Say, you," said the sergeant. "Where was it you thought you seen them stumps?"

Jimmy rose up and pointed, then stared. It was not quite dark and he could see the wire. A lane had been cut through it!

"But was them Heinies that I saw?" he stammered.

"They was," said the sergeant grimly, "and they was cuttin' the wire when you spotted them."

"But how—why couldn't we see them before that, or afterwards?"

"That," said the officer, "is the mystery, and this corner is full of them. However, you showed good nerve last night, so you come out with me now. We'll crawl out and have a look along the wire and over at the ditch."

Jimmy was tongue-tied. He wanted to object, to tell them that he had not had training in scout work, but his dread of appearing cowardly before the sergeant held him dumb, and before he realized it, he was crawling over the parapet after the lieutenant, equipped with a revolver and a quartet of bombs. The officer dragged a white tape after him and they left it strung out through the sally gap as a guide for them when they returned. In the gloom it looked to Jimmy like a slender pathway for ghosts, and he shivered as he crawled.

A heavy dew had fallen and wet weeds brushed his face like dead fingers, startling him so that he almost sprang up. The officer moved slowly, and they examined the wire where it had been cut.

A short investigation was all that was necessary. As they could easily see, the wire had been cut from the inside, judging by the way the ends were turned. It had been made ready for the quick get-away the raiders had made.

At their discovery the officer swore vitriolically, and then they crawled the length of the platoon front, watching for the entrance gap the Germans had used. To their amazement they could not find one, and after an hour of useless crawling the baffled lieutenant announced that they would go up the ditch.

"Maybe we'll catch one of them square-heads and I'll make him tell how they did it," muttered the officer as he told Jimmy to follow him.

Very lights, with their wavering silent whiteness, held them close to the tree stumps, and then the Boche began to signal. He put up red flares that made a shallow pool beside them shine like a lake of blood; then green lights went up and gave all the area a ghastly, corpse-like sheen. The officer touched Jimmy.

"Keep a sharp lookout," he whispered. Those signals mean that he has a patrol out."

They were another hour getting near enough to distinguish the German lines. Once something rustled through the grass and Jimmy held his breath until he saw that it was only a rat, its eyes gleaming malevolently as it crossed an old plant in front of him, its snaky long tail dragging after it in a manner that made his flesh creep. Nausea stirred his stomach.

Overhead a flare looped high and shed a white glow over everything. Jimmy hugged the earth and stared at the German wire. The darkness was blinding as the flare flickered out and it was a long time before they ventured to move. Then, all at once, somewhere up the cobbled road on the other side of the stump, a boot scraped on the stones. Jimmy felt a tingling sensation, a tightening of his scalp. He could scarcely keep from shaking. When the Germans had jumped down on him in the trench it had happened so quickly that he had not had time to get frightened. He had hardly known what he was doing as he had not recovered from the concussion and everything had been a nightmare. Now, as he waited, listening, his heart pounded and his pulses throbbed; his lips were dry and thickened.

The lieutenant lay his length ahead, perfectly still. They watched the bank and after a time three indistinct blurs appeared. It was a German patrol that had been on the other side of the road, on its way home. Some brigade gunner far back of the first trenches chose that moment to warm his gun and bullets zipped among the stumps. The three crouched blurs shot back for the cover of the ditch and it was pure chance that they dove for the exact spot the officer occupied.

The lieutenant shot the leader so that he tumbled down beside him, and he fired twice at the others before their Lugers barked at him. Jimmy, bathed in sudden perspiration, pitched one of his bombs at the Germans, but did it so hastily that his throw was short. The grenade burst so close that a piece of metal screamed through the rim of his helmet and a million bells rang in his ears. He was dazed, and choked by acrid fumes. He groped to find his revolver, which he had lost. But there was no need of it. When the smoke cleared, no dark form menaced him. One of the Germans lay so near that he could touch his boots, and he could see the third man some yards away, as if he had tried to escape before he fell. Both lay sprawled, inert, dead.

He turned and crawled to the officer who was moaning softly. "Are you hit, sir?" he whispered.

There was no answer. The officer made queer, stiff motions with his arms and legs and then lay still. He, too, was dead. For a long minute he looked at him, then took his wristwatch and identification disk and started to crawl back. *Crash—crash—crash*! Three shells burst in succession on the road bank. Then, three more burst in the ditch not twenty yards from where he lay. He moved back toward the German wire. The shelling continued, a methodical strafing of the road and ditch, and he crawled until he was many yards beyond the dead men and very near the enemy trench.

Hour after hour dragged by, punctuated by the shelling. Jimmy knew that the Germans must have heard the shooting and as their patrol did not return, figured that they had encountered hostile forces. The whole front wakened and machine guns clattered continually. He did not dare move from where he lay. He had seen flares go up from the Pig Stickers' trench, and expected that they were signals meant for the officer, but he knew nothing about them, and had no idea of how long they had been out.

After a second lot of flares went up the Boche redoubled his shellings; winking explosions lined the ditch until the reek of explosives drifted to him and burned his nostrils. He huddled in his meagre shelter and wondered if Pete knew that he was out, and what the hard-boiled sergeant would do if he were in the same position. Then he started nervously as a rat ran over his legs.

Jimmy did not know when it was dawn. The endless series of explosions, the nearness of the concussions, had beat on his brain until it was numb. Twice, large bits of iron had hissed into the sod beside him and a small sliver had broke the officer's watch on his wrist. He had dozed, jerking awake at times, until his sense of danger had dulled.

He opened his eyes and saw that sunrise had turned the sky pink and red. He was cramped and chilled and foggy-minded. His back was against the road bank and he had wormed so low in the ditch that he could not be seen from the German trench, though by raising his head ever so little he could see the posts of their wire barricade. He looked back. The officer and two dead Germans were lying fifty yards from him, in the ditch, but the third man had continued his struggle until he was almost abreast of him. Then he had stiffened in a death agony. He had been wounded in the neck and Jimmy could see that his tunic was saturated with black, dried blood.

His fingers clutched a stained and sodden-looking bandage.

The sun rose and after a time an aeroplane with the Black Cross on its wings circled over the road and Jimmy wondered whether he had been seen or not. He remained perfectly still, but was conscious of his thirst, and he was also hungry. He tried to imagine what Pete was doing.

All gunfire subsided and the sun gained power. After a time, Jimmy began to sweat. Buzzing flies tortured him and he had to keep turning to relieve his cramped position. A rat, a loathsome, bloated thing, slithered down the road bank and stared at him with an evil, unwinking gaze. He cursed it under his breath. When he turned, he saw the dead German watching him in a dull, listless way that made him want to yell a protest.

Jimmy knew that he would never forget that day. Each hour of it branded deeper in his brain. He thought that the sun would not move. All his thoughts were on his chances of escape, on the inquiries that would be made about the officer's death. He visioned constantly the happenings of the night, the searing flash of the bomb that he had tossed just clear of himself, the twitching of the officer as he died. He fought to make himself think of other things, and pictured the Graveyard and all its grisly horror. His nerves had been badly shaken.

When at last it grew dusk, he was almost delirious. He started to his hands and knees when he heard voices. Then he saw heads outlined near the German wire. The dead Boche had been seen and a party was coming out to get them. Jimmy pressed close to the bank and looked wildly for cover. On the road, not far from him, a shell-battered tree trunk was lying at an angle that would hide him—but every so often a machine gunner near the Graveyard raked the log with bullets.

He hesitated, then jumped for the fallen tree. Better chance the machine gun than accept the certainty of being taken a prisoner or killed.

He was not seen. The Germans grunted and muttered among themselves and worked as fast as they could, keeping a nervous watch on the Canadian lines, and no sooner had they gone from sight that Jimmy was back in the ditch. Then the guns awoke, and this time it was a battery back at Saint Pierre that strafed the road. Then salvos fell into the German front line and Jimmy saw a tangled mass of stakes and wire heaved into the air.

A shell exploded on the road just above him. Another made a geyser of black earth very near him. He was compelled to jump and run for his life. Shells were dropping all along the ditch. He headed straight for the German trench, holding his automatic ready, determined to go out fighting, as he fancied the hard-boiled sergeant would do.

But not a man challenged him, nor was there a German in sight. They had taken cover from the shelling. He raced through an opening in their wire, jumped into the trench, glanced around, and scrambled over the bags in the rear. Another few yards and he dropped into a sap, falling headlong. Two more shells whizzed down very near him and he was showered with debris. His fall into the sap had saved his life.

Someone pitched into the short trench, falling right at his feet. It was a German private, with a cloth cap pulled on in a hood fashion that almost hid his features. He quivered slightly and lay still. Jimmy touched him, and saw that he was dead. Under the arms of the grey tunic a broad white band was sewn, and he remembered being told that patrols and raiding parties usually wore such a mark to enable their fellows to distinguish them when in an enemy trench.

Two more shells dropped very close, and then there was a rush of heavy feet. Jimmy rose up, ready, but the two men ran by the end of the sap and disappeared. He just had time to see that they, too, wore the queer cap and white band. Then he had a sudden idea. If they were going on patrol he could, perhaps, slip out with them, unnoticed, provided he wore the same distinctive markings. In one minute he had taken off the dead man's tunic and slipped it on over his own. Then he put the cap on.

He waited for a few minutes and then heard feet again. Rising cautiously, he saw three more banded Germans hurrying along the trench and, his heart beating like a mad thing, his hands trembling, he fell in behind and followed them.

A few yards on, the way was almost blocked by debris and as the Germans followed by Jimmy scrambled over it, another white-banded soldier joined them. He fell in behind Jimmy, and Jimmy hoped they would not have to enter a lighted place, as his khaki breeches and puttees would give him away. They hurried around a corner and to the steps of an underground place. An officer was there and he snarled at them angrily. Evidently he had been waiting some time and did not think that the shelling should have delayed matters. Jimmy had no chance to turn back and he was sickened with dismay as he was pushed inside and had to go down the stairs.

To his great relief he saw a long passage at the foot of the steps and saw that the only light was furnished by a flashlight the officer carried, and which he flashed ahead of him. They went on, and on, until he was completely baffled. Each instant he had expected to step into a lighted chamber, but they kept on until he judged that they had covered over one hundred yards. He wanted desperately to lag in the rear but there was no way of avoiding the man behind him. Each step, he felt, took him nearer a grim reckoning.

Then he noticed that the tunnel they were in was an old one, mostly through a chalky formation that needed no bracing. Here and there were supports of masonry that had been there many years. He tried to sense their direction, and figured that they had followed the old French road.

Suddenly they left the chalk-walled portion and entered a newly-dug passage. It was much smaller and was braced by timbers. They moved more slowly, the soldiers in front of him appearing like grey ghosts in the dim light. All at once Jimmy realized that the Germans probably had a secret exit very near the wire of the Pig Stickers, and by this means had made such successful raids in that sector.

The party halted and the officer turned to flash the light on his men. His back was against the earth wall and as Jimmy, fearful of being exposed by the searching beams, tried to squeeze back of the man ahead of him, he saw the officer stiffen in an extraordinary manner. Every man exclaimed at once. The flashlight was waved in a circle and dropped. It fell so that it was pointed at the officer's face and chest. His face was distorted, ghastly. But Jimmy gasped as he saw what protruded from the chest of the grey tunic. It was a rusty bayonet point!

The man nearest the officer seemed frozen with horror. Then he leaned forward and touched the lieutenant on the arm. The dead man tumbled forward, collapsing in a huddle, and as he did so dragged with him the rifle to which the bayonet was attached—and the earth wall caved in.

Jimmy was knocked backward against the man who had crowded up to him. The party struggled to get away from the awful thing that had slid in with the loose earth, partially blocking the passage. It was a skeleton, a grisly, horrible thing, its skull rotting eerily, its bony fingers still clutching like hooks on the stock of the rifle.

The party surged back its length from the spot where the flashlight's ray played on the grim intruder. More earth rolled in, almost covering the long electric torch, and then the Germans in front doubled back like rabbits, thrusting their comrades out of the way. Jimmy was driven against the wall, was knocked about in the scramble, and for the moment could not see what had happened. Then his knees were suddenly weak and his throat so dry he could not articulate, for the second intruder was far more startling than the skeleton. It was the ghost of Graveyard Corner!

Only one man remained in front of Jimmy, and he had slumped down, shaking with fright. A tall Frenchman peered at them as he stooped and entered the opening. He was dressed in a long black coat and trousers and he wore a tall black hat. His face was a ghastly pallor, horribly unreal.

He stooped to enter the tunnel and pick up the flashlight. Then he gazed at Jimmy, and as he did there shuddered into the passage a fearful, long-drawn moan, a harrowing cry as of some soul sick with horror. It was repeated, more shuddering and appalling than before. Then the only sound was that of the whistling gasps of the Germans cowering in the tunnel behind Jimmy. One long minute, and then the man in front of him, who had been gibbering with fright, got to his feet and dashed to the rear, bowling Jimmy over again, driving headfirst into one of his mates, and screaming with fear. Then the Frenchman moved. He played the light down the tunnel on the men who remained, rested it an instant on Jimmy, and stepped toward him.

The Germans behind him tumbled over each other, gasping their fear. Jimmy himself was too paralyzed with shock to move. He had, like the Germans, had a full look at their ghostly visitant, and his blood had run cold. Over and beneath and around the eyes of the tall Frenchman ringed a deep crimson, as if the sockets were bursting and letting loose the blood behind, and, to enhance this new horror, the long-drawn moan was repeated.

The Frenchman came and placed a hand on Jimmy's arm, then turned him up the tunnel and pushed him. Jimmy went obediently, though he scarcely knew what he was doing. Everything had happened so rapidly, was so fantastically unreal, that he felt he must be having a horrible nightmare. But twenty paces beyond where the earth had fallen in he saw steps. He mounted them. Was this the exit? A wild plan entered his head. If it were, he would make a desperate plunge for escape.

The steps ended in a low wooden door that was barred. Not a word had been spoken. Only, in the passage below, there filtered again that awful screech, that made Jimmy start as he removed the bar. A cold sweat broke over him. He fumbled at the door, jerked at it in a frenzied way, got it open and crawled out the small opening—into a wrecked grave!

A corpse faced him, a hideous, huddled thing, and he leaped by it and sprang upon the bank. "Wait for me."

It was the Frenchman who spoke, the ghost who had thrust out of the opening. "It's me, Pete, don't you know me?"

"You—Pete?" faltered Jimmy, hesitating. "Wha—what—where did you get that rig?"

"Half a second and I'll tell you everything and we'll get the gang here." The pseudo Frenchman was ripping off his black coat, revealing a khaki tunic underneath. Then he sat down and tugged at his trousers. When they were removed he jumped up beside Jimmy and led the way.

They were almost to the trench when machine-gun fire caught them. Jimmy had been conquering his shakiness and thrilling to the sight of the flares and distant gun flashes when all at once there was a distant rat-tat-tat-tat, and he was almost felled by a blow on the leg.

"Beat it," yelled Pete, and they plunged ahead a few jumps and leaped into the trench. There Jimmy's leg buckled under him.

"I'm hit, Pete," he said tremulously. "They got me in the leg. Help me fix it up, will you?"

"Do what I can, Jimmy, old-timer," said Pete. "But I've got a beauty in the arm and there's no time to lose. By the look of things the whole German army was down in that hole, and they're wise to us now because they're puttin' a regular barrage on the Graveyard."

A dozen Maxims were firing from the Boche lines and bullets zipped and whined and snapped over them. Pete ran down the trench a distance and gave a long shrill whistle. It was answered, and Jimmy was on the verge of being hysterical as he saw a dozen members of his platoon hurrying toward him. His experiences and his long thirst and hunger had weakened him.

The next day at noon, Jimmy was relaxed comfortably at a casualty clearing station, gazing at Pete, who was on the next stretcher.

"Talk about luck," he grinned. "You're one man I wanted to see."

"Yeah," said Pete, with a grin of his own. "I don't mind lookin' at you for a little bit. I had you down as missin', and killed and captured. Never in my born days did I get such a start as when I saw that crooked nose of yours under that Heinie cap you had on in the tunnel. And say, I'm still shakin' yet from the scare I got when that old grave caved in and let me down."

"Shoot it," begged Jimmy. "Don't stop till you tell me everything. I don't know a thing."

"There's not much to tell outside of what happened in that hole," returned Pete. "You've been recommended for a bunch of medals, on account of your exposin' the secret of them raids and so forth. Not a word now, I'm talkin'. It was me told them how you broke out of there and hollered till I come, and you're goin' to tell them the same story. There'll be a bunch of brass hats and all that here to quiz you, and you're to side with me, unless you want to see old Pete sent down to an army clink for duration. If they ever knew I was playin' ghost, when I was supposed to be on a carryin' party, I'd sure be in Dutch."

"But—how did you know I was there?" asked Jimmy. He would help Pete on any point, but he was baffled.

"Me—I didn't. And what's more I didn't intend gettin' down there with you, didn't want to. It just happened. You see, when you and that officer didn't get back, these old-timers all begin talkin' about you bein' the cause of it. They said you was too new and green and that likely you got scared and let the officer down. Well, I didn't know what happened, but I knew that you didn't get cold feet and I got hot thinkin' about it. That damn sergeant was the worst one, but they was all chewin' the fat, and when that blasted Canary thought he had a right to sing his song too, I got wild. I figured I'd stop his mouth anyhow, because I'd seen how scairt he was of the Graveyard. The rest made fun of him, but none of them hung around that place."

Pete subsided while an orderly brought them cigarettes and helped them light up. Then he grinned and went on.

"I had a look in one of them old houses back near the dump we went to, and I found an old trunk busted open and crammed full of Frog rig-outs. Right then I had a brain wave. I remembered them yarns about the Graveyard ghost and I took the best coat and pants and a top hat back with me. Then I found an old dickey for a shirt front and I was well set. When we went back I took the gear with me and I talked all the way about a guy seein' the ghost again, right beside the trench. Every one of them brave soldiers was watchin' the place when we went by."

Pete looked out of the window beside him. "There's a car parkin' now up at the other side of the ambulances," he said. "That'll be the captain and a bunch to talk to you. Mind you tell them how you got back there by yourself, at that gate rig they had, and hollered till I come."

"Yes, sure I will," promised Jimmy. He almost forgot the pain in his leg as he thought of medals and the talk there would be in billets and dugouts about him solving the secret of the Boche raids. "But hurry and tell me what happened, before they get here."

"Well, there was no word of you and I was mad enough to take chances, so I slipped away from the party when we started out and cut ahead to where I'd hid the coat and pants and things. I left my tin lid and rifle and gas mask there and put on them things and doctored my face. Then I hustled down to the Graveyard and waited. I was stood beside the trench where I could look down on them, and just as they come by some darn fool put up a flare close to our posts and the light showed me up. I did the only thing there was to do, because I was afraid some other guys might see me—I jumped down in the trench beside the carryin' party. You never saw such a bunch in your life. They run for their lives, and two or three of them was yellin' their heads off. Well, what did one poor tripe do but hop over the side and beat it? He was sort of headed by me, and he went that way. I got scared then for fear he'd get shot in the Graveyard. You know how Heinie kept shootin' at it all the time with his machine guns, so's none of us would pry around there and find his tunnel. So I hopped up after the lad and give a yell for him to come back. He just run faster and then he tripped and fell headlong into one of them deep craters where a shell had dug up an old grave. It must have been right on the edge of that tunnel the Heinies had extended from that old passage, for when I jumped down to get him out—he was just crumpled up in there makin' a whimperin' noise—the whole blamed thing caved in. There's a bunch of bones there, an old Frog that the rats had picked clean, and it was him was holdin' the rifle. I stepped on it when I jumped down and I guess that's how it drove the bayonet so heavy into that Heinie. There's another stiff had slipped down, a big ripe one, and it had sort of covered my lad in the corner. Anyhow, he'd sprained his ankle and couldn't get out in a hurry. He was still there when our bunch rushed the tunnel. They got him out."

"And it was him made them awful groans?" asked Jimmy, shivering as he thought of them. "You bet," said Pete. "I never saw a man so scared in all my life as he was."

"He must have been," said Jimmy. "I would have been if I'd been there, but I don't think I'd a beat it into the Graveyard. But that Canary chap is like a rabbit anyway."

Pete suddenly chuckled and looked over at his chum as a file of officers entered the ward.

"You guessed wrong," he whispered. "It wasn't the Canary that I chased. It was our famous hard-boiled sergeant."

Jimmy started and whistled softly. Then a blissful content stole over him as he watched the captain approach his stretcher.

The Three Dead Germans

Angus McPhee was a God-fearing Scot who went to war with his sense of respect in full marching order. Therefore it was not strange that his very soul should writhe when he made his first trip up the line in the gory swamps of the Somme. Dead men, in discoloured field grey and khaki, lay about, half-buried in the slime, and the calloused veterans of the battalion to which he had been drafted, the "White Gurkhas," often made use of them as shell hole parapets. Angus hid his aversion for a time and then rasped a broadside.

"Gi' ower wi' sic' devil's work," he shouted at Dan Hopper, a little wooden-faced man who was trying to pull a pair of boots off a dead officer. Dan had lost his own in a mud hole the night before and had been splashing about in long rubber waders which were difficult to navigate, so he paid small heed to Angus until a second shout proved that the Scot was in earnest.

"Gi' ower, I tell ye. Ye are worse than a German tae drag aboot the dead."

"What's bitin' you?" asked Dan, dropping the officer's leg. "I lost my boots and I'm goin' to take this pair. No sense leavin' them to spoil. Look at them."

Angus looked, and saw that the boots really were a prize worthwhile. They were high-topped and laced, nearly new and of a russet grain. "It makes nae difference aboot the boots," he retorted. "Ye are dishonorin' the dead an' I'll be reportin' ye tae the captain gin ye dinn gi' ower."

"You can report to Haig hisself, if you want," snapped Dan. A comrade had called jeeringly and the taunt was all Dan needed. "Wait till yer been with soldiers a couple of minutes before you start tootin' yer horn." He picked up the booted foot again, got a firmer hold, twisted and pulled. The boot came free, but the officer was dragged farther in the soft mud.

Angus emitted a mighty roar and leaped a shell hole to attack the disturber of the dead. His plunge landed him thigh deep in the boggy trench side, and that was all that saved Dan from the assault. Before the Scot could free himself and make a further advance others had intervened and then the sergeant himself came along, a war-worn, hard-boiled South African veteran. "What in blazes is wrong here?" he demanded. "Who's doin' all the shoutin'?"

"Tis this mon here," raged Angus. "He's been pullin' wi' this dead officer something awfu', disgracefu', and I hope ye see him punished."

"What is it, Dan?" said the sergeant. "Gettin' yerself a pair of boots? Lost yours in that hole on the right, didn't you? Well, go right ahead and get this pair you're after. That guy don't want them any longer and I'll bet he'd be glad to lend them." Then he turned to Angus. "Keep that porridge mouth of yours closed till someone asks you to open it," He said harshly. "If you get nothin' moren' dead men to worry over, you're goin' to be—lucky."

Angus smothered his anger and went on with his work, but he seethed inwardly the entire trip. For everywhere he went he saw the bodies of friend and foe lying where they had fallen, or else rudely rolled into support for muddy defenses. Occasionally there were dismembered parts tossed about great shell craters, bodies that had been torn and hurled from place to place. Never once did he see a corpse receive the reverence that he judged it should, and he was certain, above all things, that Dan Hopper was as unprincipled as a savage. Dan was a machine gunner, and his Lewis gun was his sweetheart. He kept it clean at all costs, and the little man was one of the best in hitting his target. He never spoke to Angus again during the trip, though the Scotchman came near taking the offensive again when he saw Dan calmly strip back the tunic of a dead man and tear away most of his shirt, as cleaning rags for his gun.

Some months later the battalion was out for rest in a village near Mount St. Eloi. Angus had developed into a first-class soldier and had transferred to the scouts, partly because he had a liking for the work, and partly to escape Dan and a few of his ilk who on all occasions treated the dead in a very casual manner. They did nothing that drew the resentment of the sergeant or platoon officer, but simply treated every corpse as but an ordinary feature of the battleground.

They would step over a dead man every time sooner than walk around him, would search his pockets for money, would bury him, after nightfall, back of the parados, without a sign of emotion. Such treatment roused Angus every time he saw it. Then came the night of his unexpected acquaintance with Dan Hopper.

Angus was at one of the little French homes seeking a plate of eggs and chips. Being a true Scot, he was alone on his quest, not wishing to bear the expense of treating a friend who might be broke, and had ill-luck in locating a "feeding place" until he knocked at the door of Tommy Jean. "Tommy" Jean was a widow who lived in three rooms with a swarm of small children. None of the soldiers billeted in that area ever knew how she managed to keep soul and body together, nor how many of the little tots were refugees she had taken under her wing. She looked up at Angus and shook her head to all his queries, for she never served food or sold anything, and then, seeing his badges, pulled him into the house and poured forth a deluge of questions in broken French and English. She apparently wanted to know about "'Opper, ze wood face man, an' Ted, an' ze corporal."

A good fire was going in the pot-bellied French stove that heated the room and Angus made his way to a seat beside it, and there sat while the children ringed about him, staring gravely. Finally, a boy more bold than the others, put forth his hand. "Chocolay—biskeet?" he piped hungrily. "Bon soldat."

Angus paid no heed, so the inquiry was repeated. Then "Tommy" Jean tried to hush the child, though she was plainly puzzled herself by the Scotchman's actions. "What is it ye say?" he asked, as he saw that they all were watching him expectantly. "I dinna ken yer language."

Before the widow could make reply the door was opened without more than a warning knock and a quartet of "White Gurkhas" filed in. Dan Hopper was leading and behind him crowded Corporal Jack, Ted Brown, a runner, and Jerry Binks, an Irish bomber. Each man was laden with bundles and at sight of them the brood of children gave a wild shriek and rushed. "'Opper—'Opper," they yelled. "Ted—Corporal Jerry."

Such a confusion, such kissing, such smiles on all faces, such a chattering. Then the newcomers saw Angus. They stared at him, then stared at each other. They looked at the children, and the corporal suddenly spoke in rapid French. "Tommy" Jean answered him quickly, nodding towards Angus as she spoke.

The Scotchman was baffled. He could not comprehend the situation, but as he had been first in, and wanted his eggs and chips, he did not propose to relinquish his seat of vantage by the stove. Yet, as he watched proceedings, he began to realize that he had not entered a "feeding place." Dan and his pals were dividing treats among the children. They had chocolate and biscuits, canned goods, and army rations. Several pairs of stockings and some warm underclothing denoted that some of the visitors had had parcels from home. "Tommy" Jean, watching, let tears flow unashamed, and Angus began to realize what was going on. These mates of his, these uncouth, seemingly heartless men, were giving practically all their meagre money would allow them to this family of refugees, and from the way it was being received he knew that there had been many previous visits. A little girl, happy with a packet of YMCA biscuits, unwittingly blundered against him and snuggled to his knees as she ate. Then the boy who had asked for "Chocolay—biskeet," saw her. He caught her by the arm, crying some warning out of a mouth stuffed with candy, and the girl sprang away from the Scot as if he were unclean. It was more than Angus could bear, and in some way he knew he had made a mistake. He stood up.

"Dan," he said in a softer voice than he generally used, "I see ye know this place. I cam' juist seekin' a plate o' chips, but dinna care aboot them ower much. I'll be going on, for the bairns are timid, but if ye'll tak' this bit o' siller an' use it for them as ye see fit I'll be obleeged to ye."

Dan, his poker face as passive as ever, looked questioningly at his mates, and received affirmative nods. "Thanks, Scotty," he said gruffly, accepting the money. "We've been helpin' these kids ever time we're out of the line."

That was all, but as Angus went back to his blankets in the hut he felt that he had possibly been mistaken in his condemnation of Dan. He could not dismiss the matter from his mind, and the next evening hung about the little French house until he saw the quartet go again to be greeted with a chorus of shrill cries. Another night and Angus was convinced he had judged too harshly, and then, the evening they were to march back to Neuville St. Vaast, he went to "Tommy" Jean himself and solemnly presented her with fifteen francs, every centime he had received on pay day.

"Tak' this bit," he said crisply. "'Tis money I hae nae use fer. 'Twill help ye while we're up yonder."

"Tommy" Jean looked at him wonderingly, then her face wreathed in smiles. "Merci—'dank you, bon soldat," she cried, and, darting close up to him like a wren on a branch, she planted a warm kiss on the Scotchman's leathery cheek. "Good luck—'string beans'—merci, soldat," she said tremulously, and Angus McPhee had strange emotions surging within him as he trudged "up the line" in the rear of ten platoon.

Came Vimy Ridge and Easter Monday, and only Dan Hopper remained of the quartet so welcome in the home of "Tommy" Jean. So it was that the "wood face" machine gunner came to Angus and invited him to the house. "I've a bit of ham and some eats I got from the headquarters cook," he said gruffly, "and if I go alone some of these umpty-umps will be thinkin' I'm up to no good. 'Tommy' Jean asks about you every time, so come and learn to talk to her yourself."

Angus went, and before the battalion went back to battle had his favourite seat in the children's corner and had whittled them many marvellous things to serve as toys. And it was when they returned to the trenches that the company noticed the comradeship of the dour Scot and Dan Hopper. The old timers told the new men, and they whiled hours on gas guard and post sentry discussing the problem, and had much more to talk about when the sergeant saw Dan carefully circumvent a dead man instead of stepping over him. After that the little Lewis gunner never disturbed a corpse. Twice he moved to a new gun position so as to avoid shooting over one.

In July they were in the line at the head of Napoo Valley, and Dan's post was opposite the "three dead Germans." It was a point where the war had raged exceedingly bitter and No Man's Land was a fetid scar in the wilderness. The land was low at the mouth of the valley and three great scummy shell holes near the Hun lines grew myriads of flies and gave forth foul odours. At dawn a mist usually hovered over this boggy part, partially obscuring the wreckage of a part of the Hun front trench that had been abandoned. This line had been a corner, bending out in a sharp salient towards the three craters, but an hour of heavy shelling had completely demolished it, leaving only stubs and wire ends to mark where the barricade had been, and but a few mangled sandbags to tell of the German parapet. Yet, one of the freaks of war, a Hun post that had existed in the very apex of the salient, had remained practically undisturbed. Its parapet had been swept away, leaving the Maxim machine gun bare to view, and, grouped behind it, as natural as though they were alive, were three dead German gunners. Evidently they had been killed by concussion and, rigid in death and partly held by the wreckage about them, they had remained upright. So realistic did they appear that Dan loosed part of a pan at them before he saw that the bodies merely quivered with the impact of the bullets. Then Angus came hurrying along the trench to him. "Dinna do it, Dan," he said quietly. "I hae juist learned that they Germans hae been there ower a week. Nae ither but their kind would leave them there."

"I'll not shoot them much," said Dan, after a long survey, "but they make a corking good ranging mark for settin' up the gun in the mornin.'"

"Ay, they maybe dae that," said Angus, "but ye'll no be forgetting, Dan, that they be dead men."

That was all he said, and his voice was gentle as he said it, but Dan did not fire on the trio again, though he ranged his shots as near them as he could without hitting them.

That night Angus led a patrol very near the abandoned salient trench and explored the ground thoroughly. He discovered that owing to the unprotected part of low ground the Germans had never built a very strong defense to their new position. The wire was but a makeshift affair that could easily be swept aside. He reported this to Captain Mack, and the information was joyously received.

"By George, we're in luck," said the captain. "Brigade has been hinting at us getting them a prisoner. I'll take a gang over and have a go at Heinie myself, and that's just the point. Every morning there's a mist hanging over that low ground. We'd get right over before they saw us, and we'll use a box barrage to keep off reinforcements."

Angus had little to say. He had his doubts about the captain's success as a leader of raids. Captain Mack was a splendid officer, as far as attending to the needs of his men went, but as a raiding leader he had never been tried, and when he insisted that the artillery practise their box barrage a wee bit to assure him that they had the correct range, Angus made a stubborn protest. "Ye are giving they Germans warning ye are coming," he argued. "Never fire a shot till ye are going over." But he was over-ruled, and at evening, just before dark, a sprinkling of shells were placed in a perfect "box" about the area to be raided.

The Scotchman served an hour on listening post, then was relieved, but could not rest. He went to his sergeant and suggested a small patrol. "We can gae ower by the craters and hae a look aboot," he said. "We can see if they Germans hae suspeecions or no."

The sergeant gave consent.

Angus led his three men across no man's land and then worked down toward the ruined trench. They did not see or hear anything unusual and were turned on their way back when they encountered a German patrol. There was a hectic moment of Mills grenades and potato masher bombs, pistol shots, and running feet. Then flares soared up from both sides and several machine guns became delirious. When all had quieted the three men of the Scotchman's patrol crept into the trench of the White Gurkhas and reported. "Angus was hit in our little scrap," they said. "He said he would crawl direct across and go right to the RAP. He told us to tell you that everything looked Jake. We worked away down left again and come in the same way as we went out."

The sergeant cursed long and fluently. None but new men would have let a wounded comrade try to cross No Man's Land alone. He himself went out, with another, and searched an hour, but they found no trace of Angus. Then came orders to make ready for the raiding party.

Angus, with a bullet in his thigh, found crawling more difficult than he had expected. Then, in the exchange of firing that followed, a bullet struck a glancing blow on the top of his head. His steel hat saved him, but the wallop muddled his sense and he crawled in a circle until he was completely exhausted. After a long rest he thought he discerned a parapet and made his way toward it. He wormed through wire and over sandbags, then huddled and lay still a long time. He had heard distinctly German voices.

The Scotchman lay so long that when he attempted to move his thigh had stiffened so that every movement meant excruciating agony, and then the breaking light showed him where he was. He was directly behind the deserted trench and not far from the three dead Germans. A friendly crater yawned close by him and he slithered into it, for his only hope lay in rescue by the raiding party—and he was not ten yards from the new Hun trench.

After he had got his breath again and heard no alarm given, he peered over the rim of his hiding place, and got the most horrible surprise of his life. The three dead Germans had come to life!

There they were, grouped back of their Maxim, but the gun was clean, free of mud, and the cartridge belt was also ready for usage. Each man was as still as the dead men had been, but there was no mistaking their expectant crouch, the slight shift they made now and then to rest themselves.

Angus understood in a flash. The Germans had suspected something after the box barrage, and had prepared for a surprise. Knowing that this low bit was their weakest point, they had removed the dead men in the night and placed a live trio in the position. They would not be recognized until the mist had cleared from the craters, and by that time no raid could be "pulled." Angus thought of Captain Mack, so boyishly confident, and could picture him leading his wild gang in the rush across. What a slaughter it would be for the gunners at the Maxim.

There was nothing Angus could do. He had lost his revolver and could not hope to wave a warning before he would be shot down by a sentry. He trembled in his torture of suspense, was suddenly aware that the gloom had lightened, that it was within minutes of zero hour, and perspiration beaded his gaunt features. He listened for the "pop" of the flare pistol that was to signal for the barrage, and wondered if he should chance all on an attempted warning or not.

Then everything happened.

He saw the flare soar, saw the Hun gunners tauten, and heard the sharp tap-tap-tap of Dan Hopper's gun. It was the quick bark of his Lewis that was always heard as the little gunner took his post, his ranging shots, and as they came the trio of gunners at the Maxim simply collapsed as one man. They wavered drunkenly for a moment and then sank from view, one clawing frantically for support and upsetting the gun. The next instant the barrage descended, Captain Mack and his boys came charging through the mist, bombs smashed, rifles rattled, shouts and cheers co-mingled with guttural cries of "Kamerad! Kamerad!" And in ten minutes Angus McPhee was safe in his own trench.

A stretcher-bearer worked to ease his pain and gave sharp orders to take the wounded man right on. But Angus protested.

"Calm yersel' a meenute, mon," he called. "Tell Dan I want him."

Dan came, his "wood face" somewhat shameful. "I thought you had gone down to the RAP, Angus," he said quickly, "or I wouldn't have fired into those chaps. I won't do it again, and anyway they tumbled over this time. It's not that I want to hit them, but it was just a good ranging point."

"Dan," said Angus softly, "dinna mind a' a sour body like mysel' barks aboot. I can mak' mistakes, and hae done. Juist remember me last wur-rds tae ye is that a bullet wi' never hurt a deid mon."

Priscilla's Private

Priscilla could not speak when they left the theatre. She clung to Doggy's arm and followed him blindly to his car, and they were halfway home before he ventured to break the silence. "Good show, that," he commented. "Worth the price all right."

Priscilla shuddered. "The price!" she exclaimed tragically. "Don't Doggy, please don't. You—you don't understand."

He was quiet until they reached her house and then he spoke in a humble tone. "Would you rather I didn't come in tonight?" he queried softly.

Priscilla nodded, and stroked his arm with her gloved hand. "You're a dear, Doggy," she murmured. "You're so considerate of me."

Then she went into the house. Her father, J. Thomas Perley, dealer in rugs, a rotund little man, sat in his big leather chair before the fire, his hands crossed on his round stomach, his eyes half-closed, like a Chinese mandarin. He looked up at her.

"Where's Doggy?" he asked mildly. "How did you like 'Seven Days Leave'?"

"He went home," she answered tonelessly.

"That so. How's the show? Pretty good, isn't it?" He rubbed the back of one hand with the palm of the other.

Priscilla did not answer him. Her father was so—so vulgarly materialistic. She went to her room and after putting away her coat and hat sat at her dressing table and feasted her eyes on a small photo in a silver frame. It was the picture of a soldier, a private in the ranks, yet the cheap likeness epitomized to her the flower of Canadian chivalry. She worshipped the man who looked back at her from under the peak of an ordinary forage cap.

Every night before she retired Priscilla gazed at that photo; every morning as she brushed her hair she smiled at her gallant soldier. For twelve long years he had been a part of her existence, though their meeting, acquaintance, and parting had been engulfed in thirty noisy minutes at Union Station.

One paused when one met Priscilla. She was really beautiful; a chiselled blond beauty with delicate features and perfect skin; and most of all one noticed the romantic dreaminess that swam in her eyes. A thirst for romance had always been hers, had made her early one of those persons who live inner lives, and when the war came she was in an ecstasy. She looked for a brave, fresh-souled crusader who would go forth to battle as her champion.

The bands playing, the rousing parades, the fluttering flags that coloured the city, thrilled her beyond words, yet she was disappointed. She joined a band of patriotic workers devoted to entertaining the soldiers and discovered that the lads in khaki were but a plebeian herd, and she had always been fiercely anxious to divide herself from the common people. Romance, she knew, could never have birth in a drab factory or smelly farm. Then came the Adventure.

It was an evening in the early summer of '16. A troop train was leaving the city and the Patriotic Workers were serving cocoa and chocolate to the soldiers. The warm dusk had let loose the secret lure of June and Priscilla had felt a feverish thrill ripple and quiver through her as she saw a tall, lithe figure, full of grace and power, come swiftly to her as if her longing had become vocal.

"I beg your pardon," said the soldier, "but is your..."

It seemed but a case of mistaken identity yet Priscilla was sure that it was a meeting ordered by destiny. Her cheeks had throbbed and her breath had come fast. Then the band beside the train had crashed out music that drowned their voices and made it necessary for them to move closer together. Priscilla had lived years in those precious moments; she found her cavalier. He was tall and courteous, handsome and faintly smiling, and he possessed a quality of manliness that set her veins on fire. He was so gentle, so knightly, so romantic. There seemed at once a psychic bond between them, and Priscilla had suddenly realized that words were superfluous; all that either would say the other guessed; the unasked questions, the unspoken answers, there was no need to voice them. When the train pulled out amid a thunderous cheering she knew all she wanted to know; she had found a mate of her kindred and nothing else in the world mattered.

Priscilla gave a little sob as she rose and began to make ready for bed. "Seven Days Leave" had been so poignantly realistic. It was so easy to see again that tall, strong figure in the dusk. She could feel her senses rioting with the remembrance of strong, warm arms around her during that one unforgettable moment of sweet caress, the remembrance of the way his hand had slipped into hers at parting, squeezing it, while a warm flood seemed to surge from it into her heart.

She sobbed again before she turned out the light. Why had Fate been so cruel? Why had it to be that a careless maid would burn the card on which he had scribbled his address and regimental number and leave her with only her lover's name to treasure? Harold Roy Heathland—how aristocratic it sounded! She had known instinctively that he was a gentleman despite his rank.

The thought of money was inseparable from him; ease, culture, travel, privilege, spoke from every angle of his assured poise. And the faint condescension in his tone as he answered a bony, bowlegged sergeant who had attempted to hustle him back to the cars had been a final stamp of approval. The non-com had appeared completely bewildered.

Priscilla could not sleep for a long time. After she had controlled the emotions aroused at the theatre her thoughts turned to Imogene Farrel. Imogene had been her playmate in youth and had always been her rival in romance. And Imogene's mother had fought fierce duels with the House of Perley for social supremacy on Crescent Heights. Imogene was a willowy creature with a lovely brow and a liverish skin, and she had been an enthusiastic member of the Patriotic Workers. She had also captured the attentions of a khaki crusader, though her knight was harnessed in a Sam Browne, the only stipulation that her mother insisted on when the game began.

The lieutenant had been a dashing dresser, blue of eye and red of hair, with a breathless way of looking at a girl, and he had been very kind to the crushed, bewildered, and heartbroken Priscilla who had just discovered that the key to her knight's castle had been destroyed.

In fact, he had been so sympathetic that Imogene's mother, an old dame with a curving nose and a mouth for spilling bad news, had intimated to him in an intimate way that Priscilla most certainly should have been an actress—she had so much talent—and that her kind usually left their husbands or went in for bootlegging.

Mrs. Perley somehow suspicioned the confidence and at a special tea divulged that the Farrels were nice people, but that she would be extremely sorry for the unfortunate who became entangled in a matrimonial alliance with Imogene. There were, she imparted, so many family scandals that would be like tentacles, reaching out from dark corners as soon as a domestic career was begun. Mrs. Perley was grey-haired and rather gaunt. She could smile sweetly or become acid-faced, as the situation demanded, and she smiled as she breathed that in her youth her conscience would never have permitted her such amorous contacts as those in which Imogene indulged.

After absorbing all this information the lieutenant was filled to overflowing and he spilled some of it on his next visit to the Farrel stronghold, whereupon a slice of war more bitter than that which raged in the Ypres Salient was inaugurated at Crescent Heights. There were verbal barrages at close range and subtle mines were laid under family traditions. Armistice found them with battle honours about even—and the gay subaltern safely married in London.

Month had succeeded month with agonizing slowness, but no tall cavalier in general's regalia sought his lost lady in Toronto. There were no messages for Priscilla in the "personal" columns, and no inquiries were made regarding the long-defunct Patriotic Workers Association. A year passed and Priscilla pined unceasingly. She had set her heart on one of those military weddings, had pictured herself and her gallant champion passing under crossed swords held by his brother officers.

Priscilla recalled, before she slept, all that had happened afterward. The enemies had abandoned open hostilities and were, to a certain extent, friends again. But she knew that the hatchet was only temporarily buried, and that Imogene had sworn that she would some day pull a coup de grace that would leave Priscilla in languishing sorrow. Now Imogene had gone to Ottawa for an extended visit and it was hinted that she was interested in a member of the Records Staff. Was she trying to trace, locate, and of course appropriate, Priscilla's gentlemanly private?

Imogene was a persistent creature, Priscilla knew, and would go to any length to achieve her purpose, and gradually, before she could get to sleep, a cold fear gripped her like the folds of a snake. Surely Imogene had never remained single all the years after the war without some definite aim in view. Priscilla decided, as she tried to answer the suggestions that tore at her heart, that in the morning she would call Doggy.

Doggy was her mainstay. He was a faithful, brown-eyed follower, rugged and dependable as a mastiff, not handsome in any sense of the word, but a useful and passable escort and a comfort in any trouble. He had two handicaps that barred him from consideration as a life partner: First, he had not an atom of romance in his makeup; he was crudely matter-of-fact and there was no hope of his ever changing; and secondly, his name was Higgins, Henry Rupert Higgins, and Priscilla positively could not think of assuming such a surname.

Doggy had been a little difficult at first, until she had told him about her private; since then he had seemed content just to be her companion. Best of all, he had clashed with Mrs. Farrel and so had been inoculated against Imogene's deceitful charms. No, she couldn't think of marrying Doggy, but he was so useful, and one knew, instinctively, that when the time came he would abdicate generously, without heroics.

She called him in the morning. Her voice was husky. "Doggy," she implored. "Come right over. I've had a dream."

"A dream! A—a dream?" he questioned. "You're not joshing me, are you? This is my busy morning." Doggy was in the insurance business, and doing well.

"Doggy—come!" Priscilla's voice was tragic. Doggy came.

"I had an awful dream," she told him, her lips pale and drawn as she faced him in hasty deshabille. "Harold was calling me to come to him, and I couldn't answer. Oh, Doggy," she made a soft little moan and allowed him to soothe her. "I've got to find him. I know that he's looking for me. Won't you help me?"

"You bet," said Doggy, after a look at his watch. "What'll we do this morning?"

"You don't understand, dear," she said patiently, "how difficult it is. I only saw him half an hour and all he knows is that my first name is Priscilla. You see I told him I would explain all the rest when I wrote, and then the ma-maid....Doggy, what can I do?"

"Write to Ottawa and get in touch with some of his battalion," said Doggy briskly, flipping forth a notebook from sheer force of habit. "Then ask about a Heathland on their roll. You could find out..."

"I can't," she wailed. "I didn't—I don't know what battalion he was with, maybe it was the artillery. I—it was so short a time...and he looked so wonderful, Doggy, and that's all I know." She gave a tiny sob. "He wouldn't be with them long anyway," she went on, sniffing. "He'd be an adjutant or a general or something. I know he would, he had such a figure, and his profile was marvellous."

It was hard to make things clear to Doggy, he asked so many questions about silly details, but she was kind to him. Two days passed and she grew pale and thin. She stood before the mirror and viewed critically her pallid but bewitching beauty, and decided that she needed an excursion downtown. For two nights her worries had denied her the merciful anodyne of sleep. She had dreamed twice, though, of finding her princely lover, and she had had a nightmare in which Imogene had let Heathland marry her and had then tamed him like a poodle.

It was Doggy who proposed that they visit the Vetcraft display downtown, and Priscilla was grateful to him. Doggy was, in a way, sensitive about matters pertaining to the veterans. A finger lost in boyhood, the one needed in wartime to press a rifle trigger, had prevented him from enlisting, though he had tried.

In the third row, next the exhibits of woodcraft, they inspected novelties bed patients had made—and it was there that Priscilla grew hysterical. There were tea mats and dainty things made of bead work, dainty squares and oblongs and cunning patterns, and one of a delicate green shade seemed to rise up to meet her. She stared at it, and clutched Doggy. "Look!" she gasped. "I knew it—my dream—see—he's—get it, buy it. Ask the man."

Doggy looked. Across an intricate maple leaf scroll careful letters spelled one word: "Priscilla." He turned to find the attendant.

The man who came was anxious to please, and after Priscilla had pleaded with him, with her lovely face upturned to his, he promised to move mountains, if need be, in order to discover the maker of the bead mat. Then Doggy took her home.

She was radiant as she bade him goodnight. All her hopes and dreams were returning like a sunrise, and it was doubly sweet to let her mind tell like a rosary its memories of that star-like evening at Union Station. She made plans before she could go to sleep. There would be a smart suburban house, with a maid's room on the third floor, a sun porch, and a double garage. She would have a Chinese rug for the living room—her father could make it a wedding gift—and special shrubbery for the lawn. And Mrs. Farrel would be invited to the reception, it would be such an opportunity to snub her, and....

Priscilla sat up in bed and stared into the darkness as if a horrible specter had entered her room, and in truth one had. Working beads... a bed! Oh—oh—oh! Her tall romantic cavalier, so full of grace and power, helpless in a hospital bed. It could not be, it must not be!

A wan and tearful Priscilla called Doggy in the morning, but before she could spread her fears he had thrilled her with fresh information. "I'm just back from that Vetshop," he boomed. "The chap there has found out about that bead work. It was special stuff from down east."

"Down east—where?" She flung the words at him. "Away down in New Brunswick."

A short hesitation, then she spoke softly. "Doggy, will you go down there with me?"

She could hear him gasp. "Down—down there? Say, why don't you write first and find out if..."

"Will you go or not, Doggy?" she asked again, and she made her voice sound as final as possible.

"What—hold on, Priscilla. Why—er—yes, I'll go."

"You're a dear," she cooed. "You don't understand, but I do. We'll start tomorrow and it won't take long." Then she hung up the receiver.

Doggy was ready according to schedule. It was a sharp test, a strain on his loyalty, but he responded nobly and did not voice a regret as he was carried farther and farther from his business. Priscilla's cheeks grew pink as she studied a timetable. It would be noon when they reached their destination, and there should be no delay in reaching the hospital.

She tried to talk to Doggy, to get interested in the places they were passing, to do anything to relieve her of an awful premonition that she would find her knight mutilated and crippled, and her only consolation was the fact that she had never read of a general losing a leg or getting a dent in his forehead.

With every mile she grew more excited. There had been times when she even practised facial expressions in preparation for their meeting and in four hours she would be in his arms. She was sure of him, so sure, and she had so often pictured this great day, keeping the vision apart from all that was garish and superficial. She talked with Doggy to relieve the suspense.

"I feel as if I have known Harold all my life," she said, caressing the "Harold" with a soft inflection. "It was only half an hour we were together, but oh Doggy, there was such spontaneity."

He pointed to a fine herd of cows grazing in a pasture. "Looks prosperous down here," he commented.

"He was a poet," she went on as if she had not heard him. "I know he was, he had such an expression, and I am sure he can talk about the stars, that he knows them all. Doggy, he—he was divine."

Doggy grunted, and got their luggage off the carrier rack.

Priscilla could not eat after they arrived. She waited with martyr-like patience while Doggy supplied the wants of the inner man, and then they set forth for the hospital. There was a trying list of inquiries and then they were guided to the ward wherein the maker of tea mats had his bed. Priscilla paled, and asked Doggy to remain outside the door.

"Oh! Doggy!"

He plunged inside. There was that in her cry that urged him to desperate speed. Priscilla had almost collapsed. She was beside the bed of a little man with a wiry beard and a Cockney tongue.

"Sye, myte," he chirped to Doggy. "Wouldn't that can yer beans? The lidy thinks as 'ow I'm her lost boy till she sees me fice. 'Priscilla,' she pants. 'Where did yer git that nime?' Bless her heart, me mother's sister as works at Maida Vale, and a cousin in Epsom, and me brother 'Erbert's girl, the oldest one, all 'as it. I mykes them best wiv 'Polly,' coz yer can curl the y under, but I 'ates the nime. I 'ad a bit of fluff wiv that 'andle, and she let me dahn proper, she did."

"Doggy," sobbed Priscilla. "Take me away."

"Lumme," said the bead worker. "Wot do yer know abaht that?" Doggy slipped him a crisp bill and took Priscilla away.

At the hotel he tried valiantly to ease her grief but failed until he mentioned a visit to the veteran headquarters in the city. She dried her tears at once.

They found the office in an imposing building and there Priscilla completed her collapse. She really fainted and when she recovered consciousness Doggy was determinedly forcing brandy between her lips. "I put in a call for a doctor," he said. "You shouldn't have come on this trip."

Priscilla sat up and managed to smile faintly. "You don't understand, dear," she said gently. "I don't need a doctor. Tell him not to come. I just want that—that man." She pointed at the clerk who had met them. He was a bony, bowlegged fellow with one arm missing, and he bowed as she spoke.

"Glad to help you, miss," he said crisply. "Is it about pensions?"

Priscilla shuddered. "No—no, don't use that dreadful word," she begged. "I—I just want a man." They had removed her hat and her hair was in slight disorder.

The bowlegged man's eyebrows went up and he glanced inquiringly at Doggy, who frowned. "It's about an officer," he grunted.

"Oh, an officer," said the bowlegged one. "What's his name?"

"Harold Ray Heathland," said Priscilla with delicate precision. "I think he's a major or a brigadier or something. I don't know much about the army but I know he'd be away up in it."

"Hmmm," said the bowlegged man. "Heathland? Never heard of him, miss."

Priscilla was patient. "But you did," she said earnestly. "Perhaps you were offended when he—he wasn't nice to you when you were a sergeant at Union Station in Toronto, but you spoke to him. You must know him. I—I've got to find him." She went close up to the bowlegged man. "It means everything in the world to me," she said, and she touched his arm.

The bowlegged man gulped and got busy. He put down dates and asked descriptions—and got replies that dazed him. Priscilla was exact and eloquent. "The night," she said, "was mild and moist and one of those times when she felt that the stars were near. Many of the soldiers had looked nice in riding breeches but her man had towered above them all, such a striking figure, such a commanding personality, such..."

"I remember him, miss." The bowlegged man ducked from under the deluge. "He didn't go over with us, flat feet, I think it were, at Quebec, or maybe it was bunions. And now that you mention it, I seen him up north last summer. He's at Oldcastle—that's a town up there. You'd find him easy, it's not a big place."

"Oldcastle! At last! Doggy, my dream. You—you wouldn't understand, but I knew it. Thank you, my dear man. You've helped me so much more than you know." Priscilla put on her hat, and the pink was back in her cheeks again. Doggy shed a two-dollar bill on the clerk's desk and followed her to the elevator.

Oldcastle is not an imposing place and its pulpwood facilities are very prominent, but Priscilla viewed it like a promised land. She could hardly wait till Doggy scanned a telephone directory. He returned triumphant. "H. R. Heathland lives at 17 Buckingham Street," he said. "That must be him."

"It is," she quavered, and she clung tight to Doggy's arm. "I'm so excited. I—you wouldn't understand. You dear boy, do you know I've got my hope chest nearly full and all the linen is marked 'HRH' I knew all the time that distance would never keep him from me."

Doggy made no answer. He was getting change ready for the taxi driver.

Number seventeen caused Priscilla to pause slightly. She had expected an aristocratic residence in an exclusive district, and instead they were deposited before a rather dilapidated house with dull brown shades at the windows.

"There—there's some mistake," she murmured, but she went bravely to the door and rang the bell.

The remainder of the afternoon was a hideous blur for Priscilla.

A frowsy woman with darting venom in her deep-set black eyes opened the door. "Good day," she said. "What can I do for you?"

"I—I want to see a Mr. Heathland," said Priscilla. "Does he—ah—board here?"

The black eyes glittered. "He—ah—does," she said. "Are you sure you want to see him?"

"Oh, yes," said Priscilla. "Most certainly. I've come all the way from Toronto to find him, and I've been looking for him for years."

"Yeah?" said the frowsy lady. "Come in, won't you. He ain't here just now, but I'll send for him."

Priscilla went in, though she had a dreadful feeling within her, a sense of impending disaster as sudden and nefarious as a train wreck. Doggy also stepped inside, but the lady halted him. "Would you mind tellin' that taxi chap I want him?" she asked. "Catch him before he's gone."

Doggy moved obligingly.

Priscilla was seated in a fat armchair, like a portly dowager in plush. She saw a crimson-shaded lamp, a sagging sofa, and cheap bookends on a table pushing together a few offerings of Elinor Glyn and Ruby Ayres. She shuddered.

The frowsy woman returned. "And now, Miss," she rasped. "Let's hear your story. You're the fourth, if I haven't missed my count." There was vitriol in her speech.

"Fourth!" said Priscilla. "My story? I don't understand."

"I don't neither," retorted her challenger, "but I'm goin' to afore you leave this house. I've had enough of your kind chasin' my man."

"Your man!" gasped Priscilla. "It's Mr. Heathland I want to see."

"You'll see him right enough," came the grim response. "The game's up. Of all the brass I ever knowed, this has me beat. The other three telephoned from the drug store, but just because you're dolled up in city style you think you can bluff me. I'll show you..."

Priscilla struggled to her feet. "Don't," she implored. "There is a terrible mistake."

"There is," said the frowsy woman. "You made a slip this time because I've got a detective on the job. You try your bluff on him."

A thin, hatchet-faced man stepped into the room. Self-importance fairly oozed from him as he removed his hat with a flourish. He bowed to Priscilla. "What's your game, miss," he asked. "Alienated affections?" Then he added sharply. "You'd better take your seat again unless you want me to call the police."

Priscilla fell back into the plush chair. "Police!" she shuddered. "Oh, where's Doggy?"

She fought a faintness that threatened to engulf her, and the questions the hatchet-faced man poured from him rattled on her ears like rain on a tin roof. She did not comprehend one of them, and the frowsy woman seemed to be floating about the room like a great evil bird. Then, after an interval that seemed interminable, Doggy came in.

"I got another taxi," he said to Priscilla. "I thought you might want to go soon."

"The police will have a say about that," snapped the frowsy woman. "Here comes my lad hisself."

A tall, slightly haggard man in a cheap suit entered the house. He strode straight into the room and inquiry was written large on his rather well cut features. But he sagged back at sight of the group that confronted him and a grey devil of consternation harried his eyes.

"What's up?" he asked in a husky voice.

The frowsy woman pointed dramatically at Priscilla. "Her," she said. "Do you know her?"

The tall man peered at Priscilla in an impersonal way and not a trace of recognition flitted across his countenance. "No," he said in a bewildered manner. "I don't. Why?"

"She says that she come all the way from Toronto to find you and that she's been looking for you for years. Come on, who is she?"

"I never saw her before, honest I didn't, Mabel" said the tall man.

"There's a mistake, somewhere."

"That's what she said," came the harsh rejoiner. "Now look here, my lad. I've caught you three times and you know it. This time it's the police unless you talk up." She nodded toward the hatchet-faced man. "I've had this detective watching you for a month and if there's anything in this—this doll's story you're not usherin' no more in any picture palace, see."

Doggy suddenly intervened. He crossed the room and assisted Priscilla from her plush throne. "Come," he said quietly. "We've got the wrong address somehow."

But the frowsy woman barred the door. "Not so high and mighty, mister," she snapped. "Who are you? Do you travel together?"

"We do," said Doggy in a level tone, "but we don't usually land in places like this."

"You'll land in jail before night," came the hissing answer. "I know your kind wherever I see them."

"Just a minute, Mabel," said the tall man. "Where does she say she came from?" There was curiosity in his tone.

"Toronto," came the scornful answer, "and for all I know she's tellin' the truth. I been hard put to keep check on you since we was married, without tryin' to find out what you did before."

The tall man looked Priscilla in the eyes. "You're surely mistaken," he said politely. "I never lived in Toronto."

"It was at the train," said Priscilla, scarcely above a whisper. "The soldiers..." She could not say more and she was very white.

The door opened again, and she turned. A great, mustached, blue-coated, brass-buttoned policeman was standing at her elbow.

"What's all this?" he rumbled deep in his throat.

Everything spun about her, but she held to Doggy. Something in her clutch seemed to galvanize him and in one heartbeat he had dominated the room. As from far off, she heard his voice, crisp, incisive, authoritative, defying the detective, the frowsy woman, the policeman, all of them, and giving them chill warning of dire consequences which would follow any further attempts at humiliating "this lady."

She felt the fresh air in her face again and smelled the pulpwood, then she was at the hotel and Doggy was telephoning about the next train west. He hovered over her with anxious care, a faithful, brown-eyed guardian, and she still thrilled as she thought of the way he had routed her enemies at 17 Buckingham Street. Then she thought of her mother, and Mrs. Farrel, and Imogene. Wouldn't the Farrels, if they knew, sip the scandal like cream! She shuddered.

Doggy hurried to her. "That tall chap's got up here and he wants to see you," he whispered. "Will I let him come or crack him one?"

He had come, her tall cavalier! Perhaps he could explain…but did she want to know? She hesitated, then nodded. "Let him come," she said.

Harold Roy Heathland made a graceful obeisance as he approached. "I remember you now," he said softly. "It was in the moonlight outside of Union Station. There was music and the stars and…"

Priscilla had started up. She saw all at once that his hair was thin and that he had dandruff, that his trousers were baggy at the knees. Usher…a picture palace!

"I'm afraid," she said, in the most chilling manner at her command, "that you don't understand." And as she finished Doggy growled in his corner of the window.

They were on the train again and speeding home before she began to realize the extent of the catastrophe that had overtaken her. Doggy sat beside her, rugged and virile, watchful and careful. She gazed at him, and warmed to his faithful efficiency, and remembered suddenly his mention of a promotion; there had been so many other things to take her attention. Her mental picture of Mrs. Farrel began to fade. She leaned over and rested her head on Doggy's shoulder. "Doggy," she murmured. "Dear old Doggy."

He looked down instantly, questioning with his brown eyes.

"Dear Doggy," she murmured again, and she could not say that he did not understand.

Three weeks later the Perleys held a brief family conference. J. Thomas Perley, dealer in rugs, sat in his big leather chair before the fire with his hands crossed on his round stomach. There had just appeared in the city papers the announcement of Priscilla's marriage, three weeks previous, to Henry Rupert Higgins, a coming leader in insurance circles, and J. Thomas was as perturbed as he dared to be.

Mrs. Perley explained, as much as she thought necessary, dwelling impressively on the perfidy of those who wore Sam Brownes. "And," she added, "Priscilla simply had to marry Henry,"—she never used Priscilla's pet name for him, or allowed J. Thomas the privilege—"in order to prevent scandal. That's reason enough for any marriage, and I don't want you ever to refer to that—that officer again. Henry is a dear boy, and he's doing well."

J. Thomas subsided.

"Mrs. Farrel called this afternoon, Priscilla," the head of the house continued. "She was so flustered over the announcement, and Imogene's liver has got worse and she's on a diet, and she got so despondent that she married one of those Interior clerks at Ottawa. I told Mrs. Farrel that probably you and Henry would be down to the city and would call on Imogene—if you could find her. She got so red then, and wanted to know why there was so much secrecy about you getting married, and I reminded her of how romantic you had always been, and that you wanted to be married at the oldest city in Canada, and she flared again and said it was remarkably sudden." Mrs. Perley smiled and satisfaction seeped into her voice. "So I showed her your hope chest and told her how long you were getting it ready and how all your linen was marked 'HRH and she was absolutely floundered. I never enjoyed anything so much before."

Priscilla gave her mother a dutiful peck on the cheek. "You darling mom," she cooed. "We're going for a drive along the lake, there's such a lovely moon you know."

There would be, and it would be so nice cuddled close to her warm and dependable Doggy, who was never garrulous, and who was such a good driver that one could dream and make-believe all they wanted to with him.

J. Thomas stirred. In his way he adored Priscilla. "Henry's a good mixer and he's got a good line," he said, rubbing the back of one hand with the palm of the other. He wasn't—er—cut to be a colonel, but…"

"…he'll make a perfectly splendid private," finished Priscilla as she gave him his kiss on his bald head.

Sunshine

The shorter of the two dim figures in the gloom of Post Three, on the Avion sector, stirred uneasily and shifted his equipment. "Gee, Calico," he muttered, "this place makes me feel creepy. Is it always so queer-like?"

The taller figure did not turn or move, and the voice that answered was surprisingly calm. "I don't like the feel of things myself, Izzard. No, it isn't always like this, it's often worse. Fritz isn't putting up flares now, so keep your ears and eyes open."

"Gee, Calico," the voice was almost a whine, "you don't suppose anything's goin' to happen, do you? I only come up this mornin' and here I am lookin' over the top. It isn't right, Calico."

There was no answer. Footsteps sounded close at hand and another pair of dim forms hurried around the bay. The challenge given and their reply were low spoken. "See anything?" queried one of the newcomers.

"No, sir," said Calico, "but I've noticed that Heinie hasn't sent up flares for a spell."

"Hmm. Keep a very sharp watch. A prisoner, captured on our right, said an attack was due in this sector. Sergeant," he turned to the form beside him, "send those Lewis gunners to this post. This is a weak point, I believe; so be as quick as you can."

A little later the sergeant returned with a Lewis gunner and his helper. They set up their weapon directly beside Izzard, and the new man became so nervous he could not keep still. "How close can the Germans get before you see them?" he whispered to the gunner.

The fellow bit off a chew of tobacco before answering, and despite the dark the short man was conscious of scrutiny.

"You just up?" The query was grunted rather than spoken.

"Yes, I—I am," stammered Izzard. "Just got up to the transports this mornin' and they sent me right on up here. It ain't fair, is it?"

"Hardly, soldier. New guys should be broke in a bit before shovin' them in with us gunners. It don't give us a fair chance."

"W-what do you mean? Ain't fair to you—?"

Izzard was silenced by a grip on the arm. Calico had leaned forward over the parapet and was peering intently into No Man's Land, his hand upraised for caution. The gunners froze into readiness and the short man felt his limbs trembling. *Phut*! It was the dull report of a flare pistol. A light streaked high and looped earthward. Followed by a perfect pandemonium of noise. The clatter of machine guns was interspersed with the bark of Lee Enfields and soon the *ping-ng* of Mills bombs added to the din. Izzard was conscious of the deafening rattle of the Lewis gun, but his strength oozed from him as red flashes spat angrily from just beyond their wire and he glimpsed a horde of crouching forms.

For a brief second he thought of flight, but refused as he remembered the sentence given for desertion at the front. Then a German bomb landed in the trench and its explosion roused him like a heavy boot, energetically applied. Calico was shooting as fast as he could work the bolt of his rifle and the Lewis gun hardly slackened its crackling performance. *Cra-ash*! Another bomb—so close that the odour of its explosives irritated Izzard's nostrils. He sneezed violently, and unconsciously stepped back and down into the trench. That act saved his life. A third bomb landed just where his rifle had been. The Lewis gun and its handlers were thrown in a heap.

Calico had leaped to a corner of the bay, yelling and pointing to a shelf in the parapet. Before Izzard recollected that it contained the emergency bomb store the tall man jumped back on the firestep and was performing rapid overhead movements. Simultaneously came the metallic *pin-nging* of Mills bombs. In the flash of their explosions Izzard glimpsed a flying "coal-scuttle" helmet, waving arms, a face, curiously white and distorted. Despairing cries cut through the uproar.

Calico's overhand heaving ceased and he pawed wildly for his rifle. Izzard, standing as if entranced, had seen it topple into the darkness of the trench. Stupidly, he watched his mate's frantic gestures. A shouting reached him. He swung about to discern the officer who had posted the gunners, saw him pointing with his revolver, saw it spurt flame just as a huge German appeared in the haze. Utterly bewildered by the rapidity of events, the new man tightened his pressure on the trigger of his rifle that he was clutching tightly, and was started out of his inaction as the weapon discharged and a second Hun pitched forward beside the first comer.

"You got him! Great work! They're stopped!" yelled the officer. "Help me with the Lewis gun."

Izzard, thrilled by his unexpected achievement, sprang to assist, and with Calico, who had recovered his rifle, giving directions, they planted the machine in place again. The two wounded gunners were hastily bandaged and sent out of the way.

"Now boys, keep steady," the officer's voice was shrill and jubilant. "You sure saved the line here. Listen—they're beat back on each side."

From right and left came sounds of lusty cheering and the firing slackened to even bursts from machine guns. Clearly the Royal Canadians had the situation in hand. "I'll send two more gunners as soon as I can," said the officer. "Fix up your post and get some more bombs." He hesitated. "Aren't you a new man?" he asked Izzard.

"Yes, sir. My first trip in." Izzard had recovered enough to steady his voice. "By Jove! Your first trip! We need men like you. I'll be back soon."

As he disappeared Izzard discovered that his fingers were wet and sticky. He held them closer and was horrified to smell warm blood. "Gee, Calico," he wailed. "I'm bleeding. Am I wounded?"

"No," snapped Calico. "You got that blood off the gun. Both them chaps were hit bad. That was a close call—on account of you doing nothing to help."

"I—I was waitin' for a shot," stammered Izzard.

"Can that stuff," ordered Calico. "Lucky for you your rifle went off or we'd be throwin' you over into a shell hole by now. Help me heave this Fritz over. You were frightened stiff—but it was your first scrap."

Izzard seized at the relenting. "Honest, Calico, I was just dizzy the way things was happenin'. Gee, I can't touch that dead guy. Can't you drag him up the trench? If you'll say nothing about me I'll give you five francs."

"I don't want your five francs," retorted Calico. "Give me a green envelope and we'll call it quits."

"Sure thing," Izzard's voice was eager. "What's them things for anyhow?"

"Our officers don't censor them," said Calico calmly as the exchange was made. "You know I'm engaged to Arabella, and I write every Friday. Now grab hold of this Heinie." The command was unmistakable.

Izzard took hold gingerly, grew desperate as the body yielded and surged against him, and lifted with all his might. The German was rolled over the top and out of the way. Then they manned the Lewis gun. The firing had now abated to the usual night shooting. Flares were soaring up from different areas. From farther up the trench came the sound of picks and shovels. The RCRs were repairing damages. The sergeant came into the bay accompanied by two men carrying Lewis gun ammunition. "There's the gun, boys," he said gruffly, then turned to Izzard. "Give these men a hand if anything happens," he ordered, "and get a shovel. Can't you see your parapet wants fixin'."

"I'll bet it does," said Izzard, as if just remembering. "We just rolled a big Heinie out there, and there's another one beside him. Close call for us, sergeant."

"Are you the new man that put up such a scrap?" There was a mixture of awe and unbelief in the question.

"Surest thing, Sarge. Me and Calico, that's my chum there, must have killed a dozen of them Huns. We had a bellyful of fightin'."

Nothing further was said about shovels and so Izzard was still relaxing when a runner arrived, panting heavily. "Is Private Izzard here?" he asked.

"Right here, my lad," said the short man. "What now?"

"I'm one of the company scouts," panted the fellow. "Was down at headquarters and they sent for me to go out on listening post. My partner got knocked out in the scrap. The officer said you had lots of guts and said you could go with me. Come on, we're late. Put these bombs in yer pocket."

Dry-lipped, feverish with a thousand apprehensions, Izzard hustled after the man, too dumbfounded to find excuse. They crawled out through a "lane" in the wire, avoided shell holes, wreckage, brick heaps, things that smelled, listened a time and crawled again. Izzard's heart palpitated furiously. His teeth chattered as if he were chilled.

"They think Heinie might try comin' over ag'in," wheezed his leader. "Keep your eyes peeled."

Izzard could hardly navigate the last few yards that led to a small crater, too shallow for comfortable cover. "Just lay quiet and watch," were the orders given by the scout.

Flares were rising regularly from the German trenches. Occasionally a machine stuttered or a rifle bullet whined over their heads. A rat rustled by. Izzard kept watch to the left, his partner to the right. Suddenly the new man's gaze was arrested by something bunched darkly, too far away to be defined. He tensed rigid. The thing had moved—was crawling toward him! In one heart beat absolute terror had robbed him of strength to speak or move. The figure crept closer, halting briefly, but never swerving in direction. Yard by yard it advanced, and was within feet of him before sheer desperation enabled him to rouse the scout with his elbow. Then he pointed at the unknown menace. "That you, Dicky?" came a low hiss.

"Yep, Jimmy, but by old split heels you're a lucky guy. I forgot to tell this new guy you was on patrol. Great stuff, partner. Some chaps would-a shot at anything that moved."

The figure crawled up beside them. "Hell, Dicky," it complained, "you'll have me killed yet. Why don't you use your thinker? Here," he extended a water bottle toward Izzard, "have a snort. You're a good head, Mac, for a new guy."

Izzard gulped eagerly. The rum restored him. "I figured you wasn't a Heinie," he whispered hoarsely. "Anyways I had a bead on you."

Both scouts chuckled. "Great stuff, partner," they murmured.

Morning came without further incident. At night the battalion was relieved. Back in billets rumours of the new man's conduct circulated freely and several of Izzard's platoon became friendly with him. Calico said nothing, and passed almost unnoticed. The new man accepted all compliments with ready grace, and made several references to his tall chum. When that individual put on his belt and announced that he was going to the "Y" to write a letter, Izzard did not go with him. He felt it an opportunity to explain their friendship.

"Him and me's from the same little burg," he announced with nonchalance. "We called him 'Calico' back there because he worked in a dry-goods shop. He's not a bad head, kind-a slow and all that, but quite decent if you take him right. I'm goin' to kind-a look after him when we're in the line."

There was a chorus of approval and only one dissenting voice. A rough-throated, grizzled veteran spat his quid at the stove and declared that he was "fed up with umpty-ump chatter." Izzard turned swiftly to see who dared, alone, to challenge his prestige. The veteran was too husky of build, had too much bulldog in his appearance; to risk a quarrel with him was not worthwhile. The sergeant entered, and walked straight to Izzard.

"I'm sorry," he said in a low voice, "but you're down for guard. We always use the new men."

"Guard! Me? What's the idea? I'm only with you three days. Who's in charge? I'll go see him."

"The RSM is the guy to see." The rough-voiced veteran spoke quickly, "that is, if you got the guts enough to talk to him."

"You're kind-a doubtin' it, eh?" Izzard shot back. "Where is this guy? I'll show you."

A dozen voices rose in protest: "Don't go near Sunshine." "Gad! He'd murder ya." "Don't be a fool, Mac. They're kiddin' ya." "You'll be shot at sunrise."

Defying them all, Izzard put on his belt and strode to the billet that bore the RSM's shingle. In a minute he was before RSM Bricker, commonly known as "Sunshine," the pride of the Royal Canadian Regiment. Sixteen years in His Majesty's forces was Sunshine's record. His uniform was immaculate, his back hollowed with Guard exactness. The business of the trenches he regarded as temporary evils—the regulations of the parade were his Bible.

With majestic condescension he heard Izzard's tale of his prowess, his wish to be relieved of guard duty, and then, in the manner so known and feared by the regiment, thundered forth the dictum that not only would the new man mount guard, but he should do so in all the glitter obtainable by brass polish.

"Shine your buttons, your brass, your bayonet, and your boots. Wrap your puttees carefully, and never come here again with such... fool whinings. Get out."

Izzard got. And not until he was at the door of his billet again did he realize that that awful voice had ceased. It seemed to follow him. A moment he stood, thinking. So this was the reward given the man who fought in the trenches, took his life in his hands! What was this dandified personage doing to win the war? Bah! He burst inside, slammed the door, and proclaimed his righteous indignation.

Hobnailed boots sounded heavily on the cobbled road that fronted the battered brick and sandbag headquarters of D Company, RCRs. There was not a light showing from any of the ruined buildings in the vicinity, and the only other evidences of human occupation, besides the sentry who pounded the cobblestones, were voices that issued from a blanketed doorway across the street. It was twelve o'clock and Izzard was on the beat. The guard mounting had been a fearful ordeal. The corporal of the guard had used scathing language when they lined up at the billet, and the sergeant had seconded his helper's opinions. Twice Sunshine had thrust his right hand in his right tunic pocket. When that individual thrust his hand in his pocket on an inspection it boded evil for someone. In his right-hand pocket Sunshine kept his notebook, and never did he trust to a sergeant's taking an offender's name.

Izzard had sanded and polished his bayonet until it rivalled the candle that shone in the guardroom, behind the blanketed doorway. He had passed the inspection, but fires of indignation simmered within. That honest men should be subjected to such abuse, that human energy should be wasted on brass and leather at such a world crisis, were the most atrocious examples of injustice he had known. Thus he pondered as he paced twenty-three steps to the right, turned smartly and paced twenty-three steps left.

He had framed, in his mind, a letter he should send to the mayor of his home town, exposing the livid wrongs that delayed victory, when over toward Villers au Bois he heard the droning of planes. Farther back, long beams of light shot into the sky, searchlights, and he knew that bombers were abroad. Then came a series of dull, heavy explosions, and he halted, staring apprehensively at the distant village. On the instant he was aware of a rushing noise somewhere above him, and glanced up. A dark shape seemed to hover right over him and then he heard a *phew-phew-phew*, a whistling threat, horribly personal. *Cra-a-ash*! A terrific explosion. Izzard was hurled to the ground. Brick and cobblestone thudded down in all directions. Choking dust and gas fumes drifted from the corner of the ruin that bordered the guardroom. Voices were calling. There were crisp commands and startled queries. Some leather-lunged authority ordered everyone to stay in his billet.

Izzard, moaning from fright and a badly bruised elbow, was helped to the guardroom and there huddled miserably. The sergeant explained that the aeroplane had gone and that it was only a chance bomb he had dropped. The new man revived considerably as the hour passed without the airman's returning, and then, all at once, grasped the reason of his being singled as a target. He gestured wildly in the candlelight.

"What did I tell you guys?" he shrilled. "This is what comes of this blasted shining. That Boche saw my bayonet in the moonlight. He was right low over the street and there I was like a bally target. I knew it—such foolery as shining a bayonet—I—I—" He grew incoherent.

"Dry up." "Stow it." "Give your jaw a rest." Brusque and unfriendly were the interruptions, but Izzard was not finished.

"Listen," he shouted, "they can't scare me into killing myself by such foolishness. As sure as you hear me I'll get even with Sunshine. It's murder—pure murder—this shining."

"You're through, umpty-ump," the rough-voiced veteran was speaking now. "You can rest your yap. Don't kid yourself that any Heinie will ever waste a bomb in your direction. But, say, if you can take a rise out-a old Sunshine you got my vote, and the gang's with you."

"Hear, hear!" The assent was a chorus.

After guard relief Calico had to listen to a reiteration of Izzard's vow, but he was not affected. It was Friday again and he had a green envelope. Composing an epistle to Arabella required a concentration that excluded other matters. Yet he took time solemnly to shake Izzard's hand and wish him luck.

Anything new spread like magic among the soldiers. The word that the new guy was out to "get" Sunshine spread during parade, and perhaps a rumour leaked through to the intended victim.

Perhaps it was fate guided the next events.

Izzard made his second trip into the line. Under Calico's steadying influence the experience was not so bad, and three days in supports, where only light working parties were used, rendered him almost cheerful. Then the battalion marched back to billets and on the first parade Sunshine assisted with the inspection. Like an inexorable pendulum he swung around to Izzard and pulled open one of his cartridge pouches. The clips were not as clean as they might be.

"Disgraceful—this is disgraceful!" bellowed Sunshine. "How dare you come on parade with dirty ammunition?"

At the words all of Izzard's acceptance of conditions vanished. His interior became a volcano and he saw red. He would not stand further persecution. "I never heard of shining bullets," he snarled loud enough to be heard. "Do we shine the bombs, too?"

"Silence!" roared the sergeant and Sunshine in unison.

The RSM's right hand shot into his pocket and jerked forth the fateful notebook. "Two charges," he grated. "Insubordination and dirty ammunition."

And at noon Izzard was paraded before the major. The result was inevitable, for the accused broke forth in scathing comment of the diabolical treatment awarded the men who came to save their country. As D Company fell in after absorbing their mulligan, word was passed around that the newcomer had lost his first round with Sunshine, and that the loser was engaged in digging a latrine under the watchful eye of the regimental police.

His sentence had been fourteen days "number one."

The night was misty black. On the far side of Vimy Ridge moved a phantom procession. It was a ration party from the transports of the RCRs, carrying up supplies to a point near Avion, where the battalion was entrenched and where they would meet ration crews from each of the companies. Sunshine was in charge. This blackest of nights was the date of an important brigade raid, and the rest of the transports were to act as escorts for the expected prisoners. Sharp at midnight a fifteen-minute barrage was to be laid on Avion and its outskirts, and then the famous Seventh Brigade, RCRs on the right, would swarm from their trenches and assault the German lines in front of the town. All the casualties and prisoners would be hustled to the rear, as the conquerors were only to hold the captured trenches until two o'clock. The object of the raid was to get prisoners, harass the Hun, and catch his counter attack with another barrage as they massed to re-take the line.

Every man in Sunshine's party bemoaned the trickery of fate that had placed Sunshine in charge on this particular night. They were certain that he would bungle the job, as he had rarely left the horse lines and dreaded shell fire. Nearest to the RSM was a soldier whose bitterness was so great that he could scarce restrain from murder. It was Izzard, staggering through the gloom with two petrol tins of water. During his confinement he had had ample time to reflect on his wrongs, and to centre his venom on the portly brasso king who had brought him his punishment. To an unsympathetic escort he had announced his willingness to give his life for his country, if necessary, in fair battle, but it was the blackest injustice to send him, unarmed, into danger under such a brainless bungler as Sunshine. And with every step nearer the trenches his resentment increased.

Only an occasional Very Light soared aloft. They made little impression on the murk of the night and the Avion front was very quiet. Each side was depending on its listening posts. The clammy blackness and the unusual quiet produced an eerie atmosphere. Izzard felt his scalp tighten as the guide, just ahead of Sunshine, gave warning that they were almost to their destination, the support line.

The party had come overland, following a path despite the darkness, but the uneven ground had proved a sore trial to Izzard. He had caught his toes on slight rises and had plunged heavily in the depressions. He stumbled for the hundredth time and weariness had its effect; the petrol tins came together with a resounding clang. Low comments from the rear were drowned by a bellow that shattered every precedent of the trenches. Sunshine's nerves were evidently very frayed.

"Stop that racket," he yelled at the top of voice. "Take that man's number."

Whiz-z-z ba-aang! *Cra-a-ash*! *Ba-a-ang*! Three rapid explosions. A clanging of other tins. Mingled voices and cursing. A thudding of feet as the party scattered. Sunshine yelling hysterical commands. *Whiz-z-z ba-a-ang*! *Cra-a-ash*! *Ba-a-ang*! Vivid flashes that split the dark. Fumes of high explosives and dislodged earth. Far-away voices. The rattle of machine guns, warming up. A few scattered rifle shots. *Whiz-z-z ba-a-ang*! *Cra-a-ash*! *Ba-a-ang*! The chance strafing of the Hun ceased as abruptly as it had begun, but pandemonium reigned in part of the Canadian line.

Izzard had been knocked off his feet by a collision with Sunshine at the first salvo. As he scrambled up a hand gripped his belt and the RSM's voice was in his ears. Came the second salvo and he was downed rudely as the brasso king dived for cover without releasing him. Then he was jerked to his feet again as Sunshine rushed after the sounds of running feet.

"Let me go," Izzard hissed, "or I'll crown you." His words had no effect.

Number three salvo arrived. This time Izzard ducked in unison with his captor and by a clever surge freed himself. Simultaneously a machine gun clattered in their rear. Izzard's brief tour in the line had not taught him that brigade machine guns were sometimes posted some distance back, and he was vastly bewildered. Instinctively he reached for Sunshine and fastened his fingers on a much-polished Sam Browne. In turn a hand reached him.

"Stay with me," gasped the cock of many parade grounds. "We are surrounded."

Amid the clattering fire it was easy to believe. Apparently guns were shooting at them from every side. Keeping hold of each other the pair ran as fast as the nature of the ground would permit—and fell headlong into a trench. When Izzard ceased seeing sparks he disentangled himself from Sunshine, who groaned feebly.

"Where are we?" The RSM's voice was very weak.

"We fell in a trench," said Izzard. "Stop making that noise."

After much whispered persuasion he got Sunshine to his feet. They must travel; the firing had slackened, but the suspense was horrible. Sunshine was hesitant, but Izzard dare not leave him. The company of this man he so hated was preferred to being alone, and at length they commenced a cautious advance along the trench. After what seemed a mile they brought up suddenly against a cross trench and some person unseen growled, "Halt! Who goes there?"

Joyfully Izzard elbowed Sunshine to one side. "It's me, Calico," he called in a low voice. "Whow! Pull in your bayonet. How did you get here and where are we?"

"Is that you, Izzard?" The voice held immeasurable wonder.

"Sure, it's me. We go lost on a ration party. Sunshine's here with me—I mean the RSM. He's in charge."

"I am," rasped a nervous voice beside Izzard, "and you are disrespectful. What is your number?"

"Nine million and ninety-nine." Izzard slipped forward and got Calico by the arm. "Let's beat it somewhere," he whispered, "and somebody'll crown him in the dark."

His suggestion was useless. As he spoke there was a hot breath on his cheek and a hand gripped his belt. "You men take me to a sergeant at once," came the shrill order. "You are liable to a court-martial for such talk."

Izzard felt Calico turn and he grasped his chum's equipment. He must not lose him in the utter darkness and by some hook or crook they must give Sunshine the slip. "You'll have to crawl here," came Calico's warning. "The trench was all blown in here this afternoon, and there's an old CT heads into it. The wire's down, so maybe we can crawl around in front."

Izzard was compelled to release his hold on his friend in order to scramble over the debris they encountered. The earth seemed upheaved in every direction. Three times they encountered tangled wire and stakes and circled the obstruction. Sunshine puffed like a porpoise. The night was still again, but the darkness was impenetrable. After an endless crawling Calico halted.

"There's something wrong," he whispered. "We'll have to go back, for I've missed the next post altogether, and we haven't crossed the CT."

"Where are we—I mean what trench did we leave?" Sunshine's sibilant whisper came like compressed air.

"The front line," said Calico. "It's D Company's right, and I was trying to get to the next post. We'll have to go back."

Izzard's knees relaxed and his breathing was difficult. The front line! He unarmed and an attack due at twelve o'clock. Cold sweat broke over him. "Any idea of the time, Calico?" he managed to ask.

"Must be after eleven," came the answer. "The show starts at twelve and you want to get out of this."

"But how?" The query was a plea.

"You two wait till I circle a bit. It can't be far to wire or something."

"No, you don't." Sunshine's voice was raised in instant alarm. "We'll go with you, and if you get me out before twelve I'll recommend you to the colonel." He was almost whining at the finish.

More fumbling and crawling. They went to the right, they crawled to the left. There were solitary rifle shots, there were gun flashes in the distance, but they had lost all sense of direction.

"There's an awful lot of shell holes," Izzard panted during a pause. "Can you tell anything by that?"

"I would say that some shells had exploded here sometime," the rejoinder was very calm.

"Shut up and keep moving." Sunshine's contribution was unnecessarily loud, and his voice trembled. Plainly he was losing control.

The next instant rough hands seized Izzard, and there were violent struggles in the dark. Grunts were mixed with guttural exclamations. Izzard was quickly subdued and then hustled through the night by ungentle hands and thrown into a trench. As he regained his feet he was knocked aside by another person assisted by rough helpers. Bruised in every part, he hadn't time to collect his thoughts before a third prisoner was tumbled down beside him. Then husky voices gave orders and a fine-pointed bayonet enabled him to understand that they were to follow a surly-toned guide along the trench. Izzard tried to squeeze by Sunshine, who had been third to arrive, so as to avoid the steel tickler, but the RSM blocked him. "Hustle, then, you granny," he squealed.

"This guy is pushing with his bayonet. Move up."

A brutal blow with a rifle butt knocked him dizzy, but the bayonet revived him. Dimly he understood that he must not talk. He stumbled along and then flinched mightily as Sunshine halted without warning. A trickle of light shone into the trench from beneath a lifted blanket and, in turn, he saw his fellow unfortunates descend a stairway that the light revealed. He followed them smartly, his guard still prodding from the rear. The dugout into which they descended was evidently a company headquarters. Three German officers sat by a table strewn with maps and papers. A telephone was at the elbow of the most important-looking of the three, a big man with a bristled mustache. A few orderlies occupied the background. Beyond was a table piled with junk, and several bunks.

There was a stir among the orderlies as the prisoners came into the light, and suppressed murmurs of "Englanders—swine." Izzard trembled in every limb. The man with the bristle mustache was glaring at them, and the others were equally hostile. The soldier who had followed the prisoners down saluted and grunted a rough jargon. Izzard stole a glance at his companions. Calico had a black eye and had lost his steel hat, but bore himself with his usual calm. Sunshine had transformed marvellously. He seemed to have shrunken in size, his uniform was dirty and torn, his features were haggard, and a deep scratch across his bald head still bled. The lord of inspections expressed misery in every line.

"To what regiment do you belong?" The question was asked in perfect English by him of the bristles.

Izzard looked at Sunshine. "Speak up," he whispered, "or they'll kill us sure."

Thwack! Izzard groaned as he straightened from a blow that almost felled him. "Be still, little swine," snarled Bristles.

"We—ah—belong to the Royal Canadians," gasped Sunshine.

"In the trenches how long has been the regiment?" Cold and merciless was the voice that questioned.

"Ah—three days—I think," came the answer.

"Think! You do not know?" The threat predominated.

"Ah—yes, I do. It is three days, I'm sure." Sunshine's voice trembled.

"To be relieved you are when?"

"Ah—tonight—I think."

"Think you are not to say, and for the last time I tell you," came the awful voice. "Who to relieve you was?"

"Ah—I think—that is, I do not know. It—ah—had not been arranged."

"So!" Tiny veins stood out on the forehead of the Prussian and he struck the table with his fist. "You to me would lie—listen...."

Every man did, but not to him. A crashing, ear-splitting roar drowned every other noise. The very earth trembled and the candles sputtered from the jarring. The roar increased and down the entrance came whiffs of high explosive gases. The officers at the table sprang up, hate livid in their faces, and from their facial contortions Izzard knew they were shouting orders. The soldier that had followed them down comprehended, for he saluted and departed swiftly, followed by all but two of the orderlies. Then Bristles seized the phone, listened, shook it vigorously, and cast it from him. Apparently the line had been severed. Turning to the other officers he jabbed at places on one of the maps on the table and bellowed until he was heard above the din outside. The two officers withdrew. Izzard ventured to turn his head to look at the others. A heavy cuff swung him about. Bristles motioned the remaining orderlies to guard the prisoners and his glance at Izzard was vitriolic as he yanked a Luger from its holster and laid it on the table.

Izzard forgot the sting of the blow that had spun him around and his legs could scarce support him. He was shivering with fear.

Cr-r-rump! A smashing shock directly overhead sent showers of dirt from the partly timbered ceiling. Two of the four candles on the table went out. A choking, noxious gas poured into the dugout. Bristles seized one of the candles and holding it high peered into a wooden, box-like arrangement in one corner. He seemed to sniff at it and then jumped back to his maps. *Cr-r-rump*! A second shock, doubly violent, piled a confusion of broken timbers and chalky earth down the dugout steps, and instantly the crashing roar outside died to a deep rumble. They were shut off from the trench—buried alive!

The table rocked with the explosion and each man swayed on his feet. One of the orderlies sprang to save the candles from being extinguished. Bristles started to his feet and the next few heartbeats were packed with action. Izzard was just aware of a low moaning sound when he saw Calico shift forward with cat-like agility and drive his fist like a piston rod. The blow landed squarely on the blocky jaw of Bristles and the German went down like a falling chimney. In the fraction of time that he was falling the pale ex-clerk snatched the Luger from his fingers. One of the orderlies had not failed in his vigilance and Izzard saw fire spurt from his revolver. He missed his man, however, and Calico shot in return. The orderly toppled and crumpled. The second guard seemed paralyzed by the rapidity of events and made no move until Calico shouted, "Hands up—surrender!"

"Kamarad! Kamarad!" came the answer, and both candles were pushed toward the ceiling.

"Hey—save them lights." Izzard had come alive to the situation. He secured the candles, picked up the revolver the live orderly had dropped, and wrenched another from the hand of the dead one. Just as Bristles began to stir Izzard detected the maker of the moaning sound. It was Sunshine, who had slumped against the wall of the dugout and was staring about him in perfect terror. Bristles came to life gradually, but when he became aware of the change in authority leaped up like a wounded tiger, and died fighting. Calico called for him to surrender and then shot with steady aim. The moans of Sunshine increased.

"Look here, you, stop that yowling." There was undeniable command in Izzard's words.

His mind had cleared rapidly from its paralysis of fear. He realized that their situation was hopeless, but was also impressed by the fact that he was armed and was allied with Calico. The fact that they were shut off from escape sunk into the short man's mind with startling result. In one flashing survey of circumstances he recognized the factor that had placed him in this predicament, and all his animosity and thirst for revenge welled to the fore. The ever-present fears that had burdened his existence, fears of consequences if he did not obey orders, were wiped out in a breath, and his face was lighted with unholy joy. Probably an hour would elapse before they began to smother. That hour should wipe out former humiliations.

"Any chance of getting out?" he asked Calico.

"Mighty little by the looks of that doorway," was the response, "but we'll make a try for it. Come on, Henie, and get busy at this mess."

Under Calico's directions and the persuasion of the automatic the German worked lustily at clearing the debris that blocked the exit.

Izzard watched proceedings a moment and then walked back to the littered table. Its load consisted of Canadian equipment, probably obtained on some raid, and the contents of a haversack were in view. Grimly he selected the principal asset of an RCR private—his shining gear. A button stick, a can of polish, a rag, and a brush were extracted. Then Izzard confronted Sunshine. The lessening of the tumult overhead and the defeat of his captors had restored the RSM somewhat, but his hands still trembled and fear lived in his eyes.

"Come over to the table," ordered Izzard. "I've got a job for you, Mister Sunshine, and you are going to do it."

A trace of Sunshine's customary arrogance returned.

"Are you insane?" he demanded. "You have been the chief cause of our being in this place. Be calm, man, be calm. What is your number?"

"Thirteen to you," flashed Izzard, his features a fiery red beneath their coat of dirt and chalk.

"Thirteen, you blasted turkey cock, the unluckiest number in the alphabet. Get busy, you hollow-backed shino freak. Grab that brush and button stick if you want to live another half hour. I'll give you polishing, blast you."

"Hello, over there—help!" shouted Sunshine as he backed away from the automatics Izzard held. Calico glanced at them.

"I'm going to make this lousy old safety-first do some shining if it's his last job on earth," Izzard called in tense tones.

The gravity of the hour could not be mistaken, but there was an unmistakable grin on Calico's placid countenance and unmistakable assent to Izzard's plan.

"Will you get busy, or do I have to shoot?" Determination rang in the words.

Sunshine started to reply, but his words were cut short by the bark of one of the revolvers that Izzard held. The shot was purely accidental. Izzard, in his excitement, had pressed too hard on the trigger, and it was fortunate for the RSM that the weapon was not well-aimed. The bullet sped close to Sunshine's bald head and buried itself in the wall. There was no further delay. The brasso king leaped for the tools Izzard indicated and brushed furiously at the first buckles within reach. His overseer was startled by the shot, but recovered quickly when he noted its effect. And then burst forth all the rancor in his bosom. In a scorching tirade he vented with all his hatred of the RCR in general, and of this tyrant especially, and in lurid adjectives described the utter folly of shining brass at the front.

Sunshine was plainly inexperienced at the shining game, but gained remarkable speed when Izzard purposely fired another shot over his head. Evidently convinced that he was trapped by a maniac the man who had bullied thousands polished like wildfire, and assented mechanical to Izzard's caustic remarks.

The Hun had cleared the foot of the stairway. The earth was handled easily but the crossed timbers were difficult, and finally wedged planks were encountered. The force of the explosion had driven them deep in the chalky soil and their release seemed impossible. Calico informed Izzard of their problem and got little response.

"I didn't think we could get out," said the hater of drill grounds, "but this air is all right yet. I'll have a look at them beams when I get through with this brasso monkey. We've found a lot more equipment in these bunks."

They had and, urged mercilessly by Izzard, the RSM did his best to shine the dull German buckles. Any time he glanced around he gazed directly into two dark tubes of indescribable menace, and the holder of them broke forth in fresh insult. Finally the equipment was finished.

"Come over here, now," shrilled Izzard, waving his revolvers. "Shine the buttons on this bristly sausage grinder."

It was the height of cruelty. Sunshine's abhorrence for dead men was common knowledge, but in the face of certain death the brasso king yielded. The picture of fear and aversion, he knelt and applied polish to the lustreless buttons of the dead Prussian officer. Beads of perspiration rolled down the cheeks of the man who had intimidated companies, and he no longer responded to Izzard's taunts. Calico halted after an examination of the dugout and witnessed the performance.

"A little of that goes a long way, Izzard," he drawled after a short time. "That'll do for the stiff, but you can try him on this live Kaiser."

Izzard looked around. The voice of his chum had assumed a strange authority. "Get up, you shiner," he snarled at his victim, "and try the buttons of this live Fritz."

The eye of the Hun bulged. He was plainly baffled by the happenings about him. Sunshine walked up to him and daubed polish on his drab buttons, then brushed with energy, and not till all had received attention did he slacken. Izzard, tiring of his sport, waved him to one side, and Sunshine sank in a corner, exhausted, his eyes holding the expression of a hunted animal.

"What's next?" asked Izzard. "I'll let Sunshine get his wind—before I start him all over again."

"I think we can get out," stated Calico. "That box-thing over there that the officer looked into is a ventilator of some kind and we've got lots of air. I found a Mills bomb among that junk the Heinies have stole off a stiff at night, that's the only way they could have got it, and I'm going to blow these planks out of the way. We'll get the earth from behind them a bit first."

"Why not let Sunshine have a chance at the shovel?" rasped Izzard. "They always hunt work for us when we're supposed to be resting."

Calico nodded and the short man sprang into action. "Get on your pins, Brasso," he snapped, "and freeze onto this shovel. Toot sweet."

Sunshine laboured manfully, and before he had satisfied his masters was coated with chalky grime.

"Stand back, now," said Calico, "and watch a Mills bomb do its part in the Great War."

He knew that the RSM had never become acquainted with such implements of destruction, and, as if fascinated, Sunshine watched every movement as the bomb was placed. "Now we'll pull the pin that holds the lever," Calico remarked, "and when that happens you want to be out of the way."

Everyone ducked with alacrity. *Cra-a-ash*! Black smoke billowed into the dugout and bits of shrapnel struck into the walls. A cartload of earth and splintered wood slid down. Simultaneously the sounds of firing overhead came sharp and loud.

"Jake-aloo," yelled Calico, "we've broke through. Wait till the smoke clears and I'll go up first. Then send that Heinie and Sunshine up to me."

Izzard conducted his end of the programme with all the austerity of an army general. A well-like cavity merged into a great crater that rimmed a remnant of the trench. The Mills bomb had merely broken the wall of earth that separated the stairway from the crater. The night was still black and machine guns were active at various points. Izzard fancied the entire front was in combat but Calico broke the illusion.

"They're not fighting," he stated, "but just shooting a bit before they retire. It's nearly two o'clock by this watch I took off that officer. We ought to get out of here."

"Sure," said Izzard, "but which way do we go?"

"That way, I think." Calico pointed vaguely in the gloom. "I'll take care of Von Kluck, and we'll call off the rough stuff on Sunshine." He lowered his voice and drew Izzard to one side, keeping hold of the German. "Look here," he murmured, "we've got to get back to the company and we're in wrong. Sunshine'll have us sent to Rousen for life."

"He'll not," hissed Izzard. "Leave him to me. He'll promise here and now never to report us—or he'll never go back. Get me?"

"Don't be a fool, Izzard," Calico's voice raised a trifle. "You can't kill a man for that."

The short man dug Calico with his elbow. "I'll shoot him like a dog if he doesn't promise," he said loudly.

Calico started, but Izzard turned slowly. He had felt rather than seen the RSM at his elbow. Swinging his guns around he snarled like a dog. "I want to shoot you, you brasso fool, but Calico says not to. But you'll promise not to report us or I'll put lead in you right now. You'll be 'killed in action' all right. Make up your mind toot sweet."

"I'll never report either of you," promised Sunshine fervently. "You are overstrung. Just get me back to headquarters." He spoke with sincerity and pleading.

Izzard faced about. "Go on, Calico, lead on," his voice was triumphant. "Everything's Jake."

They started, but the going was difficult, and when they heard voices Calico halted. "Better give Sunshine one of your guns," he called in a low voice. "No telling who's in front of us."

A faint "plunk" in the mud was barely audible.

"I've only got one," came Izzard's reply. "I lost the other one away back." The short man was not taking chances.

One hour later they arrived at the headquarters of D Company. Two hours later their exploits were known to every man in the RCR trenches, and held equal interest with reports of the raid, which had been a success. According to rumour the trio had captured a dugout full of Germans after a desperate hand-to-hand battle, killing all its occupants but one, and had then held the trench until time to retire. Calico had said little, but Sunshine's appearance and the presence of the Hun prisoner proved the tale. The colonel sent for the three and had Sunshine retell the story. At its close he shook hands with each one, complimenting them on their bravery, and informed Izzard he was no longer a prisoner, his sentence would be quashed as a reward for courageous conduct.

When the RCRs marched out to billets Izzard was the happiest he had been in France. He was now regarded as a hero, had got the best of Sunshine, and he had an infection on his right knee that was progressing nicely. A few more days of non-attention should ripen it up for a trip down the line. Sunshine appeared on parade, immaculate as ever, with a blue and white medal ribbon at his chest. He had been awarded the Military Cross. Then came the thunderbolt.

Izzard, with the picture of Sunshine in the dugout ever before him, had confidently informed the platoon that he would never again be detailed for obnoxious duties, nor "pulled" for a dirty rifle. His suggestions were mysterious, but such as to indicate that he had personally saved the RSM's life. Therefore the jibes and jeers of his comrades were peculiarly bitter when the sergeant came around and called out his name for the next guard. Izzard resolved that a mistake had been made, until the NCO explained that Sunshine had named him in particular. At this information the short man bounded outside without his belt and marched straight to Sunshine's billet. He was ushered in by a wary batman, and the man he met was not the craven wreck he had bullied in the dugout, but the regimental sergeant-major of the Royal Canadians.

"What for you, my man?" the query was crisp and impatient. "Did you detail *me* for guard?" Izzard was boiling inwardly.

"I detailed a guard, certainly. Perhaps you are on it. What about it?" Came the challenge. "Don't you think you're going to soldier *now?*" There something dire and sinister in the *now*.

Izzard felt his ground slipping. Nevertheless he delivered the ultimatum he planned. "I'll go," he said stubbornly, "but if you don't get me off it I'll tell what happened in that dugout to the whole world—and Calico'll back me up. You hear me." The short man stalked out, and Sunshine was wordless.

Izzard hunted up his chums and told all that had been said. Calico went paler than usual. "You've done it now," he drawled. "Sunshine knows he'll never get caught that way again, and he knows that his word'll go further than ours. He's got the upper hand. Don't be a fool, Izzard. We're cooked if you balk on guard."

Izzard was obstinate. "That blasted yellow-back is never going to bluff me," he declared. "I'm just going on guard so's he'll have to get me off again. If he don't I'll tell everything, no matter what happens."

At guard mounting there were several spectators. Izzard had implied that he did not intend doing his beat, and so his fellows viewed proceedings at long range, clear of Sunshine's displeasure.

Another interesting item was the fact that Izzard was the dirtiest-looking soldier that had ever lined up for an RCR guard. His bayonet had not a semblance of polish.

Sunshine appeared in all his glory. He strutted by the rear and came around to confront the guard, his eyes focused all the while on the shortest member of its ranks. As their eyes met, his hand shot in his pocket for the book that meant crime and punishment. Then the guards, old and new, and the distant watchers, beheld the strangest incident in the history of the regiment.

Sunshine's hand remained in the fateful pocket as if entrapped, while a distinct pallor spread beneath his bronze. His voice, when he spoke, was almost unrecognizable.

"Private Izzard is to be substituted at once," he said huskily, "on account of his conspicuous conduct recently."

Shortly after the three famed adventurers were travelling, each in a different direction. Izzard went in an ambulance. His destination was Blighty, so the orderly said, after examining the infected knee. Izzard would not explain the miracle of substitution.

"Say good-bye to Calico for me," he said to one of the platoon. "He's not a bad sort, if he is a little dumb."

Sunshine went far out in the dusk, to a deep pool at the end of the field behind his billet. And all the while, since he had given his remarkable order, he kept his right hand in his tunic pocket.

Very carefully he withdrew it, exposing his fingers clasped tightly around an egg-shaped object. He shuddered as he saw it—a slightly rusted Mills bomb. How it came to be in his pocket he did not know.

This special tunic that he reserved for parades hung just inside the billet window; scores passed it in a single hour, and any man could slip the missile in his pocket unobserved by resting at the windowsill for a moment. With billets as they were, and men as they were, one had to depend on respect for authority. One thing he did know—the safety pin was missing from the bomb!

Whoever placed the bomb in his pocked had wedged it cunningly with the notebook so that the lever was held in place until one or both were withdrawn. Then.... He shut his eyes and envisioned the explosion of that harmless-looking little bomb in the dugout stairway, the awful vent it had torn in the chalk-hardened soil. Had he not climbed up the crater it had created? Had this one exploded in his pocket.... Taking a quick look around he raised his arm and hurled the bomb in the centre of the pond, then ran. Beyond a splash nothing resulted, and he slowed his steps, satisfied. It was as he figured; the fuse had dampened in time. But as he went he wrestled a mighty problem. There were more bombs, more opportunities. The despot, known as Sunshine, ceased to exist from that hour.

Calico Fuller strode in the third direction, toward Villers Au Bois. It was Friday again and he had managed to muster another green envelope and had much to say to a certain lady named Arabella. His epistle, however, made no mention of the placing of a Mills bomb in the pocket of a well-known sergeant major. Nor did he state that the said bomb had its detonator removed before being placed in aforesaid pocket. But then some of his mates said he was odd, and Izzard, from his hometown, said he was a little dumb.

Perhaps that is why he smiled to himself as he began the letter that was to skip the eyes of his regimental officers: "Dearest Arabella," he wrote, "the weather cleared favourably tonight at guard mounting. I think that we will have a spell of very pleasant Sunshine."

Sunrise for Peter

The Newfoundlanders were moving to the Somme. Three days D Company had marched through a sun-bathed, picturesque part of France, fragrant with flowers and fruit trees, pleasing to the eye. Peasant women in the fields had smiled at them, and children had clapped their hands and shouted *Bonne chance*. The soldiers had feasted their eyes on homely, chalk-walled cottages nestled in backgrounds of deep verdure, grassy gay with buttercups and poppies, rich with clover in bloom. And now they were falling in for a night move, which meant that they were nearing the line.

A ceaseless, far-away, throaty grumble of gunfire was as impressive as the low-spoken comment of the veterans, and Private Peter Teale spoke quietly to the white-faced youth beside him.

"It'll take us th' night t' get there, and we won't be for it then." The boy-like soldier looked up at him quickly, as if seeking a hope.

"But they'll shell us bad up there, won't they?" he blurted, and his voice was unsteady.

"It won't be cushy, that's sure," returned Peter, "but it'll not be too bad. There may be dugouts for the day."

The sergeant major barked an order and the men stood stiffly at attention as their company commander took over. The latter was a tall man, slightly stooped, and his voice was kind, though tense, as he proceeded, after telling them to stand at ease, to read an order. It dealt with a contemplated attack. The battalion would take over a part of the line near Bus and the company would be in Pineapple Trench. The enemy would be shelled for two hours previous to the assault, and there would be an abundance of artillery support afterward. During the actual attack each man was to do his utmost to reach the objective—the German second trench—and no one was to pause to assist a wounded comrade. Every moment would count toward success or disaster.

Men shuffled uneasily, hitching at their equipment, and a coarse whisper was audible. "What a bloody hope we got."

The company moved out on the road and swung into rhythmical step. Just outside their billeting area an old curé stood by his church, peering at them as they passed, his head uncovered and bowed, a beautiful but ominous gesture. Peter felt melancholy, and a sort of homesickness banished all the thrill that had stirred him as they fell in; he felt incoherently sympathetic for all the blurred figures about him.

They marched into open country, and as the night deepened he watched the colour drain out of the landscape, leaving all contours vague and grey beneath a pallid starlight.

"Oh, mademoiselle from Armentières, *parlez-vous*..."

The soldiers sang riotously, without attempts at harmony, seizing the song as an outlet for pent emotions. Peter did not join in. His melancholy muzzled him, and anyway he disliked the words. The doggerel ended and for a time there was only the thudding shuffle of hobnailed boots, the creak of equipment, and then someone started a similar ditty that drew mixed comment.

"...and another poor mother has lost her son." It finished like a ribald defiance to the future.

They passed through another village. A door opened and a light gleamed, then a voice asked where they were going.

"The Somme, the Somme!" The challenge was unmistakable.

"Somme. Ah, *non bon*." The voice sounded hollow, hushed, seemed to drift in the damp air, ghostlike. "Ah, *non bon*."

It was disturbing, that sighing comment, but the marching men sang louder until they were exhausted. Then came a halt, and they fell out by the roadside and cigarettes glowed like fireflies. Peter sat by the youngster, and watched him loosen his belt and twist irritably at his haversack.

"It's cooler at nights," he offered, "and there's no marching to attention."

The youth twitched again. "My shoulders are raw," he complained. "I'll be glad when we're there."

Peter was carrying the boy's rifle and extra bandolier long before they reached the dark abyss of a communication trench that led to the front line, and in helping him he forgot for a time a worry that had gnawed at his heart. He had not, however, slumped on a chicken-wire bunk in the dugout to which they were assigned, before he remembered, and stirred about until he saw the sergeant.

"Has no mail come up?" he asked.

The non-com grunted wearily. "I'll see," he said. "The limbers came behind us."

By the flickering light of a few candles the dugout looked a grisly cavern. Its roof timbers and jutting bunks made gloomy, shadow-ridden corners, and the sleeping men sprawled about as if they had been so stricken. Peter gazed at them with a return of his melancholy, and watched for the sergeant's return. Would there be a letter for him?

He glanced at the white, upturned face of Telfer, the youth, and realized that if there were a letter he must wake the lad. He could not wait until morning to have its message read. If only there had been one the previous night, when they had been rested and had had a good supper of stew and bread and hot tea. Then he would have had time to ponder each line, each phrase, like a tasty morsel, until he had imbibed the whole so thoroughly that it would have become a part of his memory.

It had been a snug billet, that overnight stopping place, very cooling and restful after marching over the hard, hot pavé. The big, stone-built barn held fresh clean straw, and in the rear were pollarded willows overhanging a little river of bright water. The splashings of many bathers and the murmur of the men's voices had but added to the soothing qualities of the scene. Telfer had rested and slept like a child.

Peter wondered how many of the men would go that way again. He wondered if he would. Such thinking was a recent thing for him, and, in a way, had gripped him. Before their last "trip" in the line there had been Simon Teale, his cousin, to talk to, to ask advice, but now he was alone save for young Telfer, and there were so many things that such a young lad could not understand. For instance, he would not know about dreams, and dreams were guides if one understood them as Simon had done.

And Simon was a home man. He had lived at Old Bear Bay just

down along from Peter, and they had fished and hunted and trapped together through many lean years. Simon was clever with tools, and he could read and was versed in many "outside" matters. Peter was more of a hunter and trapper. He knew every pond and barren and drogue all the way to Old Woman Tickle; could sense his way in the winter through dense stunted spruce where the windfalls of ages made countless pitfalls hidden under light snow coverings.

He and Simon had come to France together, and their intimacy had been a great thing for Peter. They could talk of home, and the fishing and sealing, the old folks and young folks, and Simon could read their letters to him. He also wrote to Peter's wife. It was a huge help, that letter writing, for Simon could put things in words so easily and Peter could not. He had less to write about, too, for Simon had a family, three husky sons and two daughters; Peter and his wife were childless.

Strangely, it was Simon, the family man, who had first mentioned enlisting. Peter had heard vague rumours about a war over in Europe, but his meagre geography had never caused him to think that it had anything to do with Newfoundland, and he was astounded when Simon said so. His amazement increased when within the week his partner gravely informed him that it was their duty to go to St. John's and "sign up."

"But who'll do the hunting and fishing and get the firewood?" asked Peter. Simon had upset his world.

"There'll be money from the government," Simon explained. "Wages like, that the wife will get, enough to buy 'lasses and flour. It's our duty to go, man, a wonderful chanc't, and the good Book says so."

That settled it. Peter hated to leave home but he was a pious man, a believer. He had not the religion of some of the outport Newfoundlanders, who were subject to "glory fits" and loud repentances, but he had a faith of his own, partly the result of hearing Simon read the Bible on stormy days and Sundays, and partly due to his own thinking.

Out in the vast whiteness of winter, with the glitter on the trees and an awesome silence over all, he would think and think as he visited his snares and traps, and when a perfect pelt rewarded him he would stand and gaze about him in a peculiarly reverent fashion. On summer nights, when the huskies howled and the northern lights rustled with the changing of a million tints, he had the same sensations, and would go up on the hills and rocky crags above the little bay and sit for hours alone. Mary, his wife, did not like such moods, and so he never told her about them.

"All right, Simon," he had said. "I'll go as soon as I fix for a winter's diet, but I know I'll hate the killing. It don't seem right to me."

"There was killing in Bible times," Simon asserted, "so it must have been right, and Samson slew the Philistines. 'Tis likely these Germans be the same."

So the two men had gone down to St. John's and there had become soldiers of the English King who needed them. Peter had hated it all, the bayonet fighting and bomb throwing and especially the heartless jesting. And he hated leaving Mary.

In France a discerning sergeant had noticed their silent cat-footed ways in the dark and made them his platoon scouts, which pleased Peter as much as anything could in that war-defiled country. Out in No Man's Land, lying in the stealthy quiet of a listening post, he could watch the endless flares and imagine himself back on the hills behind Old Bear Bay. Such dreamings had been easy in the sector where Simon was killed. It was rough-cratered territory in a mining region and there had been a lovely crescent moon afloat, an enchanting moon that changed the lines into soft contours until reminiscence teased his memory, for even the sombre slag heaps, huge against the luminous sky, became the dark rocky spurs that guarded his home harbour. And there had been a stillness he liked, a quiet in which he could bathe his soul as in a deep, cool pool. He had said so to Simon.

A shuddering sigh had been his comrade's first response, then came a whisper, hoarse with emotion. "It's my night, Peter. I've had my dream."

Peter had almost blamed himself afterward for letting Simon sleep. He had known, by his easy breathing, that Simon was dozing, and had not roused him, and so the death vision had come. But would it not have come anyway, or would he not have been killed without warning?

Peter knew that no man could live beyond his time.

"What was it like?" he had asked, crushing back a first urge toward pity, for it could never help a man. "What were the signs?"

"I saw my door, wonderful clear," whispered Simon, "and Maggie were in it waving good-bye. It were like daylight, all the bay, and the boys were down by the fish wharf. It were my dream."

And then, because he knew nothing else to do, Peter had held out his hand and gripped Simon's with his warmest pressure and assured him that he had one consolation—he had lived clean and honest and God-fearing, and that was a comfort to anyone.

When their hour was up they had crawled back toward the trench, and Peter had noticed how the wet weeds that brushed his face were like dead fingers. Then the Germans sent up coloured lights, and he saw that the red ones made the water holes pools of blood, and the green ones gave all the area a ghastly corpselike sheen. It did not surprise him the least when a sniper's bullet came with the hiss of an evil thing and killed Simon instantly.

Peter had helped carry the dead man far back to a little cemetery, where all the graves had white crosses, bearing names and numbers. To one of his faith and nature, respectful burial was a mighty thing. When, before they marched to the Somme, he had visited graves and seen skylarks springing up from them, flooding the earth with melody and soaring to enormous heights before dropping back to earth, he was certain that Simon was "Resting in Peace," according to the legend above him.

He was thinking of how obligingly young Telfer had written a decent letter to Simon's wife, one that she would feel was a personal message, and how the lad had clung with him since, when the sergeant returned and stared across the dugout, blinking wearily.

"That you, Peter? There was no letter. The mail's slow these times."

"It is," said Peter. "I'm a month without hearing from my woman, and the last one was long coming. I been wonderin' about my Mary."

"She'll be all right," grunted the sergeant drowsily. "The folks back home have lots to do while we're away. You'd better get to sleep. We'll be in the front trench tomorrow night and we might be unlucky."

He had not stopped speaking, it seemed, before he was snoring, and Peter blew out the candle that had been burning beside him, waxed on the top of his steel helmet. Then he lay down and stared into the murk of his corner and listened to rats in the dugout walls while he tried to visualize Mary, his wife, in the tiny garden he had made of good earth scraped from hollows in the hills and carried down in baskets, and fed each spring with decaying small fish, after which he faced again the stern fact that Mary had not written him.

Had she tried the salmon netting herself? He stirred uneasily. He had told her not to try it, for it was a man's work, and there was no need while the government sent her money. Mary! He wanted to speak the name aloud, softly, caressingly, to hear the music of it, and as he stared into the dark he saw her face, smiling, wistful, alluring, daring, gay, whimsical—she could change like spring weather—and he gazed spellbound until a thudding over-head explosion shook the dugout, and faces vanished like reflections in the still water of the bay when a ripple crossed it.

There was another jarring crash, dulled by the heavy gas blankets hung across the stairway but audible enough to rouse several sleepers. "That's big stuff," said one, and another growled assent. They listened and heard the next shells land farther away, and went to sleep again. Peter, his mind diverted, also slept.

It was afternoon and the shelling was heavy, but Peter stayed in the trench. He wanted to think and he could not do so in the foul, fetid air of the dugout. The men were boiling tea, and frying bully in mess-tin tops, and the odours of their cookers mingled with the stale, saline smell of perspiration. He wanted to inhale fresh air.

The trench was but one in a zigzag warren and had lately been German ground. A coal-scuttle helmet, daubed with camouflage paint, had been tramped into the earth, and stick bombs were piled on what had been the enemy fire step. He moved around a bay and saw a sand-bagged hollow that had been a machine gun post. A dead gunner was sprawled over his wrecked weapon and big blue flies buzzed about him. Old boots, bottles, a gas mask, were littered about, and the German's pockets had been turned inside out by some hasty souvenir hunter.

Letters, postcards, and a photo had been flung down. Peter's face set grimly. He judged it an ungodly thing to rob the dead.

He looked around. There were successive explosions in the area to his right, just where a house had been, and he saw a stretcher party hurrying away with a burden. He mused, sadly. Everyone had said that July 1916 would be the turning point of the war. It had come but nothing great had happened. There certainly was no rout. Soon the line would move on and the ruin would be but another rubbish heap; then a plot of little white crosses would be formed in what had been the garden and a signboard by the filled-in craters would say "Dangerous Corner." That was the routine of war.

He hated war, abhorred it. Over on the low ground he could see fresh graves in the swampy mud. The cross of the nearest one had been struck by a shell splinter, so that only the name remained. One name. "Karl..." And the inscription *Ruht in Gott*. Peter looked at the letters a long time, wondering what they meant, and when a corporal passed by he got him to decipher them and explain.

"Them Heinies is all Karls and Ottos," said the non-com as he hurried on. "Nobody'll ever know who's planted there."

The thought struck Peter forcibly. That was the worst part of war, the desecration of graves, of the dead. He had never dreaded death nearly as much as he had dreaded being left as a discard on a battlefield, to be rat-eaten and fly-blown, blackened and shrivelled, and at last hastily covered in a shell hole by a careless burial party. He moved down the trench to the dugout. The company was not to go forward until dark, and he would talk with Telfer, try to encourage the lad, and in the doing ease his own mind.

"What's it like up front?" asked Telfer. He was lying on his bunk and his face was pale and drawn.

"Not so bad," said Peter. "They're shelling all over but no place gets much. It's open ground in front and all trenches and wire and shell holes, same as we came through."

"We're to go up at nine," said Telfer. "The sergeant was here and told us. We stay in Pineapple Trench until five and then go over." Then, as if for something to say, the boy looked up with a feeble grin. "Did you know it'll be Sunday," he said, "and the first day of August?"

Peter felt as if someone had prodded him. He stared at Telfer.

"The first of August," he repeated. "It's my wedding day, ten years ago. Man, there'll be a letter, sure."

Then he moved over and sat beside Telfer and talked as if he were making explanations.

"It were a Sunday, too, when we were married, though Mary didn't want it. She were a great one for jolly times and there wasn't much for to do that day, but her father had his boats to see and couldn't come before. I didn't like it because she didn't, but any day would have suited me, lad, for I knew I were the luckiest man in Old Bear Bay in catching Mary. You'd never think, to see her, that she'd have the likes of me."

Peter paused and gazed at his rough hands and wrists, disfigured by sea boils. Then he shook his head in a solemn fashion.

"I don't know what she be doing now for to keep her spirits. There won't be much going on with the men away, and Simon and two others killed, and" —he glanced at Telfer— "there were no children to make her busy. It'll be hard on her, the waiting and the bad news, for Mary's not like the others. She were always a gay one, bright and joking with everybody, and there isn't her match in looks on the coast. I hope she isn't trying the nets." Peter's voice was lower. "She's not got the strength for it and there isn't the need to do it."

Telfer turned uneasily. "There's not much shelling now," he said. "Let's go and have a look. The sergeant said if it rained we wouldn't go over this time."

But there was no hope. The air was windless and cool and the sun had set with every promise of fine weather. The early dusk revealed a desolation that appalled. The trenches and dugout entrances and tree stubs were all touched with a drab greyness that seemed phantom-laden, and a faint smell, indescribable, from the unburied dead, made Telfer shiver.

"I hate it," he said nervously. "Why don't they bury them Heinies?"

"There's not the time," said Peter, "but there should be. The dead should be respected wherever they are. I hope I have a grave when my time comes."

"Don't talk that way," said Telfer sharply. "You sounds as if—you expected to be killed."

Peter's rugged features remained sombre. "I have a bad feeling," he said moodily. "In Old Bear Bay there's many has a gift of seeing ahead, and always they tell that a man's luck begins on his tenth wedding day. It's in me here"—Peter tapped his broad bony chest—"that something's gone wrong with my Mary. She were a warm-loving woman, and there's been a sickness or bad luck at the Bay. Simon told her how I keep her letters, and that I had them all." Peter unbuttoned a tunic pocket and drew forth a closely tied bundle, rather thumbed and dirty but readable. "Them 'as been a help when we're in a bad billet and there's not much to do. I know 'em, what's in 'em, every one." Then he clenched a big fist and looked over the dim snaky line of trenches. "Them transport chaps needs lookin' after," he growled. "They be careless with the mail bags at times."

"Let's go into the dugout," said Telfer. "I hate this place."

The sergeant major met them. "I suppose you're thinking of your leave, Peter," he said. "I tried to get you off this trip, but we're short of good men. You'll be away as soon as we're out again."

"Oh, my gosh," gasped Telfer in an undertone, and when the sergeant major had gone he was vehement. "Beat them out," he cried. "It's a dirty trick, sending a man into a scrap when his leave's due. Go sick or something. Don't let them fool you that way."

But Peter shook his head. "I don't do them tricks," he said, "and I won't start now. Besides I wouldn't want to go afore I got my letter."

"They're putting it all over you," insisted Telfer. "You've earned two leaves. Go ahead and take a chance. The doc won't think you're playing sick. And never mind your mail. Lots of chaps haven't got any since we started to move. Your wife's all right or somebody would have wired you. That's the way they send anything that's important."

Peter smiled in his slow way. "If my time's come, it's come," he said, "and being on leave wouldn't make any change. There's a chance a letter will come tonight, and if it's good news my luck will be all right for the rest of my life. If Simon were here he could tell you about it."

Pineapple Trench was swathed in darkness and the lines were fairly quiet. Now and then flares lobbed up and filled the night with an eerie whiteness, and when the machine guns were not shooting the very atmosphere seemed charged with expectancy. Peter was in a small trench shelter and Telfer was huddled beside him. The lad dozed occasionally and cowered in his sleep, whimpering with the poignant fears of anticipation.

Peter wished that he could sleep—he needed it, was heavy with it—but his restless memory made sleep something to be resisted. Dark thoughts tormented him, hovered over him like haunting winged creatures. What had happened to Mary? Had she been drowned, her dory swamped as she went out to look at the salmon nets? Had she slipped on the rocks on a wet windy day as she went to their little garden on the sunny side of the hill? Had some fever come into the village?

Then he remembered Telfer's urgings about getting away on leave, and pondered. Never before had he had such a dread of going into battle. What had happened to him? He was not a coward. Any native of Old Bear Bay knew that life was a precarious thing, and Peter believed that every man had his time limit set when he began living. But he dreaded being left in the wilderness beyond Pineapple Trench, an unsightly body suddenly emptied of life, at which those passing would glance with furtive curiosity. He fingered his chin and was glad he had shaved before he left the dugout.

Telfer pressed closer to him, as if for warmth, and Peter's heart filled with pity. It seemed a crime to send such a boy into battle. Then he wondered, with dismay, who would read his letters and write them if anything happened to the lad. Telfer was a find. He had been so apt in comprehending all Peter's affairs.

An hour before the barrage was to begin, Peter awoke from a short sleep and sat up straight. Telfer was aroused by a tug at his shoulder.

"I've had a dream," said Peter in a tense, excited way, "and it were something wonderful. The sun were coming up on the bald rock back of the Bay and there were a dory going ashore. A sunrise is wonderful good luck. I wish Simon were here. He'd know the signs."

"Signs!" repeated Telfer sleepily. "What signs?"

"He'd know," explained Peter, "whether it were good or bad luck."

"Dreams don't mean nothing," said Telfer, listening to shelling on their flank. "I never think of them again."

"Them as knows says dreams are signs," said Peter determinedly and with a renewal of his excitement. "Sunrise must mean something wonderful. There'll be a letter, sure."

Peter knew considerable about "signs." Simon and he would never risk a stormy passage across the Bay without giving their caps the "fishermen's toss," and the more he pondered it the more he felt certain that his dream was a good omen, so that when the barrage rocked the earth and sky he was almost cheerful. Telfer, white-faced, hugged the shelter of the sandbags. Smashing, pounding, rending explosions almost burst the eardrums, and gradually the reek of high explosives drifted to their trench.

The sergeant came along the trench, assisting an officer to issue a rum ration, and when he reached Peter he gave him a letter, saying it had come up in the night.

"It's my lucky day," he shouted into Telfer's ear. "Read it quick. We've not long now." He lighted a candle and held the stub in his fingers.

Telfer's pallor was enhanced by the flickering glow. He tore the envelope open and his fingers were trembling. Peter placed his broad back in the entrance to the shelter to keep the draught from the candle flame, and waited eagerly. "Mary would know it's out tenth wedding." His voice was strong above the tumult outside. "She have planned the letter neat to time."

Telfer nodded. He stared at the missive, his hands shaking, then glanced at Peter with the affrighted look of a cornered animal. Peter put a hand on his shoulder soothingly.

"Never mind the shelling," he said in a voice for a windy sea. "I'll stay by youse when we go. What's Mary saying this time?"

Telfer's voice was so weak that Peter could not distinguish a word, and he shouted again. "Speak up, man."

He was pushed roughly and the sergeant squeezed in beside them.

"You two come with me," he bawled. "The captain wants me to be one flank. You bring bombs, Peter. I'll use you, Telfer, for a runner."

"That'll be all right," responded Peter. "Hurry, man, and read my letter."

Telfer did not look up. He moistened his lips with his tongue, and read in a high-pitched tremolo: "My dear Peter: You must remember our wedding day and think of me. The garden has been fine. I have not gone to the salmon nets for there is no need at all. Simon's boys have a net for me. There is plenty of grass for the goat back of the hills, and I have got berries preserved for when you come home. The boats are not running so often now and my letters will be later. Write to me as soon as you can. Simon's wife is getting a pension. I love you, Peter, the same as I did ten years ago. Your loving wife, Mary."

For a full moment Peter did not move or speak and then his rugged face broke into a smile startingly alien to their surroundings. He puffed out the candle.

"Man," he shouted, "that's wonderful writing. It's the best letter I've ever had. Don't youse be feared today. Good luck's with me, sure."

The sergeant did not say anything. He stared at them both as they backed into the trench and made ready for "over the top." As the signal whistle blew, Peter patted the letter in his pocket and smiled again.

"Sunrise is a wonderful sign," he cried cheerfully.

An hour later Peter worked desperately, helping the sergeant establish a trench block. D Company had taken its objective, after heavy losses, but the enemy fought doggedly to hold a post on the extreme right. Noon found the situation unchanged and three of the flanking garrison added to the inert dead. Peter's bombs were exhausted and he was depending on his rifle. The sergeant, fighting beside him, slightly wounded, decided to send for help. Twenty yards away, across a bit of open ground, a platoon was entrenched. If Telfer could reach them...

He explained matters to the lad who crouched beside them.

"One quick rush and you're across. They'll never get a shot at you. Go on. We can't hold out here."

Peter saw Telfer gaze at dried pools of blood on the trench floor, at stained and sodden bandages beside a dead man, and knew that fear was holding him.

"Go on," yelled the sergeant. "We can't stick it here. We've got to get help."

Telfer gave him a dog-like glance of entreaty, then tried to climb to the open, slipping twice on the mud-greased bags so that the sergeant swore again. Peter, watching, made sudden resolve. Telfer had helped him with his letters; he must help Telfer. Why not attack the enemy? Only a few of them remained and they might be routed. Through all the mad fighting, the plunging, stumbling, headlong charge, the shooting and bombing and clubbing, he had had one phrase singing in his mind, carrying him, buoying him over every obstacle. "My dear Peter." Never before had Mary begun a letter so affectionately. "I love you, Peter, the same as I did ten years ago." Battered, bruised, bleeding from a dozen minor hurts, he was exuberant, exhilarated. Mary, his Mary, loved him. What else mattered?

"Wait," he shouted as the sergeant turned to enforce his order. "Youse follow me." Before they could stop him he had leaped the trench barrier and was over at the German garrison like an avenging fury.

In five minutes the German post was a welter of blood and its owners were the sergeant and Telfer, but the cost was dear. Peter lay on the fire step with a terrible wound in his side, a wound they could not staunch.

He was conscious but he could not keep his thoughts clear. There were so many things he could not understand. How had the Germans been able to strike him down, at the very last moment of fighting, when this was his lucky day? Didn't a sunrise always mean luck, and hadn't his letter proved it?

The noise that beat on his ears troubled him. Where was he? It reminded him of the storms, the tearing, slamming northeasters at Old Bear Bay. He was tired, too, as he usually was when he had had a rough time in a dory or had just got back from his trap lines. He kept his eyes shut.

When they were open he could see mud walls and broken sandbags, but when they were closed he could vision a tiny harbour with a tossing sea confronting it, and hills overhanging dark water, hills that sheltered little cottages snug on their windward side.

"Telfer!" Peter's cheeks were grey and he breathed with labour. "Read—that letter."

Telfer fumbled at Peter's pocket and then his voice rose shrill and tremulous. "My dear Peter."

Around the traverse a new parapet had been constructed and a Lewis gun mounted so the sergeant lingered and listened and wondered. Telfer's gaze was not on the writing. When he stopped reciting Peter breathed once more, a long restful sigh, and lay still. Telfer's white face strained to new lines. He made to fold the letter but the sergeant took it and read.

"Dear Peter"—the scrawled writing seemed pitifully weak—"Mary died last night. Come three weeks Sunday she were up on the rocks where you used to sit, and fell. Her wouldn't let us write before. Her been going up there since Simon were killed. The boys will tend the goats and your nets. Last thing her thought of your wedding day. Please God you don't be hurt. I had to send this word. Your cousin, Ann Teale."

He read it a second time and stared at Telfer, who was covering Peter's face. The Lewis gun barked savagely for a moment, then stilled, and the sergeant spoke.

"You did him a grand turn," he spoke gruffly to steady his voice, "but how did you know what to say?"

"I knew what he wanted, Sarge." Telfer's fear had left his voice, temporarily at least. "And if you'll let me use some of them prisoners we'll carry him back and bury him decent, like he wanted."

"Go ahead," said the sergeant. "He deserves it, and there's nothing he'd like better. But listen. What if he hadn't—what if he found out?" He glanced at the grim covered figure.

"I daren't tell him the truth," Telfer said slowly. "He's been so mighty good to me." He turned, too, and looked at the still body. "Poor old Peter," he muttered. "He thought this was his lucky day."

There was a long silence. The sergeant was reading again the letter in his hand. He stirred at last. "I believe it was," he said softly.

White Collars: A Tale of the "Princess Pats"

Outside the estaminet a huge caterpillar rumbled over the cobblestones with a long naval twelve-inch in tow; overhead droned a flight of night bombers, on their way to some German back area. Yet no one in Madame Julie's establishment was conscious of their passing.

It was one of the usual "vin blink" dispensaries that invested the partially-blighted strip back of the trenches which the heavy hand of war had but brushed, but tonight its smoke-ridden atmosphere was charged with explosive intensity, and John Renforth sat tight on his bench near the door waiting for the explosion.

The stage was well set. Fat Madame Julie, her hands clasped despairingly over her ample bosom, and fear livid in her eyes, sputtered a perfect barrage of broken French. At the same time she kept well away from the centre of a ring, which had been formed by pushing tables back to the wall. In the cleared space, swaying unsteadily, his tunic unbuttoned, his cap pushed back cockily, was a private of the London Rifles, a burly, gorilla-shouldered fellow. His features were distorted by drunken fury and he was speaking with slurring insolence.

"I sye it again, mytes," he stated. "These blinkin' Canidians gives me a belly ache with their swanks and airs. An' here's these bleedin' Pats thinkin' they've won the bally war. Twice the pay us blokes get—an' wot the hell!"

He ceased abruptly. A table had been hurled to one side, smashing its load of glass, and a great catapult shot into the ring. Renforth just glimpsed the driving fist that landed with a dull crack on the jaw of the aggrieved one, then saw him go down on the tiled floor with a sickening thud. A dozen voices betokened pent emotions, and each was flavoured with a Cockney accent. Very slowly the man on the floor revived. His legs straightened, he turned over and sat up, staring sullenly at his assailant.

"Anything else ya got to say about yer betters?" The taunt came from the human catapult, and Renforth turned to look. He could not resist a grunt of admiration. Straight, taut, and ready, stood a magnificent specimen of manhood, a superb six-foot-two of blond menace. On his shoulders were the famous red-and-white cloth markings, PPCLI: The Princess Patricia's Canadian Light Infantry had a very able representative.

"Move off, myte." The curt words were accompanied by a thrust of ungentle hands, and Renforth stood aside as the bench on which he had been sitting was pushed across the door. A table and chairs were added to the barricade, its grim significance could not be misunderstood. The fight was to be to the finish. Renforth hastily summed the onlookers. There were six more of the London Rifles and a trio of old French labourers. He was the only other Canadian present.

The man with gorilla shoulders got to his feet. Apparently the jolt had cleared his brain, for his unsteadiness was gone. His features were set with animal-like savageness, and as he faced his opponent Renforth saw that the fellow was no amateur with his fists. At the second exchange of blows the Londoner landed a straight jab on the mouth of the blond giant. It was as if he had touched a fuse. With a roar like a bull the Canadian rushed. Once—twice, his fists thudded home, breaking through his enemy's guard, and the fight was over. The Londoner crashed down under a table, and for a moment there was a stillness only broken by Madame's sobbing.

Then, like wolves, the six allies of the fallen man leaped to attack the conqueror. Madame's sobbing changed to shrieks of fright. Arms, heads, and feet whirled in a maelstrom of action. Hard pressed, but winning, the giant knocked men right and left, and soon three of his attackers were down for the count. The others gave ground, dodging, and striking from three sides. One seized a chair and manoeuvered to the rear. Another instant and the blond champion would have met disaster, but Renforth leaped, carrying man and chair to the wall. The fellow struck head on and lay inert.

The last of the Londoners went down with a crash, and the next instant the giant was guiding Renforth through a maze of wrecked furniture to a door at the rear of Madame's bar. In a trice they were outside and running. Behind them they heard a new crashing in the estaminet and many excited voices.

"Just in time, Kiddo," wheezed the big man in Renforth's ear. "Them's MPs an' there'll be hell to pay. Let's catch this lorry an' get outa town."

Too breathless to make a rejoinder, Renforth spurted and they gained the road in time to catch the rear of a large truck that was lumbering through the village.

"Where wuz ya headin', Kiddo?" The query was gasped as soon as they had found seats on the lorry's load of SAA boxes.

"I'm on my way to the Princess Pats," said Renforth. "I came from the railhead this afternoon, and have been told that they are going to Amiens. Do you happen to know where they are?"

"I should, Kiddo." The big man pushed close in the dark so that the odour of his copious perspiration was extremely unpleasant. "I belong to th' gang myself."

"I've heard of them ever since the war started," Renforth replied, "and I am proud to join them. No wonder the Imperials are jealous of their record."

"Huh, I dunno as they're much of a mob." There was no enthusiasm in the response. "They made a big name up to Ypres and was the first battalion to git in France, but that's all. They're mostly a buncha college ginks now, white collar guys, which is no good in this war."

"You mean the reinforcements they got from McGill University," said Renforth. "Why, I've always heard favourably of them."

"Look here," the voice hissed like escaping air. "Ya talks like one of them white collar guys yerself. Are ya one?"

Renforth sensed impending hostility, but he answered with courage. "I did wear a white collar in civilian life," he said calmly, "but I can't see that clothes make any difference in men."

"Well, yer th' first one of them I've seen that had any guts." The voice of the big man was friendly again in a reluctant way. "An' if ya hadn't got that guy with th' chair they'd had me purty."

"I had just come in," said Renforth, to change the subject. "What was it all about?"

"Nothin' special. I can't stand th' damn white collars in my section an' I went down there so's I could have a beer without hearin' their fool jabber. But them limeys wuz mixin' their drinks an' talkin' too loose to suit 'Bull' McCann."

It was nearly an hour's run to where the Pats were billeted for the night. Renforth's huge guide led him to a brick stable where men snored unmusically on dirty straw. He prodded one individual awake.

"This here's a new guy just come," he announced. "We're a guy short in our section, how about takin' him on?"

"Where th' devil has he been?" The man was surly as he fought his sleepiness.

"I missed my party at the railhead," Renforth explained, "while I was looking for something to eat."

"All right. Never mind yer story. You umpty-umps would git lost in a box car. You're Renforth? All right, go hit th' hay an' don't git lost again. Reveille's at five."

"That's th' sarge," chuckled the big man as he led the way to another part of the barn and made room for their bed by unceremoniously rolling a sleeper to one side. "He's a tough nut, but a good man in th' trenches. None of yer damn white collars."

"Yer in section four now," grunted the giant as he kicked off his boots and rolled out a blanket. "An' yer with 'Bull' McCann till he squares th' little account of th' guy with th' chair. I don't like yer handle, so I'll just use 'Kiddo.'"

Despite his weariness Renforth smiled at the man's blunt speech, then slept like a child till a rude hand yanked him awake. "Snap out of it," bellowed a voice in his ear. "We're movin' in half an hour. Ya would-a missed yer bacon if ya hadn't a nurse."

Renforth stared. McCann had two steaming mess tins and two tops with thick slices of bread soaked in bacon grease. Bull had got his breakfast for him, and such kindness was unexpected.

The battalion marched until noon and Renforth was glad when a halt was called. They rested until dark and then moved on till midnight. Renforth had started to ask questions at noon, but a soldier thrust a pay book in his face, opened at a page that held a newly pasted order: "Keep your mouth shut." They bivouacked in a wood and the new man was impressed by the jam of traffic they skirted. Lorries, limbers, tractors, guns, and marching men congested the roads. Near them, as they lay in the bush, were many other battalions. Everywhere was commotion, and expectancy that thrilled him.

"We're kickin' off in th' mornin', Kiddo," said Bull as he rigged their ground sheets. "Bit tough to have to go over th' first time in."

"You mean we're going to attack?" asked Renforth. "Is it a raid or what?"

"Raid!" snorted Bull. "Listen, Kiddo. Th' whole blinkin' line's goin' over, twenty miles of it. Th' barrage'll tip yer hat in the mornin'. Now sleep while ya can an' don't worry while Bull McCann is with ya."

In spite of the advice there was little sleep for Renforth. He listened to the droning planes overhead, to the booming of guns on the left, and was aware of the murmur of voices here and there in the gloom as other restless soldiers chatted of the morrow. Now and then a big shell whined overhead but he could not tell whether they were from or going to the Hun. After an hour's fitful sleep he got to his feet. To his surprise there were others about. Groups were here and there, shivering a little in the chill that precedes dawn, and the glow of cigarettes predominated. An officer came among them. "Everyone up," he called. "Zero at four twenty."

Renforth was standing by McCann when a single gun fired from some point ahead. With a jarring crash that seemed to lift him, the barrage opened. It was indescribable. The deafening clamour reverberated in a mighty unison, and it seemed as if a cataract of rushing things were pouring overhead. Far ahead Renforth saw a continuous play of flashes, and twin red lights, breaking high. He tried to ask Bull their meaning but could not hear his own voice. Through him ran sensations that cried for action, and yet his limbs trembled. A hand pushed him forward and the next moment he was in file. The battalion was moving to the attack.

Down a grade they swung, clearing the wood. As they gained the lower ground the din lessened and he could hear shouted orders. Not far from their path sudden geysers of smoke and soil puffed up and mushroomed. They reached a small river. Across it stretched a swaying pontoon bridge. Renforth slipped into position behind Bull's broad back and made the passage, his mind stunned by the awfulness of the gunfire. A grey mist enveloped them and they halted in a trench. Each man adjusted his equipment and everyone smoked. Word was passed along that they were to remain ready to advance, but that there would be a wait of twenty minutes.

Near Renforth was a scholarly looking man, whom Bull had called "Perfesser." With a few casual words Renforth found the man friendly, and they conversed until the signal whistle blew.

Renforth learned that his adoption by Bull had caused considerable merriment in the section, as the big man's aversion to "white collars" was an unfailing topic. The "Perfesser" explained that a legacy of Irish blood had made Bull too sudden with his fists; bush creeds and lumber camp jargon had not blended with the conversation of fourth-year students in economics, and the veterans of the platoon had been clannish. As a result Bull never fitted. "He hates us for being 'white collars,'" said the "Perfesser" as they stood to go. "I hope you change his opinion, for I believe he's a diamond in the rough."

The mist had lifted and they left the trench to deploy in open ground. Ahead was a slope and all at once Renforth was aware of waspy noises above his head. The line broke into a run, and then he saw, a hundred yards farther on, a grey-clad figure leap from cover to race madly up the hill. A man dropped to his knees and fired once—twice—three times. The runner spun awkwardly and tumbled to earth. Others in grey jumped up. Some halted to shoot back and again he heard the waspy singing of bullets. His blood ran quickly, his head throbbed and his heart was pounding like a mad thing; at last he was in battle.

They topped the rise and swarmed down into a ravine. Before it spread a field of grain. As they advanced a German rose in front of the khaki wave. With one quick motion Renforth threw up his rifle and fired, seeing too late that the Hun was unarmed and had his hands up.

His victim sagged to the ground, groaning. Renfoth ran to him and knelt to see the wound, but the German flinched from his touch.

"I'm sorry, so sorry," Renforth exclaimed. "I shot before I knew."

The German seemed to sense his tone was kindly for he muttered some reply. "Come on ya wild killer!" Renforth was jerked to his feet. Bull had run back to seize him and was shouting gaily. "Ya can't stop to frisk Heinies till we git th' objective. Th' white collars won't like yer bloody ways, either. We gives a guy a chance when he sticks up his fins."

"I shot too quick," blurted Renforth, smarting with remorse. "It will not happen again."

They reached the ravine. A German gun crew was struggling to take the covers off a battery of whizz bangs, but threw up their hands at the sight of the Pats. Bull charged down the bank like a runaway train and Renforth saw his goal. Two Hun officers, with helpers, were setting up a machine gun. Bull flung a bomb as he rushed and it exploded in front of the tripod. Three of the Germans and the gun went out of action. Another heart beat and Bull was among the survivors. He bayoneted the remaining officers, wrenched loose his weapon, and butt-ended a gunner. The remainder "kameraded" with speed.

It was all over in a moment but Renforth was thrilled by Bull's performance. The big blond was a war machine in himself.

The company gathered in the ravine. The battery was chalked as a capture to the credit of the University company of the PPCLIs, and the prisoners were herded back over the slope. So far only three casualties had resulted. Two men had been wounded, and on the very brink of the ravine lay the "Perfesser"—dead. Renforth turned to look at him as they moved on.

"That's what happens to these lousy highbrows," snorted Bull, following his look. "That 'perfesser' knowed a lot in books but that don't count in this war. He stopped there, gawkin', when he oughta charged down. White collars gits napooed quicker'n any others out there."

They went on but the advance had become a rout, a mere march-through. Cavalry and the tanks took up the battle and they watched from a distance. Near Renforth was a dead German. He looked down curiously at the "Gott Mit Uns" belt and the absurd-looking gas mask.

Bull watched him.

"Glad to see you've got guts enough to look at a stiff," he remarked. "Some of these white collars would get pink around the gills."

"Give white collars a rest, will you," said Renforth sharply. "You're getting monotonous."

The answer was a throaty chuckle.

Eight days after the Pats attacked Parvillers. The village had been in the path of the war back in '16 and was honeycombed with underground passages and deep trenches. At dawn a short barrage was laid down and then they swarmed into the Hun lines. As they waited zero hour a nervousness struck at Renforth's heart. The inferno of explosions was terrific, and he was chilled to a shivering point. Glancing around he saw Bull rasping the edge of his bayonet with a broken file, apparently unaware of the din beyond. The sight restored Renforth's morale.

Suddenly the barrage lifted, a whistle blew, and the Pats sprang up and over. Renforth bent low as he rushed. Bullets hissed and snapped about him. Twice he fell and scrambled up again, using some of Bull's grotesque oaths. Wire tore at his puttees, holding him back, and he tore away angrily. Bull had vanished in that split second. The next instant he plunged into the Hun trench.

It was wide and deep and as he landed a tall grey form leaped at him with bayonet extended. Scarcely knowing his actions, Renforth braced himself for the shock, parried the thrust and saw his own point go home above the German's belt. The man's hands opened convulsively, dropping his rifle, and he clawed at the steel in his stomach. Renforth surged back wildly and felt the body slide off his weapon. He leaped by to avoid the horror and crashed headlong into three Huns who were backing down the trench. His bayonet missed the first man but he swung up his butt and drove it with all his strength into the nearest face. Bright crimson gushed over the pallid features as they disappeared. So close was he crowded, Renforth could not get a blow at the second German. He was carried against the side of the trench, struggling to get his rifle free, while the third Hun gripped it and thrust moist, distorted features close to his own.

The trio had evidently been retreating from fighting farther up the trench and for the moment, in the confines of the narrow way, could not strike effectively at the Canadian. One tugged at his belt and Renforth saw a wicked-looking trench knife appear. With a desperate lunge he drove the pair backward and plunged his knee into the groin of the nearest. The fellow groaned in agony. A blade flashed and just missed Renforth's arm. Releasing his rifle he leaped backward, and tripped over the man he had felled. His hands came into contact with the Hun's rifle and he had barely time to tip its point upward when the German with the knife hurled himself forward.

There was a sickening sound and the rifle was nearly torn from Renfoth's grasp as the Hun was impinged on the bayonet. Like a madman the Canadian dashed forward and seized his own rifle again. The man he had kneed was still rocking in pain and, without taking aim, Renforth shot him.

He rushed on down the trench, crazed with the fever of battle. Rounding a corner he came into an awful carnage. There were dead men everywhere. The barrage had hit with full force, fair on the trench. Parapets were broken; debris was strewed everywhere. Near him a machine gun and its crew had been blown into the side of the trench and partially buried. A hand, dripping with blood, reached out of the heap. Over it, and amid the appalling wreckage, a furious struggle was in progress. Three Pats were engulfed in a wild melee of butts and bayonets. Dead men lay entangled with the Boche wounded, and as Renforth rushed to the assistance of his mates a stricken Hun wrapped arms about his ankles. Renforth struck savagely and the hold relaxed. He charged on, striking, thrusting, slashing, shooting. It was a frenzied survival of the fittest and ended with only one other Pat unwounded.

This chap, whom Renforth had heard discussing Religion the night before, grinned fantastically through blood streaks and yelled: "Come on, old top! It's a hell of a picnic. Let's go!"

They tore around bays and over blown-in portions until they

reached a wider part. There were more dead and fragments of dead. Standing in their midst, like a gladiator of old, was Bull McCann, swinging as a club the blood-spattered leg of a machine-gun tripod. Even as they arrived he dealt a blow that crashed the skull of his assailant like an egg shell. His steel hat was gone, his tunic was slashed to ribbons, one shoulder was completely bare, but he was drunk with the wild joy of battle. "Safe enough now, Kidddos," he whooped in his great voice. "Come right along, the main scrap's finished."

The careless derision maddened Renforth. "Hell!" he snarled as he hurled bodies to confront the big man. "This is only one corner. There's been a dozen scraps as good as this right along the trench."

Bull's grin grew broader. "Reg'lar spittin' wildcat, ain't ya?" he mocked. "If enough of ya white collars git around one Heine ya might down him."

A red mist seemed to blind Renforth. "You infernal fool!" his voice was almost a scream. "I've a good mind to—"

"What's this?" came a shout. "Here, men. Come down this way. The Boche are using underground passages and must be checked."

It was an officer. Renforth swallowed his rage and followed the others, but he resolved to prove to Bull that white collars were as good as he. They climbed over a blockade and came to where a shell had blown in a ton of sandbags, but above the debris the top of a dugout entrance was still showing, its gas alarm intact. A man could squeeze in and out of the opening. "Two of you get in there," said the officer, "and find out if it's just a dugout or a passage. The other man come with me."

Bull turned. He had salvaged a rifle and the exasperating grin still rode on his features. "Come with me, Kiddo," he said teasingly. "Ya might run into another scrap."

Without answer Renforth ran by him and slid feet foremost into the opening. A slight wriggling and he was through enough to drop to a stairway inside. Bull, grunting and squirming, followed, and dropped beside him.

"Just a sec, Kiddo," he whispered. "I got a candle."

He lighted it and they descended a stairway leading to a depth that surprised Renforth. At the bottom was a door with a sliding window.

"Wait," wheezed Bull. "There might be a surprise party here. Git yer rifle ready an' don't miss when ya shoot."

He pushed the door open with a sudden shove. Nothing happened. Candles were burning on a table in a well-finished room. There were chairs, a desk with telephone, a stove, and two beds. The place was floored with wood and the walls were burlapped. Over the table was a picture of the Kaiser and an inscription in German. On the walls were spiked helmets and caps, long coats, and tunics.

Bull stared in every corner. "Kiddo," he said softly. "This must be th' front room of old Hindenburg's layout. It's sure fixed up swell. Ah-h! Here's a door. Watch out."

Very cautiously he pushed it open. The candlelight disclosed a long passageway, lined on both sides with comfortable bunks. Tumbled equipment, blankets, and clothing lay everywhere.

Everything denoted haste and confusion. "I'll go ahead," said Renforth determinedly. "You can look over me without trouble and you can hold the candle."

Bull looked down at him quizzically. His grin was fading.

Cr-rump! The jar of explosion overhead rocked the door shut behind them and snuffed out the candle. A pungent odour of high explosives drifted in as Bull opened the door again. Every candle in the outer room was extinguished. Bull struck a light and they went to the stairway. Bits of earth still tumbled down the lower steps. Above, the passage was blocked full. They were shut off completely and Renforth realized they would smother long before they could dig themselves out. He looked at Bull. The big man's grin had vanished.

"Got to find another way out, Kiddo," he said quietly, "and not much time to waste. The air'll git bad quick."

They hurried back through the sleeping quarters and entered a long dining room that branched to one side. It was fitted with tables and benches and at the end of the chamber was the kitchen. On a table there were sausage and bread, some jellied meats and coffee. Bull peered at the smoke vent that ran from the stove.

"Must be a hole leadin' outside, Kiddo," he muttered. "We'll try it an' see."

They made a small fire but had to extinguish it at once. The smoke came back and set them coughing. The vent had been closed. They hurried back to the sleeping room and discovered another blocked stairway, then began to search for digging tools, neither speaking. Renforth took time to look in a desk of the first room and saw it contained maps, binoculars, papers, magazines, stationery engraved with the Iron Cross. A folded print was a plan of the dugout. He was studying it as Bull came from the kitchen.

"Cripes, Kiddo," he exploded. "Don't be foolin' with them things. We gotta git a move on."

"Just a minute." Renforth peered closely at the drawing. "Bring that candle out here by the bunks. Hold it up—high—along here. There—watch that flame, and you can feel the draught. That big iron pipe is a ventilator. We can take our time digging out."

Bull stared, wet his finger and proved that Renforth was right. "By gosh, Kiddo, you're correct." There was humility in his tones. "It's queer I missed it. Let's go fill up with dog meat."

They went to the kitchen and ate a hearty meal, then, after exploring both passageways, decided the one by the bunks would require less effort to clear. "First, though, Kiddo," said Bill, yawning mightily, "I'm goin' to have a laydown. There's lots of time, have a bed yourself. They can't be any lousier than where we been sleepin'."

Renforth stretched himself on a blanket-lined bunk and relaxed. The food had made him drowsy and he was more tired than he knew. He fell asleep marvelling at the strangeness of war. In dreams, he again passed through the wild frenzy of the morning, to be depressed by an indescribable menace. Something horrible and sinister seemed closing on him. He struggled and awoke. For a long breath he stared, then closed his eyes and shuddered. He must be dreaming. But when he looked again he knew the truth. Within a foot of his own was the face of a German officer, and the features were so livid with snarling hate, the eyes so animal-like, that he knew the man was insane.

For a long minute Renforth remained motionless, then stirred to rise. The suspense was unbearable and he would have chanced a blow had he not glimpsed an automatic pressed to his tunic. "Schwein!"

hissed the German. "Stupid English! You should die, but I can use you better alive. Kick this other pig awake."

Renforth was amazed at the perfect English the German used, but he made no answer beyond a respectful, "Yes, sir."

He shook Bull, who was snoring loudly, and stepped back. The big man awoke, looking fairly at the German. With a startled oath he reached for his rifle. It was not where he had left it. "Halt, pig, or die!" The words were snarled rather than spoken. "To the floor at once."

Bull, too dumbfounded for words, did as he was bidden. The officer pointed down the passageway. "Vorwarts—march!" he rasped.

Each captive grunted with surprise. The solid wall, of burlap, at the close of the passage, was swung back, disclosing a dugout of the size the Canadians termed "elephant." Wonderingly they gazed about them as they marched in, for the place was lighted by many candles. To their left was another blown-in entrance, beyond it a massive, box-like affair, with coarse wire netting over a hole in its door. Farther on were stacks of ammunition, cased mortars, bundles of flares and wicker shell containers. At the end of the place was a huge concrete vault.

Two things caught Renforth's eyes. One was the body of a German lying in state among lighted candles, the other the number of rats that scurried about at their approach and turned defiantly at holes and tunnels. They were of an enormous size, some black and some grey; all fierce-eyed and quick moving.

"Halt!"

The prisoners obeyed promptly.

"Do not move."

There was that in the harsh commands that told Renforth their only hope lay in implicit obedience, and so he did not move a muscle as he heard the false door moved back into place. Bull was as rigid as he. The German took a position in front of them and near the dead body. His automatic pistol was balanced in his right hand. He glared at his captives, then glanced at the corpse. A great black rat had stolen near enough to nibble at the hand of the dead Hun. Almost quicker than the eye could follow was the leap of the German's arm, and a streak of fire flashed from the Luger. The rat's head was severed from its body.

There were many rustlings in the corners, protesting squeals, then the officer spoke. "You are Canadians, yes. We know, for only such stupids would think to drive the famous Maikafer Guard Fusiliers from their holdings. Your dead lies thick in the trench above, yes, and already our victorious troops are repairing the trenches. Bah! What is an opening blown in? A few more dead for the Fatherland! We will survive. This Vize-Feldwebel was with me at this entrance when it was blown in. He was killed, but I am holding the position. You think I was to question you? Stupids! The German Intelligence Service knows all. For the time I spare you, yes, for I must bury this man beyond those rats. Bah! They are bad as Canadians. What is your rank, officer?"

"I am a private, sir," said Renforth.

"Schwein!" roared the German. "Do you think to deceive by uniform? I can read faces. Your rank, at once!"

Renforth remembered the old adage: always humour an insane person. "I am an acting captain, sir," he said.

"So! The next time speak the truth first. I may not ask again." The vitriolic tones of the German did not belie his statement. "Tell your man to dig by the wall, yes. And you will keep the rats from the body. Treat it with respect. That man was a veteran of the Fusiliers, and I am Major Von Sprechtler!"

"You are to dig a grave by the wall, Bull," said Renforth hurriedly. "My job is to keep the rats away. Be as quick as you can."

A dark flush had spread from Bull's tunic collar to the roots of his hair. "What th' hell!" he blustered. "Me—your man? Me an' old timer in th'—an' you callin' yerself a captain? Tell the Heinie I'm as good as—"

"For Pete's sake don't be wooden," hissed Renforth. The major was fingering his Luger suggestively. "Use your bean—if you want a chance."

Bull still muttered under his breath but he went to the pile of picks and shovels. *Cr-ack*! Renforth jumped at the sound of the shot, his heart in his throat, but the target had been another rat. Like the other, its head was severed from its body. The German's aim was very accurate.

The report startled Bull to quick movements. The floor of the place was chalky and digging difficult, but the giant swung his tools with skill born of long practice.

Renforth had to keep busy to defeat the rats. In the wall was the mouth of a wooden ventilator shaft. It had been sunk through the looser soil and all about it were rat runways and tunnels. The seam of soft earth was literally honeycombed. A black-stained plank ran along the wall to hold back the loose soil, and it was lined with beady-eyed rats, each staring unwinking at the corpse. Renforth shivered as he watched them and noticed that one grey veteran had only one ear. This brute had fiendish, ghoulishly gleaming red eyes and seemed to centre its malevolent stare on the mad major.

At length the grave was dug to a satisfactory depth. The major motioned Bull from the cavity. "It is unfit that schwein should assist in the burial of a German," he said haughtily, "but one of my rank cannot stoop to menial labour. You, Captain, shall carefully wrap Hoffmann in his blanket."

Renforth concealed his repulsion as he wrapped the corpse and fastened the coverings with wire. "Let that big pig take the feet so you may lower the body." The major's commands were as sharp as knife blades.

The Canadians lowered their burden with care.

"Ten paces—vowarts—march!" came a command.

They stood at attention while the major very solemnly recited some ritual in his own language, then clicked his heels and gave a smart salute. He snapped more orders. "Fill this grave in respectfully. It is a privilege you do not deserve."

They filled the cavity and rounded the grave with chalky lumps. "Go to the cage." The officer pointed to the box-like affair with the wire netting on the opening. They went to it. "Open the door, stupid!" roared the major.

Renforth turned the bar that fastened the door, a heavy affair in iron clasps. "In, schwein," and they were entombed in the box.

They could not stand in their prison. It was not six feet square and had no vent save the door hole covered with wire. Probably it had served to punish delinquents in the trench garrison. The major walked away.

It was five minutes before either spoke, then Bull whispered. "We're in bad, Kiddo. What's our best move?"

"I don't know," breathed Renforth. "We must humour him. Do as he says and don't talk back."

"You bet!" Bull's whisper was very subdued. "I didn't tumble that th' guy was cuckoo until it was nearly too late. I'll watch me step."

"We'll get him first chance we have," said Renforth. "I see that the rifles are all stacked back of those shell cases, so we'll have to get a club. Don't make a move till I do, though."

"If I ever git me hands on his neck I'll show him where his Cockchafers git off at," said Bull. "I'll...."

His voice trailed off. They had heard no sound, yet a flashlight sent its rays into their prison and the major peered in, his eyes blazing hate. "Schwein!" he snorted. "Fools! Gun fodder!"

He vanished and Renforth gripped Bull's hand in the dark. They waited an hour but heard no further sound save a rat scampering by their door. Then the sharp crack of the Luger startled them; a rat squealed and all was still again.

Renforth sat until he could not contain himself longer. The situation was unreal, hideous. Rising noiselessly he looked out. Candles burned around the grave and near it, seated on a box, was the major. He was smoking cigarettes and watching the rats on the black plank. Now and then he would point his pistol at them. Some would frisk back into their tunnels, but the one-eared veteran faced him with the unwavering stare that had disturbed Renforth.

Bull got up and looked but sat down quickly. "I can't watch that," he whispered. "It would set my nutty. Ugh! I can smell the rats."

It was so. Renforth slumped back to the floor nauseated by the offensive odour. His wrist watch was broken and they could only guess at the time. Bull's snoring proclaimed that he was asleep again and Renforth had another survey of the chamber. The major sat like a statue, facing the rats. For a long time the Canadian gazed, studying every detail of the dugout, trying to fathom a way of escape. Then he lay down beside Bull and slept.

The voice that wakened them was as harsh as a smith's rasp. "Stupid pigs, sleepers!" it snapped. "Outside at once!"

Renforth shook Bull and stumbled out. He was desperately hungry and stiff from sleeping on the bare planks. They were marched to the concrete vault at the end of the chamber and Renforth was ordered to unfasten its barred door. The vault was a larder with supplies enough for a regiment. Sacks, containers, cases, all with German labels, bundles of candles, and strings of sausage; food in abundance. Under the major's orders a loaf of bread was halved, a jar of meat shared, and a slice of cheese divided. "Eat it here, schwein," said the major harshly. "The rats are to be discouraged."

Renforth glanced outside. Scores of the vermin had crept near and were only kept back by the menace of the stick the major wielded. Bull finished eating, wiped his mouth and made an awkward salute. "Can we have a drop of water, sir?" he asked.

The major made no reply but motioned them outside. Renforth barred the door and the German pointed to a pipeline that ran along the wall and ended in a dripping tap. By twisting under it each man slacked his thirst. "Now," barked the major, "we will a smart drill have, yes. The goose-step, as the pig English say. Vorwarts."

Renforth had heard of the queer step but had never seen it imitated. Bull began a queer hopping progress.

"Halt! To make fun you would—bah! Schwein—I teach you! Once I will show you—once!"

Both men watched as the major, stiff and precise, goose-stepped across the dugout, but never relaxed his guard. Then they received the command to march. Renforth felt that no Boche recruit, burning with patriotism for the Fatherland, ever tried more faithfully to goose-step than he and Bull. Their knees came up in perfect time, each step was measured, and their backs were hollowed in true Prussian style.

Three times they paraded, then the major shouted angrily: "Halt! Soldiers you would never make. You are old women!"

With harsh invective he drove them back near the grave and kicked shovels toward them. "There are bags." He pointed to a heap of sacks, "take them and fill. You will build a wall here from which I will defend when you have cleared the entrance."

They dared not ask questions and his directions were not very detailed, but Renforth guessed that the crazed man wanted a defence of sacks built behind the grave, across the dugout. Bull did the shovelling and he held the bags. After filling a dozen they carried them from the entrance to the spot the major marked, and commenced a wall very near the ventilator side of the dugout. Rats scuttled everywhere as the workers went back and forth. Once the major's pistol cracked and a big black brute that had ventured near the grave tumbled over—headless. On the black plank the one-eared rat remained as steadfast as a sentry. Renforth wished that the major would shoot the creature. Its gaze was diabolical, uncanny.

As the wall took shape the German strode up and down and talked to himself. Renforth, placing bags near the dugout wall, dislodged an unnoticed section of pipe that had rested on a ledge below the long plank. The noisy clattering startled the rats, and the major shouted: "Fool! Pig! Leave it lie. You will more noise make!"

So fierce was the command that Renforth, who was picking the pipe up, dropped it again. One end rested on the bags and the other just reached the grave.

The German grew more feverish as they worked. He drove them until even Bull was weary, then gave them rations. They dare not ask for water. "Stick it, Kiddo," whispered Bull. "I'll git th' brute next time we're out or go under tryin.'"

Renforth was too tired to reply. Crouched miserably in their cramped quarters, he fell asleep. When he awoke, stiff and aching, he heard soft footsteps outside. He closed his eyes as he heard the whistled breathing of the German at the door. As softly as he had come the crazed man went away. Renforth got up and peered out. The major was at his box, toying with his Luger. On the black plank sat the one-eared rat, watching. There seemed to be hundreds in the rat army that peered from holes and tunnels.

The scene was fascinating in its weirdness. As Renforth watched, shivering with horror, an idea flashed into his mind, a chance of escape. He saw that the pipe rested as he had left it. Soon the major should have trouble with the rats.

Bull coughed and roused. The major rushed over and unbarred the door. "The captain only," he snarled. "one at a time shall work."

Renforth felt that their fate rested on his nerve. To his surprise he was marched to the vault and allowed to get rations for Bull as well as himself. The major was so occupied that Renforth managed to slip a slice of cheese in his pocket without being detected. Bull asked for water as he received his supply. "Shortly you will not need it," was the German's snarling response. "The food is also wasted."

As he filled bags Renforth watched the major. Back and forth the officer strode, halting now and then in a listening attitude. Then it came. *Crr-ash*! The jarring explosion was directly above. *Cr-rump*! The second report was not so near. A third was still farther away.

For five minutes the major stood rigid, his pistol ready, then he whirled. "Over to the wall, schwein!" he yelled. "Make it higher at once. The fight is on."

As he worked Renforth managed to get his hand in his pocket and broke off a piece of cheese. Watching his opportunity, he rolled the fragment into little pellets. Then came the crucial test. He manoeuvered to get near the pipe and luck favoured him.

The major began to walk about, chanting some tirade regarding the Guard Fusiliers. Twice he shot rats. As he turned the last time to kick the victim aside Renforth shot a handful of pellets into the open end of the pipe. The major paused by the grave and began to sing "Deutschland Uber Alles."

Renforth rolled a second handful of tiny yellow cheese balls into the pipe. He saw the bits jump from the lower end of the section and disappear into crevices on the guarded grave. Presently a rat darted forth and caught at a pellet that rolled to one side. The taste was enough. In a moment he and a score of his fellows were digging furiously to get at pellets among the chalk. *Cr-rump*! Another heavy explosion overhead, echoed by the fainter ones.

The major's song died on his lips. As he saw what was happening at his feet he screamed like a wild thing. A perfect fusillade of shots rang out and a dozen rats lay kicking. But others swarmed from their tunnels and with a horrible cry the German flung his pistol at them and snatched a shovel.

His blow killed one or two but a score took their place, regardless of the frantic human. Renforth cast caution aside and tossed a fistful of cheese on the grave. Rats poured from their places—black ones, grey ones, lean ones, and bony ones. The major struck wildly, but they bit at his feet, lacerated his hands, jumped on his legs. Yelling like a fiend, he slashed and struck. The huge, one-eared veteran left his post on the plank. Running swiftly he leaped—at the major's neck. His long, grey body flashed over the pack. Renforth saw the blood spurt as the rat bit the German's chin, saw the madman drop his shovel and claw his assailant loose, saw other rats swarming up his limbs. There came an awful cry, then on the grave writhed a mass indescribable.

Renforth ran to the box and released Bull. He explained his trick, then spoke of the explosions overhead. "Them's salvos," blurted Bull. "An' it's out artillery, too. We're Jake if we can git outa this mess without them rats gittin' us as well. Kiddo, you're th' white-topped boy of this brigade."

They could not bear to look at the happening by the grave but Renforth saw a quick end to it all. The wall they had built was not substantial as it had no supports or braces. "Put your shoulder to the other side, Bull," he cried. "We'll get back of it and surge a few times."

The giant planted his feet firmly and placed his back to the bags. Renforth added his strength and they surged in unison. At the third sway the structured toppled, falling almost intact, and smothering completely the milling mass over the grave. A few rat survivors hustled into their holes.

Cr-rump! Again the explosions overhead.

"Th' battery is right in th' trench," said Bull with conviction. "Let's git busy and dig out."

There was a tremor in the big man's voice and his bombastic arrogance had vanished. "This place is full of rats," he exclaimed. "Look over there."

A score of the creatures were ranged on the black plank. More were squeaking in the walls. "Where's that door in the wall?" asked Renforth, his own nerves taut. "What's the quickest way out?"

Bull found the door and forced it open. In the first chamber they felt calmer and selected the first entrance for digging. "Let's send smoke up the ventilator." Renforth assumed charge and his authority was not questioned.

Bull tore up some magazines, placed them in a pan, and lighted them with candle ends. The paper was damp enough to smoke properly and he held the pan below the big pipe vent. One lot had burned out before Renforth felt a jar on the pipe. In an instant he had snatched an entrenching tool from some German equipment and was tapping on the iron tube. *Tap-tap*—a pause—*tap*. He was using Morse code. Bull stared stupidly. Again and again Renforth rapped his message: "Canadian—trapped—in dugout—help."

"Say, Kiddo, what's th' idea? Th' smoke's goin' up all right." Bull was perplexed and the gentleness of his tone implied that he thought Renforth was losing his nerve. "Come and lay down a bit," he pleaded.

Tap-tap. Renforth continued his efforts, and at last got an answer. "Who is it?" came the tapped inquiry. "Two Pats," he telegraphed back. "We are digging now," came a moment later.

Renforth relaxed and explained his signalling. Bull was amazed. Suddenly he thrust out his hand. "Kiddo," he blurted. "I'm a plain damn fool and I knows it. Fergit them things I said about white-collar guys. Gosh, we'd never got outa here if you hadn't had th' old bean workin.'"

Renforth could not expect a more handsome apology. He gripped the proffered hand. "I knew you were just kidding," he answered. "White collars are all right, but you're a whole platoon yourself."

Bull was content. A flash of his old self came back. "Gee, Kiddo," he boomed. "We'll sure make some team for th' old section."

The men who finally crowded down a hastily dug shaft listened with awe to Bull's account of what had happened. He led them to the false section of wall and pushed it inwards. A few candles still burned and they saw scores of eyes peering out from shadows, heard the pattering of many feet. "Let's get out of here, quick," said the leader of the rescuers. "You're lucky guys to be alive."

"You bet," Bull responded. "But when one guy's a hundred percent brains and—"

"The other one is one hundred percent guts," Renforth cut in.

"They take some stoppin,'" Bull finished, grinning delightedly. Then he added, "And listen. We belong to th' white collar section of th' Pats, th' dude college guys. Git me?"

Perhaps it was his size that drew their respect—perhaps they were sobered by what they had seen. At any rate, there was no sarcasm on the faces of the rescue party as they all emerged into the sunlight and brushed from their uniforms all traces of the tomb of Major von Sprechtler, late of the Berlin Guards.

Eyes! Eyes! Eyes!

It was when the "Prairie Squirrels" were at Parvillers that Pete Mullins was sent down the line as a shell-shocked case, with every man in the platoon knowing that he had not been near a shell explosion. Yet none of them derided him, or said he was swinging the lead, for he was, for the time at least, as pitiful a physical wreck as one would care to see.

He kept hiding his face with his hands, and shuddering, and when they got him to bed at the hospital he lay for six days with his face to the wall. When they spoke to him or tried to get him to turn all he would say was "Eyes, eyes, eyes."

Ted Hiller was with Pete all that terrible day when he saw the eyes, and it was Ted who told me the story.

It was the morning after Parvillers was captured, he said, and Pete and I were out in a sort of foxhole we were using as a listening post. We figured that we were about halfway across No Man's Land, but things were in such a jumble down there that we couldn't be sure. It was a jungle of old wire and trenches where the fighting the day before had been bloody and hard, and where our guns had smashed things completely.

The hole we were in was a pit like a well, deep enough for us to stand in, and big enough to let one sit down when he was on watch. There were big weeds and thistles all around the hole and we could look through them. I thought it was as good a place as any for the day, but old Pete was nervous. In the attack on the 8th, Pete had been nearly shot by one of our own boys who mistook him for a Fritz when he tried on one of their pot helmets, and the old man's nerves hadn't got over the shock. Our section was about thirty yards behind us, in a stretch of old trench, but Pete thought they should be nearer.

When it got real light I got up and did first sentry. I reached out and made little lanes through the weeds and we had a corking good field of observation. I watched the right for a while at first, and it was one grand mess of rotting sandbags and jumbled timbers and old trench revetting and broken brick. Old Pete got to his feet after a while and started to stare out on the left. Then he gasped and grabbed my arm. "Look—see," he gurgled.

To the left of our pit, seated in a hollow, was a Heinie. His steel lid lay at his feet and his face was a grey colour that matched his tunic. He was sitting among a rubble of splintered plank, braced there as rigid as if something had taken his attention, but stone-dead!

There was a blood-clotted bandage lying beside him and we could see that he had been trying to dress an awful wound in his thigh. He must have died of shock as he sat there, or else a bullet had got him through the heart. His eyes gave me an uneasy feeling. They were dull and unobservant, but curiously disturbing, for they seemed to be focused full on us, as if he were watching us in a disinterested fashion. Pete insisted on changing sides with me at once. "I can't stand the look of that man's eyes," he whispered, and his whisper was shrill.

I'll own I found it a test myself. I couldn't seem to avoid them, and their dull, unwinking stare was enough to give anyone the creeps. I tried looking away beyond him and studying other things. I tried to pick out Heinie's new lines, to see a machine-gun post, to watch for aeroplanes, anything I could think of, but in five minutes it would be as if I were simply forced to look at those wide-open, expressionless eyes.

Finally I made myself look at the wreckage of a machine-gun emplacement. A big shell had made a direct hit and sandbags and timbers and steel rails were scattered in all directions. A sap had led to the post, and it was blocked completely. Where it entered the main trench the parapet had been blown away, and as I watched I saw a man raise his head. It was a Heinie, and I knew by the way he got up and looked around that he had no idea where we were.

I watched that place for over an hour and in that time saw eight or ten Germans. Then an officer came and got up and looked over our way. After that I couldn't see anyone except a sentry who had stayed in plain view. It was very quiet. Not a plane was over and none of our guns were firing in that sector. The war was away over on our flanks.

It began to get hot. There was no breeze at all and the sun was blistering hot, choking hot, in our burrow. Sweat scalded and blinded us. After a while the distant guns seemed to tone down until the quiet itself was irritating. Then flies, those big blue ones, began to buzz around the dead Heinie, and we noticed that there were dreadful smells. My stomach almost turned.

It seemed an eternity before noon. We had sneaked out to our pit before it was light and there was no hope of being relieved until it was dark again. We had only a little water with us and it had got so warm and brackish that we couldn't drink it. The German sentry at the sap-head got himself a plank seat and sat on it as he watched our way. I had my field glasses and focused them on him. He was staring in a vacant way, and was dirty and not shaved and very tired looking.

All at once Pete grabbed me again. "Eyes!" he hissed, in a way that made me jump. "Just eyes."

I squeezed over beside him and he pointed at the debris near us, where crossed rails, tangled in a V, seemed to cover an opening of sorts, possibly a small crater. There was a narrow, dark opening down beneath them. "There were eyes in that hole," he whimpered. "I seen them."

I watched and watched, and the minutes dragged by. I was fighting flies all the time and I was acutely aware of the dead German. I was cussing all smells and was properly fed up with everything—when I saw them. My scalp seemed to crawl and I fairly froze. Two eyes had certainly appeared in the gap under the rails, and they had simply glared into mine. I felt as if I had had a look at some weird underground monster. One instant was all I saw them, then they vanished.

It was all so utterly unreal that I leaned back and wiped the sweat from my forehead and eyebrows, and then I looked again. For a long time I couldn't see a thing but that black, narrow space under the wreckage—then the eyes were there. They seemed to leap into the place, and I couldn't make out a face to fit them into. They stayed longer that second time and I flinched from them in spite of myself. I never saw such a mixture of fear and hatred and madness in eyes of any kind as in those faceless orbs under the rails.

My first impulse was to take a shot at them, and then I realized that it would be suicide to do so. Old Heinie could snipe us if we tried to leave our hole, and if we fired a shot he would know where we were. Then I wondered if the eyes belonged to a German scout who had made himself a listening post under the debris. No man could possibly have wormed down between the steel rails, which were crossed, and I was certain that the eyes did not belong to any sane person. All at once a Heinie machine gun opened up and its bullets were cracking and snapping over us for five or ten minutes. Pete was sure that Fritz had discovered us, and he begged me to throw a Mills bomb into the hole when the eyes returned.

I talked to him and quieted him but he kept whimpering every once in a while and pushing against me so that I could feel him shaking. That place was enough to try anyone's nerves, but he got my goat and I talked to him rough till he stopped his whimper. I had the safety of my rifle released all the time, and a couple of Mills bombs ready to throw. A bunch of aeroplanes droned over us, but there was no other sound. The machine gun had stopped firing as suddenly as it commenced. The sun got fair overhead and the heat in that hole was suffocating. Flies had come in clouds and they were all over the dead Heinie, at his wound, in his ears, clustering in his hair and around those eyes that watched us. A rat appeared and went over to him and nosed the bloody bandage, but those dull, unintelligent eyes looked at me all the time. I had to shift over to the other side of the pit.

The eyes were there in that dark hole again! They appeared as if my glance had called him. For a full minute they looked straight into mine and I felt as if I were being mesmerized, then there was nothing but the void between the rails. I wondered if the sun was playing tricks with us.

There were heat waves dancing all over the wreckage. I watched a long time, but could only see the black gap, and was feeling quite relieved—when they popped up again.

An hour went by. I had been looking at my watch every twenty minutes since morning. Sometimes those eyes were there, sometimes they weren't, until at last I felt that I would get as bad as Pete. He wouldn't try to look over at all but stayed huddled down in the hole, making funny little noises like a hurt thing.

The Heinie sentry stayed on his plank and stared in his stolid way. He must have been tortured by the heat, but he never moved other than to scratch himself regularly. I ducked down beside Pete and tried to eat my ration of bread and cheese, but had such a nausea that I couldn't swallow a bit. Pete wouldn't try to. He just moaned and wanted to know how much longer we would be there. I stood up, and those livid eyes under the rail seemed to almost jump at me. It gave me such a queer sensation that I had to squat down again. When I rose up they were still there, and more malignant than ever. I prodded Pete. "You get up and take a turn," I said as savagely as I could. "I'm tired of looking all the time."

He got up, looked, and ducked, white-faced and trembling, and I had to clap my hand over his mouth to keep him from crying out. He had looked out his own side, at the dead German.

"He's moved—he's moved," he gulped through my fingers.

The sweat on my skin turned cold and goose flesh was all over me. Pete was telling the truth. That Fritz *had* moved. He had shifted so that his hand had dropped down, black and curled like a hen's foot, and his tunic collar was tight under his chin as his head tipped forward. He seemed nearer to us.

I tried to soothe myself, for I was getting mighty shaky. There was some explanation, surely. It was only three o'clock. Five hours to go before we could expect a relief. I squatted down again.

"You've got to look over part of the time," I growled. "It's too hot for one man to keep his head up all the time, and if we don't watch the Heinies are liable to sneak over on us."

He muttered about something, but got up. Then he shot down again, gasping. He sobbed with fear and he caught me around the knees. I grabbed a bomb and jumped up. A pair of small, beady, blood-red eyes were peering through the weeds not a foot from mine. It was a rat! Ugh! I spit at him. Those eyes were cruel, foul glitters.

Pete whimpered and clung to me and wouldn't listen to anything I said to him. Our long day of fighting, and the killing, had shaken his nerves badly. We had taken the ground we were on the previous day and it had not been a picnic. The eyes under the rails drew mine every time I looked over. They had a sort of fascination, there was something uncanny about them. I squirmed around Pete and looked over on the left, at the dead man. One long look and I was almost as bad as Pete. I pulled him to his feet. "Look over there," I said. "I'm going to beat it before something else happens. That Heinie's moved again."

Pete stood and shuddered and licked his lips. "He moved, he moved, he moved," he whispered in a sing-song, and then he began to blab about eyes.

The German *had* moved. One leg, the unwounded one, was almost doubled now. Not a shot had been fired since noon, and there had been nothing to move him. I stared around, felt dizzy. The sun blazed down unmercifully, and I felt that all around us there were eyes and eyes and eyes, staring, glaring, beady eyes, dull, unmoving eyes, eyes without faces; eyes...eyes...eyes.

Then I yelled, and Pete caught at me like a wild man. Flies had swarmed all over the dead man's nose and as I looked I had seen his eyes close!

Pete caught at me again, but I fought him back and jumped out of the pit. I never thought of the German sentry at all. I jumped a shell hole and hopped over old wire and slid into the trench where our section was—and was lucky not to get shot. Our chaps had been half asleep and they had all seized their rifles. Then Pete came tearing in, and he ripped his puttees off his legs on the wire.

I told our chaps what I had seen and then we had to take charge of Pete. He got to shaking so that he couldn't stop and we had to send him back to the transport lines. He got worse all the way back.

Our corporal was hard to scare and my story made him curious. Not a shot had been fired at Pete or me and so he crawled out through the wire and put up his tin hat. Nothing happened and so he went on till he reached our pit. He looked over and couldn't see the sentry I had told him about. So he signalled us to join him.

Half an hour later we had worked around till our platoon was in the trench where we had seen the Germans. They had beat it. We looked at the dead man. His eyes were closed, and they wouldn't believe me when I said they had been open. Then I showed them the gap under the rails and eyes looked up at us!

"Who the hell are you?" yelled the corporal. "Speak up, or I'll heave a bomb down there."

He would have, too, but just then our officer came and took charge of things. We told him about the eyes, and he set us to work pulling away the wreckage. After we got the top stuff away we found that there was only room enough for a man's head to show in the hole. We pried the rails apart—and there was our German!

He was a pitiful figure. Evidently he was one of the German machine-gun crew and had been buried by the shell that wrecked the post. He was so badly shell-shocked that he had lost his voice, and his mind was affected. He would only glare at us. Our stretcher-bearers doped him and they took him away.

Then one of our chaps crawled into the cavity and explored. He found a timbered passage that led under the refuse on which the dead Heinie was lying. The shell-shocked man had tried to force his way out there and his efforts had moved the corpse. As the dead man's head tipped forward the stiff collar of his tunic had pushed up the skin of his face and closed his eyes. The corporal pushed his head back and they opened! Ugh!

You know these advance advertisements they throw on the screen at the movies, how the eyes sometimes appear first? Well, I didn't go to the pictures for three years after I came home for fear I'd see them.

Pete was never sent back to the battalion.

The Laughing Jackass: a Tale of the RAF

The air under the low-hung clouds raved and moaned as it was split a million times by tracer bullets and plunging planes. Four black-painted Sopwith Camels were fighting desperately a dozen blood-red Fokkers, and scarlet tongues licked from the muzzles of Spandaus and Vickers. Lieut. Jimmy Murdie hardly knew what he was doing. Twice, within thirty seconds, death had breathed in his face, had almost touched him with grisly fingers. Just by a flicker he had missed crashing side on into an enemy plane, and then bullets had ripped the shoulder from his flying jacket.

Grimly, he held to his tactics. It was not the first time death had jibed at him, and he was wildly eager to acquit himself well before Jarvis, his new flight commander. At mess, the night before, it had been whispered that Jarvis was not cordial with Canadians, did not consider them cool fighters—and Jimmy intended to give him an eye-full.

He zoomed suddenly, gained the position he had risked all to reach, a place under the tail of the most belligerent red machine, and pressed both triggers. The cockpit of the Fokker was shattered. Flames licked out. In a heartbeat the black-crossed ship was a fiery comet.

Jimmy's speed shot him up into the low cloud ceiling and before he could turn he was engulfed in slow-moving banks of grey mist. He swore and set his teeth. The glimpse he had had of the blazing Fokker had dazed him, and he had gone high into the mists. He wheeled at once, circled and darted downward, feverish with sudden panic. There was nothing above earth he hated as much as he did a heavy fog bank. *Wheeee*...He gave the gas full on and his machine roared and trembled as he swerved through space. At any split second he might collide with a zooming plane from below, and he set himself to regain his balance when he shot from the clouds.

Sixty seconds after his gun had ceased shooting he glanced at his instruments, and nausea gripped his stomach. He was lost again, was in a spin. His one and only weakness was having another inning. The fog had bewildered him once more.

Two months of hectic service had not helped him; if anything, had made him worse. Given a clear sky, he had no superiors in the 27th Squadron; in a maze of mist he invariably lost all sense of direction, grew panicky, and almost lost his nerve.

He braced himself angrily, gritted his teeth. The frenzy of fighting had not cooled and he was wildly anxious to reach another Fokker. One more sweeping rush, and he shut off the engine. His altimeter showed immediate loss of height. Five thousand, four thousand, three, two... He hurtled downward and at last dropped from the swirling canyons of damp cloud vapour. Tense, heart-stopping seconds followed, for he was nearly to the ground before his sense of balance was restored and he could right his machine.

Soaring, he looked around. Not another plane, Fokker or Camel, was in sight. Jimmy's emotions swung back to anger. He maintained his vicious climbing turn until he was very near the fog ceiling again and then swung back over Zillebeke. He had lost touch of his fellows, lost all chance of a double kill. Would they think he had dodged into the mists to escape the fighting? No, he knew that Hart and Barry would never hold such an opinion, but what about Jarvis? What would he think? Jimmy's interior was burning with chagrin. He wanted to scream curses at his diabolical luck.

More fog, lower still. How he loathed it! His instruments glowed dully, their phosphorescence wavering a baleful greenish-yellow up at him from the crowded dashboard. It was bitterly cold, a miserable, soggy October day, and yet his veins grew more heated. The more he scanned the empty sky the more his chagrin grew. If only he had not got mixed in the mists.

Suddenly he swung crazily on a wing tip and dived wide open with wires tautly screaming. Just across the lake, a lone Fokker was streaking homeward. It had probably fallen away from the fighting and was trying to avoid meeting more of the enemy.

Jimmy squeezed trigger and the sharp crackle of the twin Vickers broke high above the crescendo of the engine's roar. The lightning trail of tracers shot from between the propeller blades like a succession of red-hot needles. They reached the fuselage of the red plane, and it swerved adroitly so that the smoking path of the incendiaries was without a target.

The German was a master flier. His Fokker behaved like a thoroughbred, swooping, climbing, rolling, banking, and zooming, but Jimmy's nimble Camel was swifter in evolution. Gradually he gained advantage, reached a deadly firing position. Only a few bullets had snapped near him, and he wondered if his adversary were waiting for close-in duelling. If he were, he should have his chance. Jimmy was vengefully resolved not to miss his quarry. At the same time, through all his rage and determination, something whispered to Jimmy that his foe's manoeuvering was not according to Hoyle. The red machine was not crippled in any way, was clearly handled by an expert, yet it did not try for positions as all other Fokkers did.

One more breathtaking zoom. Jimmy was as taut as the wires of his plane. Up, up, and then his guns were spitting venomously, raking the struts and fabric of his red enemy.

Up, around and over—there was the red devil, billowing smoke, dropping earthward. And even as it broke into flame Jimmy guessed the reason that his victory had been safely earned. Once before he had seen such a happening, one of his own comrades trying every stunt of flying, every possible trick, doing everything but shoot—because his guns were empty!

There was no doubt about it. The delirious dogfight had been a prolonged affair, with the Germans trying desperately to best the quartet of Camels, and his victim had used up all his ammunition, then had broken away from the fighting in an attempt to sneak homeward. His reserve, fired as Jimmy first dived on him, had not exceeded one dozen rounds. It had been a "cold meat" kill.

That night Jimmy sat uncomfortably silent in the mess while wine-loosened tongues chattered around him. He was listening, trying to learn whether or not his fellows thought he had dodged purposely from the fight. It did not seem possible that they would, and yet... This new man, this Jarvis, seemed a sinister influence. Jimmy did not like him.

He knew, as he tried to eat, that it was mostly his own fault that he was feeling so miserable. If he had talked out straight as soon as he reached the 'drome it would have been different. He knew he should have told then and there just how he had got lost in the fog, how he had swerved and dived and swooped about in the mists until he had got clear away from the combat. They would have believed him, then, and the confession would have been a wonderful help. A dozen times he had been on the verge of telling the others about his weakness, and yet he had never done it. Some foolish pride, or fear of pity, had stricken his tongue.

Jarvis accepted his terse report without comment, and had not spoken to Jimmy after. He was giving all his attention to Willow, an officer of his own type. Each moment became more unbearable to Jimmy. He could not eat. Some instinct told him that Jarvis had talked about him, or that Hart and Barry had told how he had disappeared. It was possible that he was a victim of his own imagination, but he did not think so. He put down his knife and fork, gave up all pretence of eating.

The door opened. He jerked around nervously. It was Captain Hendricks, their squadron commander, who had been called away on a message. He seemed excited and he headed straight for Jimmy's chair.

"Murdie," he called jubilantly. "Congratulations. Your work caps the day. This squadron is making a name for itself. Old Heinie will be shivering each time he sees these old black boats of ours in the air. That message was from brigade headquarters and they have a full report from artillery observers at Zillebek who watched your fight with Captain Karl Allmeder...."

"Allmeder! The 'Red Devil'!" Every man in the mess was shouting excitedly.

The squadron commander nodded. He help up his hand. "Listen, gentlemen," he called. "Murdie was very modest this afternoon. He didn't report that when he left your flight he was chasing Allmeder. The artillery chaps saw them break from the clouds just over Zillbeke Lake and they say the red machine was full out for home, streaking it like a pigeon trying to get away from a hawk. Murdie headed him and out-manoeuvred him and shot him down. Three of the artillery officers witnessed the whole affair and they've sent in all the verifications needed...."

Every officer jumped to his feet. Murdie, flushed scarlet, perspiring, his throat full, could not make an explanation, was not given the chance. Jarvis was leading the cheers.

"Here's to the man better than Allmeder," he called. "Everyone drink to our own Hun-killer, our Johnny Canuck." The cheers were generously given. It was an opportunity for everyone to relax nerves that the afternoon had tensed. They shouted cheers until the dishes rattled, they whooped their praise. Allmeder had been a dread name among all fliers of the Twenty-Seventh.

Just as the shouting died Jimmy regained partial control of himself, and the humour of the situation reacted on his suspense-ridden nerves. Before he realized it he had thrown back his head and was relieving himself in a whole-souled shout of laughter—and at that very moment the rest of the mess had stilled.

Each man had stiffened and all heads turned toward the doorway. There stood a stout, bristly moustached major, with a protruding stomach and a protruding sense of importance. Behind him a pair of red-tabbed satellites stood in respectful attitudes. Jimmy's laugh seemed to re-echo, then there was absolute stillness. The major's face was a brilliant red.

"Who," he barked, "is that damned laughing jackass?"

The CO hastened to explain that someone had just told a very funny joke, but it was difficult to soothe their visitor. He had evidently had a bad day somewhere and had come to the 27th to release some of his venom. He snarled and raged and tramped about and declared that he was sure that the laugh had been at him.

"Murdie," said Captain Hendricks, after the major had gone. "That old bull was in a bad humour and I'm afraid he may turn down the recommendation I'm sending in. What in the world made you laugh like that when he was coming in?"

It was the chance for Murdie to explain everything, but at that moment Jarvis joined them, and offered personal congratulations. He talked sincerely, and Jimmy was so jubilant to know that he had impressed the man that he simply could not spoil the hour by telling about his helplessness in a fog bank. The next day would do.

The next day, however, gave no opportunity for any explanations or confidences. The weather broke clear and every hour was filled with action. For a week the Squadron scarcely knew rest or relaxation, and its record grew. Berry downed three Fokkers in three days and Jarvis added a couple to his record. Then Hart was shot down in flames after a terrible battle with overwhelming odds. Jimmy's flight almost lived in the air in the week that followed, and they took a toll of six black-crossed machines to avenge the death of their mate.

Then came a day when the air was bitter cold and not a Hun was in sight. Jimmy was thinking only of the fire and warmth of the mess when he heard the peculiar *flac-flac-flac* of bullets hitting his machine. He swerved sharply, and saw that they were being attacked by a flight of Albatross D 5's, powerful machines, faster than the Camels but slower in turning. In one lurid instant Jimmy was whirled into the wildest fight he had ever experienced.

Back and forth he dodged and darted, in and out and around and around and over, his engine roaring and moaning, the wires screeching madly. Diving, circling, and diving again, red planes and black ones went through all the manoeuvres known to skilled pilots, and at a tremendous speed, with each spitting death at the other. The wing of one red ship broke off and the plane went down in flames, a great torch falling far to a muddy field below.

Then a black plane lurched, side slipped, and fell after the blazing one, and Jimmy knew that Berry had met a flier's finish. A terrible anger cooled his fighting fury, made him a calculated killer. He was determined to get a German victim.

A sudden burst of bullets ripped the fuselage beside him. Turning, he saw an enemy on his tail. He kicked his machine to the right and found he could just keep clear of the fixed guns of the slower Albatross by circling. Around and around they went. He and his enemy were alone in the world. Around and around and around. It must end.

A desperate hope flashed into Jimmy's mind. He knew that the heavier red machine could not loop as close to earth as he could. He kept circling, but went lower and lower. After him roared the vindictive Albatross. Jimmy looped. It was a nerve-racking stunt for he was very close to earth. He shot up—behind the German.

It was a clear shot. His opponent's only hope was to escape by sheer speed, and he could not avoid crossing Jimmy's sights. One short burst sent him down in flames. Jimmy swerved, wheeled to rejoin his flight. It was not to be. Another red fighter had come behind him like a great hornet, roaring, spitting bullets. Once again he circled madly, around and around and around, closer and closer to the ground. Again he made that dangerous loop, so close to earth and with a bullet-riddled machine, and again he was where he wanted to be and had added another victim to his tally.

That night the survivors sat moodily about the mess and heard Captain Hendricks speak with strong emotion of the part they had played in preventing enemy domination of the air. It did not stir Jimmy. He felt that his whole being was numbed, deadened to any feeling. Good old Hart! A champion in any corner! And Berry! He remembered their first flight into the blue, an escort for observers. It seemed hours and hours after Hendricks was speaking that someone clapped him on the shoulder.

"Wake up, you bleary owl." It was Jarvis, trying to speak in a bantering fashion. "Haven't you been listening? The captain says you've been handed an MC."

Jimmy looked up gravely. He dragged his feet together and stood up. "Thanks, ever so much, sir," he said, as if he were speaking to strangers.

Then he sat down and Jarvis went back to his seat. There was considerable pushing of chairs, and swearing, and hard drinking, but little talk the rest of the evening.

A few days of bad weather rested the squadron. Jimmy began to regain his composure, to get back his steely control. Then the captain brought information that made all the mess howl disapproval.

"The major's coming over Tuesday night to present the ribbons," he said. "Decorations have come through for Deane and Jarvis as well as Murdie, and he's going to have a whale of a time making speeches to you. For the love of salt petre, don't get his goat. I think he's half-sorry about the way he raved when he was here last time, and probably he'll try to act the other extreme. Be good little boys and he'll likely trot off home by ten at the latest."

Tuesday morning was dull and Jimmy was elated when he found he was to be excused from the morning's flight. Then Hendricks sent for him. "I didn't want anything to happen to you on the day you get your ribbon," he said, "and so I've landed you a cushy job. You're to go to St. Omer and bring back a new scout they've sent over. It's a snappy little machine, according to reports, and you'll have a sporty trip."

Jimmy thanked him and hurried away. The weather might grow worse.

There seemed to be a conspiracy against him at St. Omer, a plot to keep him from getting into the air before the mist thickened. When at last he was away he was so filled with impatience that he at first lost his bearings. Veering, he ran into a fog, which seemed sweeping to meet him, a solid wave of thick grey vapours.

He dived with his engine full out, then zoomed abruptly. He had not escaped the fog and his altimeter had shown him that he was not four hundred feet above the ground. Crawling, drifting mist walled him in on every side. He could see nothing but dim greyness, above, below and all around him. Desperately he climbed, up, and up, until the fog thinned into lacy layers and at last he was in daylight.

Jimmy flew in a straight line, watching his compass, resolved that he would not lose his head and that his best plan was to outfly the fog area and land wherever he could see ground. And, once down, he would make a clean breast of everything. No matter what the result, he would explain his weakness to Hendricks.

The crawling banks of mist slipped under him endlessly; the mist seemed to extend in every direction. He dived at last, watching his altimeter. Down, down and down, until he was dangerously near the earth. He soared up again. Tree tops or telegraph wires were treacherous things to hurdle. On and on and on he flew. He began to have dreadful thoughts. How far had he flown?

If he were drifting to the eastward he would be over the Hun lines before he knew it. Or it was possible to get over the water, the Channel. What lay under that floor of mist? A feeling of sheer helplessness seized him, gave him wild impulses. He wanted to dive straight down, to crash any old way so long as he was on solid earth again. The mist had become a deadly thing, a maddening, terrifying thing; something he must escape, outwit.

Calming himself with effort, he nosed downward, plunging and flattening out, watching his altimeter. At last he shut off the engine and went down in a long glide. Five hundred, four hundred, three, down to two hundred feet he went, and still the swirling greyness. He opened up his engine again, so as to keep his flying speed, but shut it off at intervals and glided, straining his eyes on the vapours, listening for sound of anything but the whine of the wind on his wings and wires.

It seemed useless. He grew panicky, jerked his throttle wide open and shot up, up, suddenly, steeply, the deafening roar seeming no louder than the thumping of his heart. Then, abruptly, his panic fled. He regained control of himself. Down, down again. Down, still down, his hand ready on the throttle. This mad game could not go on forever. He must land.

Down, down, steadily, gradually, down, and down...down... down.... He knew that all depended on what sort of surface lay below him. If it were a field, well and good. He would make a half-decent landing. If it were a village, a camp, he must catch his speed again, soar up and away before he was wrecked.

Down, down...the mist *must* clear. Down, lower...only feet above the earth...down. A warm moistness broke over Jimmy's body. He almost went limp. It was impossible, unbelievable. He wanted to scream, to yell so that all France could hear. Daintily his plane took ground, ran along gracefully, a perfect landing, and he sat, limp, in the cockpit. It was a miracle! He had actually landed at his own 'drome!

It was so screamingly funny that it weakened Jimmy. He could hardly credit his eyes, his senses. But there was the dim outline of the hangar, and the huts, and the broken lorry...wait...how, had that lorry been moved?

Jimmy stiffened as if he had had an electric shock. A dog came into view. It was a strange-looking, low-set creature; dachshunds, they called them. He switched on the engine, breathing fast, with whistling intakes. A man ran from one of the buildings, pointing. A whistle shrilled.

It seemed an hour, but it had not been sixty seconds since Jimmy landed. He swept over the field but his machine appeared to have lost power, response. More men appeared, and some were very close. Another few seconds...He thought feverishly, wished for a weapon. Ah, the bottle of "icicle" wine in his pocket that he had bought for Hendricks. He wrenched it free and hurled it with a swinging motion. It went over and over in a high spiral. The running, grey-clad men ducked, plunged for cover. Jimmy took the air, his plane rose gracefully. *Crack-crack-crack*. Rifles, somewhere, then machine guns. They were too late. He was into the mists. The last thing he saw was the dachshund running in circles.

Up and up and up. What! Sunlight. He tingled with new emotions. Perspiration dampened his clothing, but he felt as if he had escaped a precipice. And...the mist was thinning rapidly.

He throttled the engine to slower speed, watched his instruments and compass. The seething banks of vapour became more and more transparent. He dived through them, cut into them, tore them apart, drew them after him...he wanted to cheer. He could see earth.

In two minutes he had picked out his direction and in twenty minutes he had crossed the lines and was circling down to his own aerodrome. No one made particular mention of the mists, and he did not. He could not trust himself to speak about them. His nerves were so jangled that it would mean a sobbing breakdown, a holy show of himself before the crowd. Everyone was talking about the evening's celebration, and the major.

The major liked his liquor. Jimmy, that evening, saw him empty three glasses without so much as a gurgle. He was in great good humour, and was actually smiling at Hendricks. Everything went smoothly. The three men to be decorated were seated together, and Jarvis had placed himself beside Jimmy. During the first lull he turned and smiled.

"Do you know, Murdie," he said, "that I'd give anything to have one gift you've got?"

Jimmy could only stare at him. He had come to like this rather austere English chap, who surely was a master airman.

"I mean your gift of getting through those blasted fog banks and mists. I hate them, and I'm helpless in them."

Jarvis shivered visibly. Jimmy felt a queer tension creep over him. Now was his chance to tell the truth, but if even his life had depended on it, he could not have confessed. Some inexplicable revulsion sealed his lips. He said nothing.

"I think the way you followed Allmeder through the fog over Zillebeke was one of the best stunts of the war," Jarvis continued. "I don't believe there's another man in this squadron who would have even tried it."

Captain Hendricks rapped on the table. "Attention, gentlemen," he said. "The major has a few words to say."

Jimmy sat as if he were rigid. His skin was burning and he had queer sensations. What a fool he was, what a consummate ass. This had been his best chance to explain himself, and he had muffed it hideously.

The "few words" were expanded to a bombastic speech. The major was proud, very proud, of his men. They were "his boys," he loved them like a father. It gave him great pleasure to be able to bestow a few medal ribbons. He regretted there were not more, so many were deserved. The squadron was the finest in France, undoubtedly so. The Germans dreaded its black-painted machines, had reason to.

He was in splendid humour, and he finished with a humourous

story. "You all need a good laugh," he wheezed. "I'll give you one. A German airman was brought down just at dark this evening in the Bethune sector. He had a marvellous tale about an English airman landing at their aerodrome while the mist was on and trying to set fire to it, or some such stunt. The fellow was not clear on that point. He said that they hadn't really known what the chap was going to do, and he was discovered before any damage could be done. Now listen, gentlemen, here's the richest joke I've heard. They asked the German if the Britisher shot at them, and he said, 'No, but a bottle of wine was at the men thrown.'"

The major laughed, and all the mess joined him, except Jimmy. A thousand emotions had paralyzed him. He was seeing again that queer-shaped dog…those running men…the mists… "but a bottle of wine was at the men thrown!" Blast this pompous old brass hat. What would he have done in such a place? Jimmy's resentment flamed within him. He saw red. Then, as if the lights in the room had changed, another feeling surged over him. He pitied the paunchy old meddler. What did he know about war, flying…mists?

"Did you ever hear anything funnier?" The major was mopping his red face. "Imagine an Englishman throwing a good bottle of wine at a beastly Hun! Pow! Haw-haw!"

The major haw-hawed and chuckled and the mess gave him considerate accompaniment, all but Jimmy. He gazed around the room at his fellow officers, watched their simulated laughter, and something seemed to give within him. A full realization of the situation struck him, prodded him. He leaned back in his seat and simply exploded hilarity, a wild, free-lunged hee-haw roar that dominated.

The major's eyes widened but he graciously overlooked the discord. "I hear my friend, the laughing jackass," he called good humouredly, "and I like to hear him."

Jarvis laid a friendly hand on Jimmy's shoulder. "Hold in," he whispered. "There's really nothing to laugh about." Anxiety was written large on his face.

And the mess decided, after the major was gone, that Jimmy was really a bit of a jackass, for he had laughed more shrilly than ever.

The Russian Coat

Private Otto Kettner slowly opened his eyes. He stirred in his bunk, shivered, and spat; there seemed to be a bitter taste in his mouth. Along the dank passage, which held other bunks and makeshift beds, the mutter of voices sounded like a prolonged growling. Many of the men were coughing with dismal hacking sounds. He pushed back the foul blankets under which he had huddled and put his feet to the floor. Ugh! The place was beastly cold. The stove ten paces from him was red on its sides, yet the icy cold dominated.

He went to the light of a small Hindenburg lamp and looked at his watch. It was seven o'clock. It was his turn, too, as senior private, to go to company headquarters and get the rations for the day. Also the mail, if any. The hope of a letter aroused him. Then, too, there had been a rumour that they were to be relieved and taken back to a town in the rear.

No one spoke to him as he bundled himself preparatory to leaving the tunnel-like space which had been some sort of storehouse before the Russians had fitted bunks into it and established a stove. They had been lucky to find such a billet, Otto knew, and it had been a simple matter to oust the peasants who were occupying it.

Otto pushed the door open and closed it quickly on its screeching hinges. He gasped as he met the sharp air that swept the open, and then hurried through a path in the snow to a cottage that looked sunken in the frozen landscape. He pushed into the porch and opened the door quickly, to confront a hungry-looking fellow with a long cold nose.

"Are the rations in?" He asked the question before the sentry could complain about his abrupt entrance.

The fellow flicked a drop from his nose and shook his head. "We will have to eat the same rotten bread and carrot jam. There is no mail, of course."

Otto shrugged. "This could be yesterday or the day before. Why are you so cheerful?" It was a joke he had used often. "You have a soft job here, and the best Russian coat in our company. What more could you wish?"

The other resumed his hunched apathy. "Perhaps you will be cheerful," he said, "when you hear the message from our officer."

"Come along," a voice said roughly. "Why chatter with that dolt?"

It was Demming, the platoon sergeant, who spoke. He sat in an inner room attending to the stoking of a stove with a broken top. "There are the rations for your men,"—he pointed to bundles on the table—"and be thankful they are not less. It is a miracle that we have food at all."

"Of course." Otto said it mechanically. "Is there any word of relief?"

"The word is," snapped Demming, "that we are to remain here another week. The fools think there are some of those cursed Russians roaming about this area. They do not seem to realize that we are forty kilometres from the reserve lines and that not a dozen buildings remain standing in that distance."

"There are the paratroops," Otto shrugged.

"So! We have heard that song for months. Where would they be? Are they invisible?"

Demming snorted and kicked the stove. He had become very irritable.

"There is the forest?" Otto said it mildly.

"The forest! A wilderness in which not even a wolf could survive." He paused and looked at Otto, then put more mockery in his tone. "Do you wish to earn a leave to your home town? Search the snow banks until you find a Russian soldier and you will be permitted to go at once. Our new officer promised it. Also there will be an Iron Cross. Imagine!" The sergeant rubbed his chest violently as if the heat of the stove had roused body vermin. "It was hard not to laugh in his silly face when he gave me such word last night. Russian soldiers! Does he think we are magicians?"

"Did you ask him about a coat for me?" Otto tried to keep the whine out of his voice. "This one I am wearing is thin as paper. Did you tell him?"

"Of course not," shouted Demming. "Look after yourself and salvage a coat. That's all anyone can tell you. Go."

Otto gathered up the rations. Demming was always like that, getting to screaming when you asked him to do something. The sentry was moaning softly to himself like an old dog in misery and Otto went past without looking at the fellow. The outside air made him flinch. It was a cold that penetrated, that brought an agony above the eyes.

As he arrived at the platoon billet some of the men on the floor cursed savagely at the inrush of cold. The rest lay and shivered, huddled against each other for warmth.

"The orders?" a voice in the gloom croaked.

"The usual," Otto said dully. "No fresh rations. No mail. We are to stay another week."

He put a kettle on the stove and when the water boiled they made barley coffee. It seemed more bitter than usual but he drank three mug-fulls in an attempt to get rid of his chills.

Someone blundered against the outside door, and Otto opened it. The sergeant stood there, beckoning.

"Come with me," he said swiftly, and Otto closed the door behind him and obeyed.

"There is no need to spoil the morning of those shirkers in there," the sergeant went on. "You and I can do what is to be done, and forget it."

"What is it?" Otto asked. "I have not eaten yet."

"It's that sentry we had. He went to the latrine as you left. I heard a sound and went out. He had shot himself."

"Shot himself? Why?"

"That is a simple question to ask. How do I know? It is probable that he has done too much thinking, and it is not good to think in this place."

"Now," said Otto, recovering from his bewilderment, "I can have a warm coat."

"Not so quickly," snapped Demming. "The officer has ordered that such matters must be settled by a drawing."

"But I have not—"

"Stop it," grated Demming. "There will be a drawing. Say no more."

They carried the body to a drift in the open. The sergeant had a spade and with it he cut the snow crust. "You may have his ration for the day," he said.

Otto helped with the rough burial although he was almost stiff with cold. He carried the Russian coat as they went back to the platoon billet, and felt in the pockets. They held nothing of value. There was but a sheet of paper with two words pencilled at the top: "Dear Mother."

Had the poor fellow been interrupted as he began to write or had words failed him? What was there to say? Otto stared at the inky lettering, then shredded the paper into small pieces.

The men in the billet stared at the coat Otto carried and the sergeant told them, tersely, of the suicide. "Now bring me bits of paper," he finished. "We are going to draw for the coat."

A slip of paper with a number marked on it was given to each man, and the corresponding pieces were placed in a cap by the sergeant. He shook them well, then ordered Otto to take one from the cap and announce the number.

Otto nervously made the drawing, and called a number. It was held by Private Suhren, a youngster with a too-ready tongue. He took the coat gleefully.

"But," Otto protested, "he already has the best coat in the platoon!"

"Then beg it from him," said the sergeant roughly. "You had your chance," he went on in a lower tone. "Fool! Why did you not call out your own number?"

Otto waited until everyone had eaten and the men were quiet again before he went to Suhren. "I have ten marks," he said. "I will give you them for the coat."

"Keep your money," sneered Suhren. "I will not sell."

"Then," said Otto desperately. "I will give you five marks for your old one."

"Too late," grimaced Suhren. "I have already given it to another man."

Some of the men were wrapping blankets about themselves to go outside and all were cursing the cold when the door was thrown open and the sergeant shouted "Attention!"

The officer had come to inspect them and they stood, woodenly, where they had arisen, waiting. "No one would know we are at war," the officer had come lately from Berlin to stiffen the morale of the company, "if he were to see such a rabble as this. Who is the senior here?"

Otto saluted. "I am, Herr Lieutenant."

"So, and what are your duties?"

"We are to watch for enemy planes during daylight, to keep an eye for any civilians who may move about, and to collect fuel for the fires."

"It is daylight now," rasped the officer. "Who is watching for planes?"

There was an exit at the opposite end of the building and Otto had seen one of the older men scurry outside as the sergeant fumbled with the door latch.

"Private Gresser, sir."

The sergeant looked relieved. "Show me," said the officer.

They went outside and Otto led the way to a square space they had cut in a drift so as to get shelter from the wind. A soldier stood there, gazing at the sky. He was ragged and dirty but he was clearly on duty.

"Do you have," snarled the officer, "but one man to watch for both planes and peasants?"

"It is very cold," Otto said mildly, "and it is but a few steps into the billet to report anything."

"There are only seven peasants in all the area," added the sergeant, "and they are old ones."

"Bah!" snorted the officer. "You are all becoming better at making excuses than anything else." He glared at Otto. "You are too much by the stove," he went on. "Take a man with you and make a scouting trip. See if you can locate any of the enemy. Get ready and go at once."

As Otto turned to obey he pointed to his thin greatcoat but the Sergeant's face was as stone and not a word was said.

Otto thought of Private Suhren with the warm coat, and ordered him to make ready for the patrol. Rage set Otto's breathing faster. Such beastly unfairness. The officer would hustle back to his cosy billet and stay there, and the sergeant would sit by his stove.

Otto shook himself and coughed as they climbed a snow bank. The walking was heavy so that the first efforts caused a small pain in his chest and he coughed again and again.

There was not a sound in the landscape. The few ragged silhouettes of destroyed buildings seemed one with the billets of their company. To their left the forest stretched like a great dark barrier and as they veered toward it to rest their eyes against the glare of the snow Otto noticed several gaps in the blurred mass of evergreens. They were small glades, he knew, offering shelter from the biting little gusts of icy air, and he led directly toward them.

He had another fit of coughing as he hurried and resented instantly Suhren's suggestion that they ought not to tramp so fast.

"What's wrong with you," he demanded, "that you want to go slower? Don't tell me that you are cold."

"I wasn't thinking about myself," said Suhren easily. "I can follow without trouble. But you are much older than the rest of us and you don't look well."

"I am well enough," Otto said shortly. "We will get among those trees and be away from the wind at least."

"It is quite a distance!" Suhren was startled. "I thought we would not be away more than an hour?"

"Fool!" scoffed Otto. "The officer expects us to patrol this entire area. It will be easier to rest among the trees than to keep tramping."

Suhren was short and stout and the Russian coat made him appear as broad as he was tall. He shook his head as Otto had another fit of coughing. "You should report to the doctor the next time he comes to the company."

"Fat good that would do," panted Otto, "and if you are so concerned you can let me have that coat in exchange."

Suhren made no answer and they trudged on until they had passed under the first trees, then he paused.

"Have you a compass?" he asked.

"For what?" queried Otto impatiently. "Are not our tracks enough marking to guide us back?"

"To be sure," grunted Suhren. "I had not thought of them. I would not want to lose my way here."

Otto's hatred of their futile errand increased as he plodded through the loose snow but he kept on and did not halt until they had reached a small ravine. There he stopped by a pine windfall and began breaking its brittle branches.

"We can build a fire here," he said, "and the smoke will not rise enough to be seen back at our billets. See, I have brought my pan so that we can make some of that miserable coffee."

They built a fire and huddled beside it on seats of brush. The blaze seemed fierce but after an hour it was not enough to banish the chill from Otto. His breath formed icy particles on the collar of his greatcoat. Cold stole up his body from the snow. Cold stabbed down at him from overhead. He knew that he had not eaten sufficient food in more than a month and that he was not a well man.

The nagging cold was too much for him. He piled on brush extravagantly until the flames leaped high but warmth still eluded him. "One side may roast," he cried, "but the other side of me is freezing. Put in the coffee. The water is boiling now."

Suhren dumped in the coffee and stirred the mixture. Then he stared upward.

"Look!" he said in alarm. "Snowflakes! A storm is coming. Let us get from here. We do not want our tracks to be covered."

Otto gulped the coffee. The drink ran through him like fire. It raced through his veins in a scorching flood and he welcomed the stabbing pain. But a moment later he was shivering.

"No," he refused, "we will stay here for a time. It will take plenty of snow to cover our tracks and there is no hurry."

"You forget," argued Suhren, "that it is not only the snow that falls that covers the tracks, but the loose snow will drift. Listen, and you will hear there is quite a wind. We are rested now. Let's go."

"I am in charge," rebuked Otto. "We are going to stay for an hour more at least. Make a second fire so that we can stand between them. I want to get thoroughly warmed."

"Don't be a mule," said Suhren harshly. "You know that you cannot get warmed outdoors. See, the flakes are beginning to come quite fast."

"You are like a boy." Otto was angry. He did not want to tell Suhren that he was tired but his weariness was so great that he intended to rest for a long time. He tried to make an excuse for delay but his attempts to think clearly resulted merely in a more complete fuddling of his mental processes.

"It will be hours before our trail will be covered," he muttered. "Get some more wood and pile it on."

"There isn't much more that I can break with my hands," Suhren said impatiently, "and I cannot move the windfall. The cold has made you stupid. Come—stir yourself."

"I'll report you for disobedience," threatened Otto, all his former dislike for the fellow welling within him. "Get more wood."

His distorted thinking played with the fact that Suhren dared to dispute authority with him and he became more incensed.

"Always," he announced, "you have had too much to say. You will obey my orders. If you were decent at all you would let me have that coat. Hand it over now. You can wear this one back to the billets and see how the wind goes through it."

"You are crazy," retorted Suhren. "I got this coat in the drawing and I will keep it." He threw the last of the fuel on the fire. "I am going back before the storm gets worse," he added determinedly. "You can do as you wish."

Otto threw up his rifle. "Give me that coat," he ordered grimly.

He had taken Suhren by surprise but the fellow, instead of obeying, rushed at him, and Otto pulled trigger. There was no response from his weapon save a dull click, and the next instant Suhren had crashed him backward into the snow.

"Everyone at the billet has been saying you were losing your mind," gasped Suhren, wrestling the rifle from him, "and now I know they are right. You fool—you would have killed me."

He jerked back the rifle bolt and peered, but the chamber and magazine were empty. "On a scouting patrol without loading your rifle," he jeered. "That is proof that you are crazy."

Otto put all his strength into a desperate lunge, and again he caught

Suhren off guard. His shoulder struck the fellow in the middle and threw him down. Then they rolled in the snow and Otto beat at the fellow's face and drove his knee into Suhren's groin. Their heavy clothing hampered them but they struggled and fought with surprising fury until Otto weakened and was beaten down under a rain of heavy blows.

He never knew when Suhren left him, and when he had recovered sufficiently to sit up the fire had burned low. He groped for sticks but his sluggish stirring failed to rouse him until he discovered that there was no more fuel. He flung the brush they had used for seats onto the embers and as they blazed tried to push the fire to the fallen tree. A terrific fit of coughing seized him and there were buzzing sounds in his ears. But he finally got the fire licking into the windfall. Then he broke frozen branches from the nearest trees and flung them into the flames.

They blazed with gusto and smoke clouds billowed aloft.

When he had imbibed some warmth Otto stood and gazed about him. A little whispering wind struck at his exposed cheeks like needlepoints and a whirl of driven snow came among the trees. A shudder ran through his aching body, then he squatted by the fire and spoke aloud.

"They are all against me," he complained. "They know I am sick and that this coat of mine is like paper, but who is there to care? The sergeant has not helped me. I will report to the officer myself. I will tell him...."

His voice trailed off as stupor possessed him. He stirred drowsily, knowing he should attend the fire. Then someone was shouting at him...commands. Dazedly he put his hands up in surrender. Figures were all about him, men dressed in greatcoats such as Suhren was wearing.

He was dimly aware of some words in awkward German and then a flask was held to his lips and he drank eagerly. A fiery liquor rushed the blood in his veins and before he could be sure of anything he was being hustled along the ravine to where the snow was packed like a road. Then he entered a tunnel leading into the ravine bank and was pushed and guided into a chamber where such heat met him that he became dizzy.

An hour later he sat and stared at the strange faces about him, and wondered if he were dreaming. But the food in his stomach and the heart-warming liquids he had drunk assured him that everything was real. These men about him were Russians all right, and they looked like seasoned soldiers. They had their place fitted up like a barracks, too, and everything in order.

It amazed him that they were so kind to him. The sergeant had said that the Russians killed every man they captured, that they tortured their prisoners. It was all lies. He could not wish for better treatment. They had spared no pains to get him warmed. They had given him great helpings of a meaty broth, and cheese and black bread, and then, when he could eat no more, they had given him cigarettes.

"I cannot understand," he said to the one who acted as interpreter. "We were told you killed prisoners."

"Of course your officers would tell you that," the Russian agreed. "They do not want you to surrender. Have another drink and tell us about this place and where your platoon is billeted. We are newly arrived at this post."

Otto blinked, tried to concentrate his thinking. "How did you arrive?" he blurted.

"By plane," said the Russian, as one comrade to another. "Our supplies were dropped with us. We have been here a week. How many men are at your billets?"

"Too many, for the rations we have. And no mail has reached us for two weeks." Otto let loose all the bitterness he had felt through the long shivering nights. He told them about the officer from Berlin who had sent him on a fool's errand. Talking of the errand made him remember Suhresn and although his mind was becoming confused he told them of the unfairness he had experienced over the Russian coat.

"Feel my coat," he insisted. "It is thin as paper, and his was warm. Yet they let him take this other one. Is that fair?"

"You are a little drunk," the Russian said.

"Not too drunk," returned Otto. "I wish you had arrived sooner so that you could have caught Suhren as well. There is a matter I want to settle with him."

"Later will do," soothed the Russian.

The room had become hazy and Otto wanted to sleep. He felt that he should not have talked so loosely but Suhren had hurt him, and no one had sided with him at the billets. Let them stew in their own juice.

When he awoke there was only one man with him, an older fellow who had served the food. "Where are the others?" Otto asked. "Is it morning?"

"Not yet." The fellow's German was difficult to understand and he appeared very sleepy. "The others have gone to visit your comrades."

"To visit them!" Otto's head was aching but his mind had cleared and a vast uneasiness possessed him. He had babbled too much. "When did they go?"

"They will be there at daybreak," said the Russian, "and it is snowing. It will be an easy matter."

Otto visualized what would happen, and was jabbed by a thousand accusations. He pretended to doze again until he heard the Russian snoring.

Then he glanced about him. His equipment and greatcoat were piled in a corner back of the Russian but his cap and gloves were near him. He arose softly, snatched up the blanket that had covered him and, after some moments of anxious groping, found the exit.

The air that met him was razor-edged but he threw the blanket over his head and shoulders and rushed into the darkness. Twice he tripped and fell, and each time he found it more difficult to get up. A frightful fit of coughing seized him so that he had to pause to get his breath. The cold numbed him, made him leaden in his movements. He should have had his greatcoat. The blanket was like nothing.

Thinking of the greatcoat drove his slowing mind to remember Suhren. He stopped, and turned. "He is so smart, that one," he mumbled, "and the sergeant would not speak to the officer. Let them all be surprised."

He kept on mumbling about the officer from Berlin, and the fool's errand he had been sent on...a warm coat was what a man needed...he would get that one from Suhren...there was no hurry....

There was a moment when he knew he was lying in the snow but the Russians would be coming that way and they would give him a coat, one of those warm Russian greatcoats. It was the last thought he had. The snow sifted over him and the breath of the storm hardened him like iron.

The Finer Instincts

Sergeant John Keene watched the prisoners file by; men in field grey, shuffling down the dusty road, plodding in dully apathy, indifferent as tired cattle. He turned to the man beside him.

"Those," he said, "are the real German type. They're stolid, unimaginative, coarse-minded animals, beasts with women, beasts in war, and bovine in peace."

Corporal Ashley's dreamy eyes filled with protest. "You're too wholesale," he objected. "You've swallowed too much propaganda. I've got no use for their professional soldiers, but the rest of them are not much different from us."

Keene's eyes flashed impatience as he moved away. "You've been soft-hearted about them ever since you saw their Red Cross men bring one of our boys out of the shelling at Vimy," he retorted. "What they did to Belgium, and with gas at Ypres, and what they're doing with their zeppelins and submarines, doesn't count with you."

"You don't get me right, Keene." Ashley looked back at him and smiled. "Their leaders have different ideas of warfare, that's all. In Canada we're all British but don't we have different religions and politics?"

It was Ashley's same line of argument. Keene flung his final retort. "They're Huns, Boche, killers, brutes, raiders, and always have been. They're mechanically clever and systematic, but they're totally devoid of the finer instincts of the white race."

He hurried away to his hut. Every time he argued with Ashley he got hot, his blood boiled; the man was so infernally narrow-minded. He had seen Red Cross Germans do one kind deed and he has made it a halo for the rest, an excuse for clinging to exasperating asinine viewpoints.

Their company marched over the Ridge at dusk, back to the line again, to do another routine tour in front of Avion. Keene, at the rear of his platoon, watched the wide arc of Very lights rising and falling over the plain, the red flicker of distant gun flashes, and felt unutterably miserable.

Back to the front again, more war, more casualties, more shelling by the Hun; how he hated it!

Down in the long communication trench leading forward their progress was painfully slow. Enemy whizz bangs had broken down the walls, smashed bath mats, tangled wires, and a litany of monotonous warning travelled along the column. "Hole under foot...wire overhead...step up...step down." Reliefs were just as tedious, for the shelling had not spared the front. The out-going men carried wounded comrades, and the stretcher parties had strenuous times getting around wrecked bay and traverse. It was midnight before Keene's unit, the "Prairie Wolves," was completely established.

"We've got a good dugout this time." Corporal Ashley's soft drawl reached him from the shadows. "It's a Heinie one but they've changed the entrance so it's Jake for us. There's pictures on the walls, a real bed and stove and chairs."

"Stuff they've taken from French houses," said Keene bitterly. "They steal whatever their shells don't smash up."

He went down the new stairway into a dark underground, pushed aside a heavy gas curtain and entered a board-walled chamber. A bedstead heaped with dirty linen faced him. To one side were chairs, a table, and a pot-bellied French stove. A wire strung with stick bombs stretched beside the entrance. A German greatcoat still hung from a nail in one corner. On the wall were newspaper pictures of Hindenburg and the Kaiser. Everything exuded the faint inexplicable characteristic odour of German occupation.

Keene sniffed the close atmosphere. "Phew!" he said disgustedly. "The smell is too much for me. I'd sooner sleep in the trench."

"You'll change your mind after a few 'Minnies' come over," said the corporal. "I'll take the gas blanket down and let some fresh air in."

The sergeant went back up the steps and visited the machine-gun post, a sandbagged emplacement in the corner of a stone wall. He inhaled the night air. Despite the aroma of chloride of lime and rotting handbags it seemed heavy with the scent of roses. The guns were quiet for a moment and overhead stars sprinkled a velvet sky. Around the jagged rib-like ruins of Avion soft flares shot up and unfolded like flowers from a world of ghosts.

Crack-crack-crack. The weirdness of the scene was dispelled by the bark of a machine gun. Bullets snapped over them and jerked Keene back to grim realities.

"Smells like there's flowers somewhere handy," grunted the Lewis gunner. "Roses, I'd say."

"That's what they are," said Keene. "It's a wonder the Hun missed them." He spoke ironically.

He was restless until morning. The perfume-laden night air had wafted him back to a June that seemed to belong to a remote past. If only the gaunt skeleton-like trees between the lines could take on greenery, if only those palpitating glows that rose and fell so intermittently could become fixtures among the trees...Years and years ago there had been soft perfumed evenings with smooth lawns, jewelled flower beds, gay lights, happy voices...The rose scent brought it back, set his whole being seething with longing.

He slept fitfully on the tumbled bed and went up to the trench at stand-to. Birds were chirping in a remnant of hedge near the garden wall. The sentries were huddled on the fire steps. Others paced the hard-packed trench floor. The east was shot with crimson. Over on the Somme the guns were grumbling throatily. Elsewhere it was quiet. A light mist hung over the hollows near Lens, making the slag heap dank islands in a woolly sea. All at once sun rays glittered through them, gave a glisten to the dew-wet wire and weeds in front of the parapet. Men moved about briskly, looking expectant. An officer came along with the rum issue. After he had gone there were odours of tea and bacon from the dugouts. Another day had begun.

It was an hour later that Keene heard the sharp spiteful crack of a sniper's rifle, and a choking cry. He hurried along the trench. What new deviltry was afoot? Scared-looking men were grouped about the Lewis gun post. "It's Jim, Sarge," they said. He pulled away some of the bags and crawled out under the wire to get some of them roses. Some dirty sniper plugged him."

Jim sniped! Jim, the best gunner in the company, out since '15, sniped because he tried to pick a rose! Keene's veins swelled and pounded. Hot rage and grief welled tears to his eyes. The dirty, despicable cattle. Sniping a man because....

"I told him not to try to get them when he talked about it at stand-to." It was Ashley's quiet voice. "Fritz wouldn't know what he was after."

Crash! A rifle grenade exploded just outside the bags and scattered chalk fragments over them, causing each man to duck and crouch.

"Damn them!" Keene bellowed curses as he took cover. "The dirty dogs. Send word to our Stokes men. They're trying to batter Jim, to blow him to pieces." He glared at Ashley.

Crash! Another grenade. Two more after that, and then all was still again. Keene raised his periscope carefully. Jim's body lay sprawled half under the wire, his head rolled back, his dark hair matted with blood. He had reached the roses, had plucked one and fastened it to his tunic, but it had wilted, looked crushed, smothered.

The sun grew hot. The Stokes crashed their hate in the Hun lines, and quieted again. A few planes droned overhead and circled amid the resulting puffs of white smoke, the "Archie's" protests. The Hun shelled ground he had lost near the Triangle. Every now and then there would come a great rushing sound, and the brick-strewn earth would erupt in geysers of black smoke and debris. Keene looked in the periscope again. Big blue flies were buzzing about the dead man. They sickened him, and he went along the trench.

When he returned a limp form, covered by a ground sheet, lie on the fire step. He looked at the sentry enquiringly. "The Corp got him in," said the fellow. "He stuck up a white rag on a stick, left it up five minutes and then stepped right out to the wire and pulled Jim in. It was takin' chances all right."

A white rag! Keene hadn't thought of trying that, and, anyway, he wouldn't. Then he started. The sentry was a big-mouthed, coarse-looking man, unshaved and unwashed, and—he was wearing a wilted rose in a buttonhole.

"Where did you get that?" Keene pointed a finger. "It's the one Jim had," the fellow mumbled.

"Take it off. Blast it, man, haven't you got any sense of decency at all." Keene was furious. He stamped down the dugout steps. Ashley was sleeping. On the table were rations, rifle rag, and a letter—his.

He tore it open and his hands trembled slightly. "My dearest John," it began. "I think of you more than ever now that everything is in blossom again...."

Three times he re-read the close-written pages, and then he looked at the sleeping man. He'd like to talk to him, tell him about his letter, picture the gardens and field and orchards in Canada, but he couldn't. Ashley was not the right type. He had been a clerk in some big shipping firm and, probably, a careful methodical fellow, a decent chap, clean-living, but, queer, narrow-minded on some points, especially thick-headed about the Germans; he hadn't discrimination, a sensitive intellect.

Keene could not rest. He went back to the trench and with his binoculars scanned the Ridge and its surroundings. He had had the feeling that they had made a mighty advance into the enemy territory, but now as he gazed it came to him that it had been a paltry step, futile towards hastening the end of the war.

He adjusted the range of the field glasses. Currents of heated air from debris vibrated in tremors that confused his vision. Scars of old trenches on the distant slope showed raw white. A black puff of smoke dislodged two crows from some putrid feast on hidden ground. Far back, huge sausage balloons rode lazily in the blue, like question marks against the horizon. All peaceful, yet ghastly, mocking. He loathed the landscape, hated it with an intensity that startled him; it was as if he were struggling against it, and did not know how to escape it.

The heat was sickening in the narrow confines of the trench. The sentry at the periscope was chewing tobacco. Now and then he pursed his lips and expectorated into the corner of the bay. His partner on duty was slumped on the fire step with his tunic and shirt open, searching for vermin. The stale, saline smell of his sweat-dried clothing added to the conglomeration of sun-roused trench odours. Keene felt a nausea stir his stomach. He went below again and flung himself down, determined to rest.

Sleep would not come to him. He had a nagging, gnawing, sense of futility. Heat, smells, horror, death, clamour, shelling, marching, the soldier's existence was all a torture, and yet he felt that there lay within his reach some quality, some tangible, obtainable magic, some knowledge, that, could he but attain it, would reveal new vistas of hope, provide a merciful anodyne for shattered nerves.

The greens and balmy breath of June had not brought it. Slush-filled and rain-swept trenches had seemed an agony that made warm sunshine a manna from heaven, but heat brought stench and dust, fine powdery dust that clung to their khaki and skin and tormented their nostrils. Rest billets in war-battered villages meant sleeping in stables, noisy evenings over beer in sloppy estaminets, wearisome drill and routine details. And always there were rumours; another attack was to be made; a thousand tanks were to break through; the division was going to Egypt; the airships would bomb Berlin.

Rats scrambling back of the board walls interrupted his thoughts, and while he listened he dozed and slept.

Ashley woke him for stand-to. "It's another Jake night," he said. "We'll have it easy, and this is a short trip. The sergeant-major says we're going back to practice a kick-off from this trench we're in."

Keene sat up and stared at the corporal. "Kick-off," he echoed. "What's the idea? We're only just back to strength from the Vimy show."

"They want us to take a slice off of Avion, that's all the SM told me," said Ashley, "and if our artillery put down a decent barrage it hadn't ought to be much of a job."

"No? It'll just mean more work for the pioneers, making more white crosses, another draft to the company, that's all." Keene's voice was bitter, hard.

"Stand-to." A voice shouted down the stairway.

Keene went up sullenly. It was the sergeant major who had called. "Another nice evening," he said pleasantly. "The major wants a patrol to go out and see if they can get information about the machine-gun post near that brick heap straight over there. Ashley can go. Tell him to take one of the scouts, that's all."

Keene hated to tell Ashley. He hated patrols himself, and there seemed a sinister threat about the German line. It lay among too many cellars and brick heaps. But the corporal seemed cheerful. "I'll be out among the roses," he said. "There are quite a few near the German wire."

He had been gone an hour and Keene was listening anxiously when there was a sharp report, the bark of an army revolver, near the Hun line. Then there came sounds of plunging, running men, and Ashley and his scout slid under the wire. They were not a heartbeat too soon. Maxims raved and bullets hissed and swished over the ground they had passed.

"One lone chap came outside their parapet," Ashley panted. "I shot him and tore off his shoulder straps so's to get his regimental numbers. That ought to be good information."

It was, but Keene stared. It was hard to visualize Ashley shooting a prowler in cold blood. Why... Ah, that was just the reason he made such arguments and never understood talk about the finer perceptions. He was devoid of them himself, so how could he see their lack in the Teuton make-up? Later, when he came back from making his report, Ashley paused and looked over the wire a long time.

"It's just come to me," he said softly, "that that poor beggar might have been after some roses. If I had thought that I couldn't have shot him."

Keene, in the shadows, grimaced, and spat at a rat.

Dawn brought another glorious morning. Keene went up into the trench to get his lungs full of fresh air, and a sentry beckoned him to a periscope. Its glass showed him the bigger brick heap near the Hun trench. A grey-coated figure lay sprawled there, a pot helmet nearby. As he peered Keene saw a head upthrust from the German trench, a head that rose and withdrew several times. Then a German soldier scrambled over his parapet and crept out to the dead man. Every move was hurried, furtive, fear-ruled. He seized the inert form by the arms and dragged it back the way he had come, through a gap in the wire. Then he jumped down into the bay he had left and tugged the corpse in without exposing himself further.

Keene looked around. Half a dozen men were peering over the top and had watched the German. Not one of them had reached for his rifle. Somehow, he felt proud of them.

It wanted only three minutes to zero-hour. Keene looked up and down the trench, at the different expressions of the men. Some were white-faced, tight-lipped holding themselves as with a leash.

Others showed unmastered fear, sheer terror. They were the ones with too vivid imaginations, going through all dangers twice, and the non-coms had to watch them.

He smelled the morning and its dewy dampness. The odour of disturbed chalky earth was not obnoxious, but he hated the sight of flies buzzing around newly-emptied bully tins left on the trench floor. Flies, he hated them.

Crash! The barrage! A smashing, tearing roar of guns. A flash of explosion in front, lurid lights, smoke. *Crash—crash—crash*. Three upheavals of soil just in front of them. Mushrooms of drifting, acrid smoke and fumes. The first retaliation. An officer looked at his wrist watch and held a whistle to his lips. The pounding gunfire increased. There was a red spurt of flame in front of a traverse on the right, and shrill cries.

"Stretcher bearer—stretcher bearer!"

Then they were over.

Somebody pitched down at the cut wire and Keene tripped over a rolling tin hat. He plunged on without looking at the fallen man, drove on, leaping shell holes, seeing dim figures in smoke flurries, hearing the *pin-ning* of Mills bombs. He saw the scarlet of an explosion near him, heard a man scream in death agony, then...a searing white flame blinded him, hurled him to earth...oblivion.

If only the clanging, banging bells would stop ringing...They did, but the slamming roar of guns jarred his head, made it ache with splitting violence. He tried to move, put down a hand, feebly. It touched earth, loose, soft earth, wet earth. Something hurt his neck. It was the edge of his steel helmet, twisted back, the strap under his chin holding it in place. After a tremendous effort he loosened it, let it fall away from him. Queer how such a trivial thing would be so difficult. He must be hit somewhere, wounded.

It was hard to think. His head throbbed, burned; he was weak, too weak to move. Vaguely, he wondered where he was, what had happened. Oh yes, the attack. He must be hurt. Why didn't someone come? Where were the Germans? Someone touched him and he looked up slowly—he could do nothing quickly—and saw a stretcher-bearer place his sack of bandages on the ground, on the rim of a crater. Funny, now, that he didn't remember that crater. Where—

"Don't try to move, Sergeant." The stretcher-bearer was speaking needlessly. "You're lucky to be alive if you were here when that shell burst." The man pointed to the new shell hole. "I'll turn you a little, there. Hold still, now, when I pour on the iodine. Perhaps you won't feel it, though. You've got a bad one."

Keene watched the fellow dully, then flinched as the sudden red-hot needles lanced his leg, pierced his flesh.

"Easy, man," he tried to shout, but his voice was faint and husky. The man seemed to fumble a long time, to be doing an endless amount of wrapping, then he gave Keene a drink of water.

"We'll get you in as soon as things get settled," he said. "Heinie's putting up an awful scrap over near the houses. I'll prop you up and then I'll have to leave you."

He pulled Keene's equipment back off his shoulders and scooped loose-flung earth from the shell cavity into a supporting pillow. "Don't try to move," he added and was gone.

Keene could see the rear of a ruin, shattered brick, a splintered beam, and a dead man on the ground near him. Sunlight on the man's bayonet caught his eye first, and then his gaze travelled over an outflung arm to a face that was turned toward him as if in repose. "Hul..." He had tried to whisper, to speak to Ashley, and then he remembered that the man was dead.

Why didn't he shut his eyes? Keene didn't like their dull, unseeing gaze. Why wasn't Ashley tumbled about, twisted, bloodied? He lay there as if having a rest, and, somehow, he knew that the corporal would die like that. He was never headlong, excited, emotional; he wouldn't even get angry in an argument. Arguments...hmmm...now it was too late to convince the man.

Keene wanted to protest such unfairness. How could anyone die thinking that Germans were....

He couldn't think. The world was all noise, indefinite noise. It was all blue overhead, clear blue...no, something obstructed his view, wavered there. A man, what...it was a German.

The fellow's dirty-grey tunic looked so—so unsoldierly, his tin gas mask dangled in a silly way. What hideous uniforms these men wore!

He looked at the man's face, scanned it incuriously. In a way, it wasn't so bad being hit—one lost all fear of the enemy or anything; funny, that sort of feeling. The fellow muttered something, seemed to be pleading. He had his hands up, was stupid with the shock of being taken prisoner. A Hun! The forehead was too wide, the complexion too pasty, except...aha, he was wounded too. One ear was almost torn from his head, shredded, and blood clotted on his neck. Faugh—it was sickening. Keene shut his eyes. When he opened them the man had gone.

He wished he had talked to him, asked him something, heard him speak...it seemed so long since anyone had been near, anyone but Ashley. Ashley...if only he had been able to see and understand for just a few minutes. A few words with that wounded Hun would have been enough, one could see that he was the "type," a war cog, incapable of fine reasoning, intuition; just a number in the ranks; one more "goose stepper," capable of any bloodshed, minus all thinking principles.

The shelling had stopped. He must have dozed, for he couldn't remember its cessation. What time was it? If only he were nearer Ashley. There was a watch on that hairy outflung wrist, and it would be the correct time, the corporal was so careful, clerk habits, of course.

What...stars overhead. Flickers on the ruin, noiseless, flighty fingers, never-resting. Flare reflections. Night...why didn't they get him? Ugh! What was that? Something cold touched his hand. He turned his head. It was a rat, a black, bloated thing, scuttling away.

"Scat!" He tried to call out. That foul crawler mustn't go near Ashley. Ashley—blast it—was his friend.

Keene felt the rush of cool air as his stretcher swayed and jolted. There were murmurings, voices, near but indistinct. Ouch...the ambulance rocked, bumped, jerked him cruelly. Pain jabbed him, tore at him, knifed him, seared him, cut him...At last they had left him alone....

They had seemed to probe at him for hours, that doctor and the square-shouldered nurse who had just gone. They had muttered, talked incoherently. If only he knew what they had said. His leg, his left leg, yes, his side, too, were hurt. But, how badly? One thing was sure—they should not operate in France.

He had had that on his mind ever since he had seen the stars the first time. There had been chaps put on the table in France who lost legs through hurried work, quick work without proper precautions. No slip-shod treatment for him. And—the biggest thing—he wanted to get across the channel. To get away from the war, that was all he wanted, away from those twisting, raw- white trenches, from guns and shells, and ruins, and flies, and smells and rats. Once he had prided himself on being a good soldier, a hardy one; now he only wanted to get away, he had slipped from under all other ambitions.

The nurse came again, with two men who carried a stretcher. Keene held up his hand. "No, sister," he said, slowly, stubbornly. "You're not putting me on a table over here. I'm for England. I refuse."

"But your leg. It is serious!"

"I—refuse, you hear me, sister."

There were whisperings and then the two men went away again and took the stretcher with them. Keene gloated in his victory. England... no more France, and war.

His leg and side pained him so that he could not sleep and he wondered fretfully when they would take him away. Then a nurse walked through the ward. She was a slim, dark-haired girl and she was carrying a violin and bow. A violin! Keene had not seen one for years, ages, eternities.

Music! It began with a low fluting note, clear and yet soft, a tremolo that both stirred and soothed him. It woke memories long dormant, flooded him with them, calmed him with them. Music!

Golden, soul-pulsing music! Exquisite harmonies that built exquisite pictures in sweet bewildering procession. Sunrise on the lake at home...a flashing splendour on still water...sparkles on a thousand rushes. Sunshine from a cobalt sky, shimmering over a greening countryside, on trees in bloom, hedgerows in colour...dandelions... buttercups...daisies...gay colour...sky larks springing up from poppy-spangled old graves across the Ridge, thrilling the air with melody and soaring as far as his eye could see...Sunset and amber haze, heart-swelling beauty...the sea, cool, murmuring, the lap of little waves.... beach fires and scented dusk...the twang of a guitar...soft voices, singing. Music—

The doctor returned. He looked haggard, worn, but he spoke patiently to Keene as he tied a fresh tag to his cot.

"You'll be moving in an hour, Sergeant," he said.

Moving—leaving that music! Keene felt his throat suddenly go dry, feverish. His fingers plucked at his cot.

"I—you can do me here, doctor," he said huskily. "Go ahead—anytime."

It was another evening when Keene was strong enough to watch for the girl with the violin. There had been a few days, he knew, that he could never count, but he had not lost out. There would be more music.

The square-shouldered nurse was beside him and he looked up at her. "I stayed here because I wanted to hear that violin," he whispered weakly.

The nurse's face did not express much emotion. Perhaps months of hard days had dulled her; but her voice was kind.

"It saved your life, then," she answered. "If you had gone many more hours it would have been too late. Gangrene had commenced."

Gangrene!

Keene kicked his lips and did not try to speak again. That was a near go. England—and a grave. If he hadn't seen that violin, heard it... The palms of his hands were moist with perspiration.

Then she came, the dark-haired girl, passing quickly, but carrying that which he most wanted to see and hear.

The music again. After its first throbbing sweetness it swept him away to far-off places, away, away, up, up, swirling, turning, gliding, until he could look down with elation on long valleys, rivers, tree-lined highways. A wild jangle of notes, fervent, stirring, tugging, drums and bugles...then the gliding, dipping, swinging turns, up, up, up again, and over....soothing, stilling, smoothing hands...soft lights, low murmurs, scents and perfumes, stars and a crescent moon...peace, quiet, tranquility, content, and love....

He never knew when the music stopped. It was day again and the square-shouldered nurse was busy among the beds. A screen had been placed around one in the corner and he saw the two carriers come again with their stretcher, felt the hush that settled on the ward as they bore their burden outside.

If he hadn't heard that violin, that wonderful, speaking music, there would have been a screen for him, and what difference if in an English hospital? The thought stayed with him, dominated.

What a debt he owed to that girl! Gangrene—a grave, a wooden cross. RIP.

He shuddered, and remembered the graves he had seen at the Souchez end of the Ridge, French graves. "Mort pour la Patrie," and dark, crude crosses bearing the inscription, "Ruht in Gott."

"Ruht in Gott!" Were Germans Christians?

How Ashley would have answered that question; pale-faced Ashley, the clerk, lying with his head on the sod so comfortably, so placidly. Poor fellow, he never understood Keene's arguments. Strange, too, for he seemed intuitive in other matters. If only he had been wounded instead of killed, if only he had come to the hospital and heard the violin—then it would have been easy to convince him.

That slim, swift-footed girl with the dark hair had all those finer instincts, the perception that elevated the human race and put man on his highest levels. Only those so endowed were capable of such music, and—the thought struck him with delicious force—only their kind could understand it. It was as if they shared an almost visible aura of fellowship, figuratively touched hearts.

The music that evening began on a sadder strain. It seemed as if the player were tired, perplexed, lonely, but after a time courage crept in, courage that was contagious. It was penetrating. Keene was a soldier again, ready for those chalk trenches that had become grey ghosts, nerved against the thick blackness of any night. Then the sweeping melody changed, toned to subtle, easy rhythm that seeped all Keene's bitterness and animosity, expanded him, warmed him to contrition. He wished that Ashley had not been killed, that he had never argued with him.

The girl with the violin paused. "I want so much to thank you," Keene whispered. "You're wonderful. I was starved for music, sick for it, and it saved my life because...."

"Wait, listen to me." The girl shook her head. "This is my violin, but you didn't hear me play it. I take it to a poor chap in the next ward who has an ear almost torn from his head. He's a marvellous player, he seems to know just what will soothe the patients, and he's a German prisoner!"

An ear almost torn... *German prisoner*!

How...what...Keene's lips were working but he could not articulate.

"Isn't it wonderful," said the dark-haired girl, "that he has such intuition, such sympathy?" Keene's lips moved a little, but they made no sound.

"Don't you think," said the girl as she moved away, "that all our finer instincts are alike, whether we're British or German?"

Keene nodded, and smiled.

When he slept he dreamed of whispering to a calm, white face resting on sod back of the new line at Avion, and the face smiled, restfully.

If You Were Me

Part I: November 10

The dawn spread out, sickly and menacing, over a low, ragged sky. An ominous quiet brooded over the sodden woods. Ahead, blocking the only opening, a group of dead trees cowered like grey skeletons twisted in a final agony. Crumpled figures, men in soggy, mud-stained kilts and khaki, were squatting among the thickets, making a hasty breakfast of bread and cheese and cold bully. It was the autumn of '18 and the soldiers were a company of Canadian Highlanders. They were pursuing the Hun through wooded territory, a part of the Raismes Forest, where French nobles used to go boar hunting.

"I dreamt last night that the war was over," said Roberts, a tall, fair-haired man who was digging bully from a tin with his issue knife, "and they wouldn't let us go home because we were lousy."

"Another one of your blasted dreams!" The speaker who spoke so irritably was Milton, a thin, nervous fellow. He stood up to eat and kept peering through the brush. "Give us a rest. I hate this 'war over' guff," he added savagely.

"It's got to end sometime, kid," said Bill Hilder, a big, bony leathery-looking man who sat on a pile of dry brush. "And we've come a long ways from a trench, ain't we?"

"You're right, Bill," said the fourth man of the group. "I thought the thing would never end, but it's looking different now. Old Heinie's on the run this time."

"Rats! It's nothing but another game to get us into a hole. Everybody said the same thing when he pulled back off the Somme."

Corporal Morton, the man who had championed Hilder's speech, looked sympathetically at the nervous youth. "Don't be a pessimist, Milton," he said kindly. "A couple of weeks ago you wouldn't have believed we'd be having a picnic here in the bush."

"Some picnic," shot back Milton. "Wet from head to heels, half-frozen, not a drink of tea since yesterday morning, and Heinie shooting from behind the trees. He picked off two C Company men yesterday."

"That's because they don't know the bush," said Hilder, the leathery man. "If you'd been a lumberjack like myself you'd be tickled pink to get in under these trees. And we've got as good a chance as Fritz to shoot from back of the bushes."

"Get your gear on, fellows." A sergeant had come through the trees. "Same orders as yesterday. Slow advance. Scouts in front. Keep touch with your flanks. Be ready to move in ten minutes."

The quartet was ready in less time, and Morton looked around. "Who's coming with me?" he asked. "Two of us till noon, other two till night."

Bill Hilder stepped forward as he gave his equipment a final hitch. "I'll go with you, Corp," he said quickly.

The two men, Morton leading, pushed through the thickets fronting them and shoved forward until they were in line with the other platoon scouts. There they awaited the signal to advance.

"You needn't of come, Bill," said Morton. "It was Milton's turn."

"I knowed it were," said the lumberjack with a grin, "but the kid's got his wind up in this bush, and I'd just as leave be with you anyhow."

Morton tingled at the words. He and old Bill Hilder had been army chums since Passchendaele, and the woodsman was at his best in this French forest. He seemed to find his way by instinct.

As the whistle sounded they moved on, but separated, Morton going to the left. They parted undergrowth and waded hip-deep through ferns that soaked them anew, always peering, listening, watching for skulking figures. Then came a knoll with a clearing in the centre. There was a faint toot of a whistle far over on their right, the signal for a halt to even some part of the line, and Hilder snorted his disgust. Morton looked over at him and saw the woodman's face expressing his disdain.

"Same as yesterday," he called through cupped hands.

Morton nodded and grinned. Then he sat down on a log and waited. What a change in one month! Four weeks ago they had attacked the

Hun in an old battle area, a zigzag warren of trenches and dugouts, had routed him from it and spent hours in looking, curiously, about his abandoned stronghold. There had been his spades, with saw edges, his round water bottles, field-grey greatcoats, queer-shaped shrapnel helmets, goat-skin pouches, his rifles, gasmasks, Gott Mitt Uns belts, and awkward-looking long boots. And over all that inexplicable characteristic smell of German occupation.

He remembered Old Bill sniffing and spitting and refusing to drink from a German bottle, Milton looking for hidden explosives, and Roberts dreamily fingering a discarded guitar. His own feelings had been beyond words.

Then the rout had begun and everything changed. The battalion marched endless kilometres, but only men like young Milton complained. Morton thought that after a year in the trenches a man could have no new emotion, but he had found himself eager, strangely eager, and anxious, and fearful by turns, always absurdly impatient to "get along."

All in the platoon were the same. Every man, no matter how far they had pursued the enemy that day, thought only of the morrow. And they had charged every rear guard with which they came in contact with a ferocious eagerness.

"Fritz is beating it," they chorused. "Keep him going."

But in the forest it had been different. More than ordinary caution was needed, for contacts with the flanks were difficult, and the enemy snipers were particularly dangerous. So nerved up had Morton been that he had lain awake half the night, conscious of the mysterious hushed silence of the woods, the steady hiss of rain among the branches, the bent, silent figures of the posted men, the huddled, rubber-sheeted forms under the trees, stirring and muttering in their sleep as drippings from overhead caught their faces.

Crack! Wheee! The report of a rifle—the whine of a bullet in the brush. A sniper had fired from the other side of the knoll and he had not missed Morton by many inches. The corporal ducked low at once, and he heard sudden low calls of warning in the woods behind him. He looked to see Hilder, but the woodsman had disappeared. He came in sight a moment later, squirming along on his stomach, working to the right. *Crack*! The sniper fired again. Another bullet split leaves over Morton.

Hilder paused a moment and looked back, then wriggled on, keeping low. *Crack*! A third shot, then a fourth. The sniper was evidently trying to keep Morton pinned to his shelter. Hilder became anxious, too eager to make a kill. He half-rose and ran as a skirt of low bushes hid him. In a moment he would have a chance to spot the sniper.

Crack! A nearer, sharper report. A more snarling, whip-like sound to the bullet. It came from the left this time and Morton heard the thud of Old Bill's body as it struck the earth. He knew the woodsman must be badly hit to drop so abruptly, and he crawled to him in fierce haste.

Hilder lay on his back. His steel hat and rifle lay apart from him, where they had fallen, and he was plucking feebly at the strings of his respirator holder; his face was a ghastly grey.

"They got me, Corp," he muttered, "they got me dirty."

"I'll fix you up, Bill," breathed Morton, snatching out his field dressing, but he knew as he spoke that it was but a matter of minutes.

"You—can't." Old Bill spoke with effort. Beads of perspiration gathered on his forehead and lips.

Morton tore away the respirator holder, pulled back the equipment, opened Bill's tunic. The shirt underneath was soaked with blood; blood seeped everywhere. "Don't bother, Corp," the whisper was panted. "Git them—dirty Boche—won't you?"

"I will, Bill, I'll shoot their hearts out." Morton's lips trembled with emotion. Nothing in the war had touched him as much as to crouch there and watch the veteran relinquish life. Hilder was rough and uncouth, but he was as "white" and "square" as a man could be. "Bill, I'll get them some way," he went on, not knowing what to say, desperately striving to make clear his loyalty, his affection for the old fellow. "The first Heinie I get my hands on is going to pay for this."

"Corp..."

"Yes, Bill?"

"Same—as if—you—were me."

"The same—I will, Bill." The words were half-sobbed.

Hilder closed his eyes, opened them. A last flicker of understanding, and he was dead.

Morton looked around. He saw a head poking through the brush and at once signalled the man to keep low, then he crawled back.

"You chaps spread out around this clearing," he ordered. "There's a pair of dirty devils on each side. They tricked Old Bill into chasing to the right and then the guy on the left plugged him. He's dead."

"Old Bill dead!" Milton's voice was shrill with horror. "Is he dead—sure?" The youngster's face showed his distress. "Good gosh, Corp, I—you know it wasn't his turn."

"Never mind that now," said Morton curtly. "That was just a matter of luck. You chaps put some rifle grenades over and then sneak around on them quick. Get them if you can. I'm going to get Bill's pay book and disk and stick his tin hat on his rifle so's the burial party'll be sure to find him."

The men wormed their way through the brush, muttering revenge. Presently there came the sharp metallic *ping* of a grenade, then another, and another. There were quick rifle shots, then all sounds were farther away. The Highlanders routed the snipers. Only one man came back to have a last look at Bill. It was Roberts, the whimsical dreamer, whistling softly in his quiet way. He leaned on his rifle and looked a long time at the still, blood-soaked figure, then went away without saying a word.

The days that followed were hectic ones. Long marches, occasional skirmishes. They drove the Hun from the forest, but they had to advance slowly on account of the flanking battalions being more or less "in the air." In the villages it was pleasing to witness the thankfulness of the people released at last from the long paralysis of the domineering men in grey. At one place there was a hysterical rejoicing at a large brick farmhouse. An odd-looking man was shaking hands with everyone. He had the strange waxen colour of death. Three years he had lived in the cellar with the Germans overhead, and they had not found him.

Each day the tension showed more on the men. Was this the end of the war? Never had rumours raced more wildly, never had hopes ran as high. And even Milton had ceased to complain as they chased the enemy over farmlands and through villages. At long last the tables seemed turned.

"We been three years holdin' water-logged ditches for the king and Art Currie," said one lean hound of a fellow. "Now this here's a vacation."

"Vacation nothin'," snorted another. "It's the bloomin' end of the war, and the next war, me lad, you'll have a hard time gettin' me..."

"Can it," yelled a chorus. "Next war! What in hell are you givin' us?"

And so it went. Morton never joined in their talk. He and Roberts shared their blankets and rations but they did not converse much; it was as if they understood each other. Milton clung to them, always making his bed next to theirs, watching their faces, smoking cigarettes continually. Saturday evening, November the ninth, they marched after a hard day, into the little village of Jemappes, and just before midnight the three men were in blankets in a small room in a snug house. They had had an excellent supper of bread and coffee and fried potatoes, and Milton was flushed and eager with his good news.

"A runner told me that the war's going to be over on Monday," he said. "He's from the brigade, so he should know. Gosh, I hope it's true. We'll be here tomorrow, anyway, resting up, and there won't be much doing the next day if it's the end."

Morton said nothing. But he lay awake long after the others were sleeping soundly, thinking of Old Bill gasping out his life on the wet leaves in Raismes Forest, of the promise he had made him. "...same as if you were me." Not once since he had pledged his word had he got near a German! He thought of other chums he had had, of the mad, bad days in the Salient, of the whole tragic devilishness of war. Then he slept fitfully, and when he awoke Milton had brought him his breakfast.

"Cook kitchens came in last night," said the boy excitedly. "Here, Roberts, I got yours, too. Get up, you thickheads. It's a perfect morning. The church bells are ringing and there's not an order at all. I don't believe we'll do another tap till the war's over."

In spite of himself Morton grew eager. He ate and dressed hurriedly and went out in the yard. He was going to seek the sergeant and find out if anything definite had come through or not, but he halted. Why push the thing? The luck might not hold. He sat down on a sun-warmed doorstep and smoked. Children came around, eyeing him curiously, then Roberts came out. In a moment the tall fellow had two of the youngsters on his knee and was trying to talk Flemish to them.

Milton came back, and starting walking to and fro, smoking furiously. "Oh, boy," he chortled. "One more day. Say, who'd ever have thought this spring, that it would be over so quick? When I get back I'm not going to do a thing for six months. What about you, Roberts?"

"Me?" The whimsical look flashed back in the dreamer's eyes. "Me, I'm going to have a home right here in Belgium. I'll settle down somewhere in the Salient, a broken-tiled floor, sandbag walls, corrugated iron roof, rats running free, a manure heap by the window, gas alarm at the door, an estaminet right across the street...."

"Morton!" It was the harsh voice of the platoon sergeant that interrupted, and there was something in its tone that made the corporal get to his feet in chilly expectation. "Get your section ready at once—battle order. Leave your other stuff in your billets. We'll get it after."

Milton had stopped his pacing. The cigarette in his fingers dropped to the flagged walk and showered sparks. The lad's face was like that of a man in a trance.

"What's up?" Morton heard himself ask the question, he had not known he spoke. "Mons." The sergeant's voice was a snarl. "Get your men ready."

"But—wait, Sergeant." Milton had thrust off his daze. "We're not going into a scrap, are we? The war's over tomorrow, I got it straight. There'll be no fighting now, will there? What are we to do?"

"You're goin' to do just what you're told, me lad," came the answer. The sergeant's face was pale and set. The harshness in his voice was unusual. "You don't know anything about the war being over. That's all from the horse lines. Go on, get ready."

Roberts put the children from his knee, then called one back, a little girl. He coaxed her for a kiss and she gave it to him shyly.

"There's my luck," he smiled. "See you later, mademoiselle." The little girl laughed at him.

When the platoon formed up every man was irritable. They swore over trivial matters, they hitched and changed position, they looked at their watches. One or two were cursing, with frightful emphasis, the ones responsible for the new orders.

Morton said nothing. He gazed moodily beyond the village and saw a few long-range crumps leaving black smoke trails away to the left. When the order came to proceed he fell in with his section, last in the platoon. They wound around a corner to the Mons road and marched up it a distance, then entered a field.

The Hun began to shell them with shrapnel and gas, but the shells did not drop close enough to do damage. They crossed a deep ditch by using a stretcher as a bridge, and an hour later were at a building that proved to be a brewery. A shell or the soldiers had started one vat leaking and there were many rough jests among the Highlands as they sampled the beverage. But in the building the sound of the shells was more alarming and several HEs came very near the entrance.

Roberts filled the top of his mess tin with beer. He raised it to his lips. "Here's to the day we go home," he said as he drank.

"Blast you, keep your trap shut or I'll shut it." It was Milton, his eyes blazing, his thin form taut, almost crazed with fear and anxiety.

Morton had to step between them. "Cool your head," he snapped at the youth. "What's the matter with you?"

They left the building and went on. The platoons were now scattered and soon they were advancing by sections. Morton saw his officer and sergeant lead along the bank of the main highway. Machine guns were firing from the first houses in Mons and he saw three men of C Company become casualties. Then shells began to drop in quick succession. They fell between Morton's section and the rest of the platoon. "Come on, fellows. We have no cover here," Morton called. "Let's run for that building ahead."

A small brick outhouse was near the bank of the road. "Let's get over the bank," yelled Milton. The youth was white-faced from fear, and starting at each explosion.

"You can't," called another. "Look—see?" They saw the officer and a man get wounded as they tried to cross the highway. It was plain that the Hun had a machine gun placed so that he could sweep the road with bullets.

They reached the outbuilding and took refuge behind it. *Whammm*! A shell dropped within yards of them. Another came, another and another. Shrapnel moaned and sang about them.

Milton tried the door of the building. It was locked. Beside it, however, was a long plank. Two of the men seized it and used it as a battering ram, breaking the door inward. The five men in Morton's section crowded inside. Roberts sat on a box by the door, whistling softly in his calm, meditative manner. Milton stood well back in the shed and the others found seats along the side.

They waited a time and the shelling slackened, then the shells began dropping nearer the town, on soft, open ground. Morton got up and went to the door. "We can get to the houses now," he said. "Let's go. I can see C Company men there already." He pointed to suburbs over on the right.

Crash! A terrific, ear-splitting report. A blast of air, awful concussion! Overhead shrapnel just above the door, almost in the door. Morton and another man were knocked down, but not hurt. Then low cries.

"Look at Milton."

The corporal got to his feet. Milton had staggered back against the wall. Every drop of blood seemed to have drained from his face. His eyes were fixed. He did not speak. Then they saw that his wrist had been almost severed, that there was a dreadful wound in his stomach. They had not lowered him to the floor before he was dead.

Morton turned to speak to Roberts, and froze with horror. The dreamer had never moved from where he sat. His head was forward, his hands still circled his rifle barrel, but from a ghastly wound in his temple blood dripped in a dark, thin stream. He, too, was dead.

The men looked at each other, but no one spoke. Then Morton

looked out again. "Come on, boys," he said, in a grim, strained voice, unlike his own. "I'm going to get one of them Heinies if it's the last thing I do."

They filed outside and in a straggling line ran for the nearest buildings. They kept inside the field and had the protection of the high road bank and in a short time were in a cellar. It was filled with frightened Belgians. Men and women and children were crowded into the underground chamber and near the door a young fellow sat with a girl on his knees. An old man caught Morton's arm and pointed to them.

"Just married," he said in English. "Just married."

Morton tore from him, from all of them and went upstairs from the cellar and into a yard. From there he led a wild dash across the road. Snipers shot at them and missed and the machine guns awoke too late. On the other side they found that they could work forward through gardens, if they used caution. Then the sergeant called to them from a cellar.

"Keep low," he said. "We're into the town, but the Germans are hidden in the houses and we can't take chances. The word is to sit tight till dark."

Morton's men left him at once and got into a cellar.

Ahead, sheltered by a clump of small fruit trees, the corporal saw a bomber. He crawled to him.

The fellow had a grenade cup on his rifle. "Let's work ahead to the corner and get a chance at that machine gun," he said.

The man grinned, and exchanged rifles. Morton went on and the bomber followed.

It seemed hours before they reached their objective, a pathway with banked sides by which they could reach a forward cellar. The householder of the place was a nervous Belgian who would not speak louder than a whisper. He was in terror of the shelling he had heard and begged Morton not to look out of his windows or doorways. If the Germans thought he had helped to fight them....

"But we've got the Germans on the run and they'll never get a chance to hurt you,". said Morton impatiently. The man shut his lips tight, shook his head and refused to accompany them upstairs.

Morton found his way up but saw there was no chance to use grenades effectively unless they were nearer their target. It meant more detouring through gardens, more risk from snipers. It was growing dark and they had not eaten since morning. But they went on and on and at last were in a garden very near the enemy post. Very slowly he crept to a fence corner, put a grenade in the cup, then fired. The Mills bomb looped high and descended exactly as he wished. It was a perfect hit on the house corner where the Maxim was established. He waited a moment, then sent a second, a third, and a fourth grenade. Then a voice called from a cellar, and they saw an excited Belgian. "You got the Boche," he called jubilantly. "One is dead, perhaps another. They are gone, like sheep. Bravo, English."

"We are Canadians," said Morton.

"Canada! It is so! Bravo again. I am glad you have won. Was it not a fierce battle?" The bomber grinned. "Not much," he said. "Just a workout for us guys."

The Belgian frowned and did not answer him. He turned to Morton. "The Boche are in some houses," he said. "You will need to be careful, but there are not many. All their officers have gone."

Morton went to the cellar and asked for something to eat. The Belgian quickly got them bread and potatoes and a bottle of wine. They ate without saying much, but the Belgian and his wife were much excited. They pointed at the kilts and gas masks and steel helmets, and jabbered rapidly in Flemish.

As soon as he had finished eating, Morton went out again. It was dark enough to move unseen in the shadows and he and the bomber made careful reconnaissance. They found that the enemy had flown. Then they went on, very slowly, wary of traps, Morton burning with a desire to meet a skulker. He fixed his bayonet on his rifle.

There were sounds from the next street. Men were on the move, a big platoon of them, and the company commander was leading. Morton and the bomber joined them. They went direct towards the station. A spray of bullets hummed and sang down the wide way, the last salute of the fleeing gunners. That was all, and shortly the platoons were on their own, scouting the streets and lanes.

Part II: November 11

When dawn came Morton had not found a German. One of his platoon reported shooting one in a yard. Another had seen two grey figures running down a distant street. Nothing else had happened. And the sergeant had sought Morton and informed him that the war would be over at eleven o'clock. Morton had turned from him and cursed so luridly that he had been ashamed of himself. The war was over. Who cared? He hated everything.

He went into a house, urged by a vociferous Belgian, and accepted a cup of coffee and some fruit. His head was heavy. It ached and throbbed. He was tired, utterly weary all at once; he was bitter, a burning sense of grief, which he felt could never be stifled, made him sullen. He was curt in his answers to a deluge of questions in Flemish and bad English.

Then, as he sat with his coffee, he saw the window of a house farther up the street raised quickly. A head thrust out and tunic of field grey was exposed. It was a German soldier seeking to escape, and he was certain to be caught. The fellow dropped to the ground, then looked up street. Morton guessed his intentions at once. A trio of officers were in front of a fruit store, conversing. The Hun intended to surrender to them and thus ensure himself a fair treatment.

In an instant Morton crossed the room and picked up his rifle. His host uttered a startled cry, then all the family rushed to the window. Morton released the safety catch and made sure the weapon was loaded. He was tingling all over. Here was his chance for vengeance, vengeance for poor Old Bill, for Roberts and young Milton, killed in the last hour. By heavens, a Boche should die at the last hour.

He was forced to wait until the fellow reappeared at a gate leading into the street, a high, door-like affair. Then, as he watched, he tensed. An elderly Belgian had suddenly appeared, a thickset man with a sledge in his hands. He hid behind the open gate. The German came forth, watching the officers. The Belgian struck from behind. His sledge crushed the man's head like an eggshell, seemed to drive the body into the walk. There were shrill cries from the street, from open doors and windows, shouts from the officers. Morton looked away. He was sickened. He rose and left the place, turning instinctively to streets that seemed the most deserted. How he hated everything!

No man was with him as he walked on and on, heading, without knowing it, back towards Jemappes. He started as he saw the little brick building beside the road. Immediately he hurried over. Soldiers were there, a party under a sergeant, and they were reverently removing the dead. Morton watched them and bared his head as the bodies were carried by him.

"Know them?" asked the sergeant.

Morton nodded. "I was with them here," he said.

"Phew!" whistled the sergeant. "Close enough. Well, considering everything, we got off pretty light. And now she's ended. They're going to give those boys a bang-up funeral and..."

"What good'll that do?" Morton snarled the words. He was on fire inwardly.

The sergeant looked at him closely. "The best thing you can do," he said slowly, "is to go and get some liquor and go to bed. The big brass hats are coming to town as soon as it's safe and there'll be a lot of ceremony, and all that."

"I'd like to shoot every blasted one of them," Morton grated the words as he walked away. He knew that the sergeant stared after him, but he did not look back.

In the main square were men of his company, haggard, red-eyed for want of sleep, almost despondent in their attitude. Belgians were around them, chatting, pointing, laughing, offering drink and food, cheering. Morton did not stop there.

It was late afternoon before he awoke and had a real meal. He was in a house on the outskirts of Mons, the farther side of the town, and the old couple who served him were very kind. They had beckoned him in from the street. They could not speak English, they were deaf and they lived alone, but they wanted him to rest on one of their beds. Morton, feverish, heartsick, no fit company for anyone, was glad of the privilege. He had slept like a child.

He promised the old lady he would be back and then went out

on the street. Lights were everywhere. There were sounds of singing, shouting, riotous rejoicing, but the world was queer. Something was missing. It was the dull thudding and drumming of the guns that had been in his ears for two years.

He went along the street and met soldiers. They were not members of his battalion, but others who had marched up during the day and were in for a celebration.

"Come on, Jock," they called. "There's an estaminet near here where they've got the real goods. We'll wet you in good style."

They were loquacious, gay, wine-mettled. They told him how the brass hats had posed for pictures in the square, how the pipers had played, how the Belgians were honouring the Canadians, and then related all the rumours about the Kaiser and the German navy.

"Nothing ahead but home now, Jock," shouted one excited lad.

Home! Morton scowled at the word. What had home to do with the war? Home was something remote, something connected with the past; he could think of it later. Just now there were Old Bill, and Roberts, and Milton, and the Hun with his head smashed in. He refused them sullenly.

In one hour he was back in his room. He kicked off his boots and sat on the bed, thinking, thinking.

His mind went back over the years he had been at the front. He remembered his first trip in the line down Arras way. He had been so eager to see the war, to feel it, to sense it. He had stared in a box periscope the first morning, looking over the top. There lay the enemy trenches winding a white snaky wriggle over the face of the slope, and beyond were the ruins of a shell-broken town. He could see gaunt ribs of shattered roofs, the sunlight catching bits of glass that remained whole. The front was quiet and a strange feeling had possessed him. Was this the war? Then, some yards outside the wire barricade, half-hidden by old grass and debris, he had seen a skeleton. The uniform was rotten and indefinite. Friend or foe? Who could say? And, as if an icy hand had gripped him, as if a fleshless finger had pointed—he saw, understood. That shrivelled, nameless, unknown corpse spelled war!

Other things had startled him afterward, but that first sensation had lingered, remained with him. War! For seemingly endless time it had meant inhabiting the underground, damp, ill-smelling, rat-ridden dugouts; an existence amid mud; mud and rusting wire, mud and rain, mud and slimy sandbags, mud and mire, always mud. War! Brick dust and ashes and broken timbers, and twisted iron and gateways into houses that were not there; gaping cellars, bedding and toys and clocks and cradles in a chaos of destruction; a lone crucifix at a crossroads where all else was ruin. War! A plot of white crosses sandwiched among heaps of rubble, and a signboard saying "Dangerous Corner." A wet wood, dripping trees....

"Same as if you were me."

The words came back to Morton as if they had been whispered out of the shadows. He started and clenched his hands. Old Bill, grey-faced, stiffening on those wet leaves.

Strange that such a picture should come back so vividly. Had he shirked his promise? No, every time there had been an enemy in range he had sought eagerly to get at close quarters, had thirsted for his chance.

Old Bill. What a "square-shooter" the old fellow had been! He had borrowed money once, to play crown and anchor, and had won, and had made Morton take half his winnings. That was his type. He had—

"Kamerad!"

Morton raised himself, stood up. A closet door he had scarce noticed was suddenly ajar. He strode to it, flung it open. There, blinking in the lamp light, cringing, white-faced, stood a German!

He was a young fellow, as young-looking as Milton had been, and his eyes held the fright of a hurt animal. Morton did not speak. "Kamerad!" It was barely a whisper.

The corporal clenched his hands again. He drew his breath in a long whistling intake. At last! "Same—as if—you—were me." The cowering man huddled back, gasped. "Kamerad!" His whisper was shrill. He tugged off his grotesque red and grey cap and offered it to Morton. "Souvenir—kamerad." Morton made a stern motion for him to put it on again.

They stood looking at each other. From the street came ribald shouts, a rollicking song: "I'm out to catch a Hun, a Hun, I'm out to get the son of a gun; And when I do I'll bet he'll rue The day he left the Rhineland."

The German, listening intently, whimpered his fear. Morton shook his fist and placed a hand over his mouth, signalling silence, then he sat down on the bed again. The fugitive stood watching him, dry-lipped, wide-eyed, and terror-stricken.

The war had ended at eleven o'clock. It was a fact Morton could not evade, and how he hated it. Yet, he raged within himself, if only this German had been a husky, defiant fellow—one of those arrogant, supercilious officers he had seen captured at Amiens—then he would not have recognized armistice. This young fellow looked like Milton.

Morton thought of the prisoners he had seen during the autumn drive. Somehow it seemed they were more like humans than he cared to admit. Roberts had spoken of it in his whimsical way, after he had shot a gunner in Jigsaw Wood.

"I'm glad that chap's got a grey uniform on," he had said, "for if he were shaved I'd swear he was a cousin of mine."

This trembling lad scarce looked an alien. It was easy to see that he was nervous, had probably bolted into the house in a panic as news came of the advance at dusk. Dress him in a kilt and khaki and wipe the fear from his eyes, and no one would call him a German. But—poor Old Bill! They had shot him dirty. Morton's anger leaped within him again, but it was weaker and cooled quickly. After all, wasn't all war "dirty"?

"Kamerad?" Morton shook his head. No use to put the chap into the street. That wine-crazed mob of singers would tear him to pieces. Even the Belgians would kill him. He waved the youth to a chair.

An hour passed, then another. Morton was hardly aware of their flight. His brain whirled with a kaleidoscope review of the war as he had seen it. Old emotions revived and waned. He knew now that he could not harm this German, his first impulse had fled, never to return. The crowd had gone. It was midnight and the town had grown quiet. A long day of celebrating had taken its toll. The corporal got up and the youth rose hastily from the chair into which he had slumped.

Morton looked into the closet. It was partly filled with old clothing. He probed and brought forth a long, blue coat and a soft cap, and handed them to his visitor.

The German looked at him, then his eyes lightened with a wave of gratefulness. He understood and at once slipped the coat over his tunic. It fitted well, and he put on the limp cloth cap. The change was effective. He appeared a young Belgian and would never draw a second glance. It was only a short distance to the open, and then there were the outposts, scattered, relaxed with the excitement of the day ended. It would be easy to escape them.

Morton opened the door of his room. The old couple had retired. He went on to the street door. The way was clear, and he gave an imperative toss of his head, the order to go.

The German stepped out hastily, with a nervousness exactly like young Milton, then hesitated, turned and slowly, awkwardly, held out his hand.

Morton drew back, then relented. What did it matter? He gripped the hand kindly.

"Kamerad," said the German in a soft guttural.

"Good luck, kid," said Morton.

Then he stepped back hastily and went to his room. For a moment he was torn with a desire to shout an alarm, to recapture the fellow. Had he been disloyal? The thought, after the deed was done, seared him. But—the young lad had been so like Milton.

He wondered why he had shaken hands, then knew, and warmed to the thought. Long contact with Roberts, good old whimsical Roberts, had made him. The tall fellow would have shaken hands with the German and blessed him.

"As if—you—were me."

Very carefully he considered the words, then started up, thrilled, relieved, at last happy.

Never before had he fully grasped it. Old Bill's last wish had been that he "play the game." He had not wanted any "dirty" work.

Corporal Morton lay down to sleep without a dread of the morrow.

A Soldier's Place

The last heat of the afternoon sun warmed the corner in the pasture gully. It was floored with stone and withered grass, and Bill Green sat on an old board he had carried there, leaning his back against the gully side. He was lanky and red-haired, dressed in a worn grey suit and a blue roll-neck sweater. His old felt hat lay beside him but he had no overcoat or gloves. All his possessions were in a battered army haversack with "W. Green, A Company" lettered on its flap. His companion was a small brown dog.

Green was watching a blaze of broad splinters and twigs over which he had suspended a small pail filled with water. Presently the water began to boil. He sat up and took a paper bag from his pocket. Left-handed, he poured tea from the bag into the pail, and let the blaze die to embers.

While the tea cooled he sliced bread and bologna taken from the haversack. Then he looked at the dog.

"Okay, Sarge. Dinner's served."

He ate slowly, sipping his tea and pausing to feed the dog slices of the sausage. Finished, he gazed dreamily at the coals, fanned by light airs, until they were ashes. Then he shivered, and stood. His skin was reddened by exposure to wind and sun but, shaven, he would have been good-looking for he had blue eyes and his features were well-shaped.

"We might as well start marching, old timer," he observed. "It's going to be too cold to sleep out."

The dog ran up the gully bank, hobbling, and lame in the hindquarters.

"You're not fit to travel," Green shook his head. "You need to rest somewhere."

They reached a surfaced highway and occasional traffic rushed past them. Green tramped steadily, the dog at his heels, and it was dusk before they reached a village where the first lights of evening were winking yellow eyes.

"We've got three things we can do here," he muttered to the dog. "Get a job, catch a southbound freight, or find some money, and to begin with we'll strike off finding any money."

Lanterns glowed beside a concrete mixer and building materials, and Green walked faster. A warehouse was being enlarged and there might be work he could do.

"Any chance of a job here?" he asked a man near the lights. The man held up a lantern. "Where you from?"

"West and north. How about it?"

"No." The man put the light down. "I thought you was somebody else. We only take men that belong here. No outsiders can get a job in this country."

"Grub and sleeping's all I'd ask for a few days?"

"No use. You don't belong here."

They stood, Green gazing at the streetlights and conscious of the other's scrutiny. Then the man spoke again, and kindly. "I'm the watchman here and it's warm down in the boiler room. Want to rest there?"

"Thanks. I'd be glad to. We've been on the move all day. Any freights going south?"

"Freights? Don't you know the railways have put on special police this month? Steer clear of trains unless you want trouble."

"Well, I'm glad you told me." Green wearily followed the man to the rear of the building. "Here you are. You can use that cot and welcome. Which way you from now?"

"West of here. I was working on a farm all summer and had a stake to take me south, but some guys ganged me last week and took every cent."

"Say, that's bad! Nothing you could do?"

"Nothing. I wouldn't know one of them in daylight. My dog tried to help me and they nearly killed him. His hip's still swollen."

"There's all kinds of guys on the roads now." The watchman shrugged. "But the police are picking them up and taking them to camps. You don't want to hang around this section."

When he had gone Green removed his socks, washed them in hot water from the boiler and dried them by the furnace. Then he slept soundly on the rough cot.

It was breaking light when the watchman aroused him. "Give us a hand, will you?" he asked. "It's starting to rain and I want to get the new cement covered."

Green hustled briskly for half an hour and the watchman insisted that he accept half a dollar. "It'll get you something to eat," he said, "but don't stop here to get it. You'll get picked up."

At noon, in a railway culvert, Green and the dog finished their bread and sausage. They ate it cold because there was no dry fuel with which to make a fire. It was too chilly to rest long and by night Green was utterly worn, footsore, and stiffened with cold. They came to a small town, and he read its name on a signboard: "Lappan." At the outskirts he paused to look in a restaurant window. It was a small place with only one waitress and there were no customers. A stove in the centre held further appeal. It would be warm in there and they might be able to rest a long time.

Weariness was ground into Green until his marrow ached. He ordered beef stew and ate it slowly, feeling its warmth circulate through his aching body. He cooled the coarser lumps of meat and fed them to Sarge. The waitress, sharp-eyed and attentive, stirred the fire.

"You look chilled," she remarked.

Green prodded his brain to respond. He knew the girl wanted to find out who he was and where he was going, and he felt that he could remain in the place as long as he dallied with her small- town curiosity. "I've come a long way," he said.

He had a second plate of stew and mashed potatoes and vegetables, then deep-dish apple pie and coffee. He was very hungry. He fed Sarge rolls dipped in the stew, and the girl smiled.

"I'll bring him a bone," she said.

Green thanked her and, speaking slowly, told her of his being robbed and the manner in which the dog had tried to defend him.

"Wasn't that tough!" she sympathized. "I knew by your look that you'd had hard luck."

She brought a big, knobby bone and put it under the table. "Your dog'll be all right under there with it," she said. "There won't be anybody in."

"No?" Her tone caught him. "Why won't there?"

"Haven't you heard? There was a holdup in the next town last night and a guy was killed. They've got the two men who did it cornered in some woods over the river tonight, and everybody's gone to the bridge. They're sure the police will bring the men in that way."

"I see." The warmth had loosened the tight lines in Green's face and he had relaxed. The girl took away his dishes and he reached for a paper that was on the windowsill, and began reading. He didn't want to talk further.

The newspaper was old but he didn't mind. One bit of news was as good as another to him. Nothing mattered that happened outside his world. Then he tensed and almost spoke aloud.

He looked around. The waitress was eating her own supper and had not heard him, so he re-read the filler on the editorial page.

"John Green, of Lappan, Scott County, still believes his soldier son will return. The boy enlisted in '16 and went overseas with the Canadian forces. He was posted 'missing, believed killed,' after the battle of Passchendaele, and no further information was received by his parents. They were living on the Pacific coast at that time, but removed to Lappan after the war and resided there. Mrs. Green refused to believe that her son was dead and until her death, two years ago, kept a place for him at her table and a room ready for his occupation. Mr. Green, now in failing health, maintains his custom his wife established, and their faith has never failed to stir the emotions of those who visit the home. 'He was a good-looking boy,' Mr. Green told a reporter last Armistice Day. 'He was red-headed and left-handed, and we called him Bill.'"

Green looked down at the dog. "Some guys would try and ring in there," he muttered. "I've got red hair and I'm left-handed, and there must be hundreds of Bill Greens. But you and me stays on the level, no matter if we get picked up."

"Were you saying something?"

Green started. He had not noticed the girl come over. Then she looked at what he had been reading.

"My gosh!" She saw his name on the haversack. "Is your name Green?" He nodded.

"And—you're red-headed. Were you in the war?" She was quivering with excitement.

"Don't get stirred up." Green shook his head. "I'm not that boy. I'd know it if I had people like that."

"What do you mean—you'd know it? Don't you know who you are?" The girl dropped into the seat opposite him.

"I know I was in the war." Green felt that he would have to talk to get her calmed. He thought, too, that if she were real interested she might tell him where he could find work, or a place to stay overnight. "All I remember about it, though, was being in a trench. That part like one flash you'd see of a picture, and no more. There were coloured sandbags tumbled in a corner and an officer lying on them. I guess he'd been wounded. Beyond the trench there were shell explosions every second, and whistles were screeching. The officer was yelling at me to get him a drink, but I wasn't looking at him. I think the Germans were coming over and I was watching, ready to shoot. That's all I can remember, but I know I saw that."

"And you don't know about any of the rest of it? I mean about something hitting you? Or your being in France?"

"Not a thing. Only what I've told you."

"Then you must have got hit on the head?"

"Likely I did. I can't remember."

"But what about afterward, when you came home?" She was avid for every word.

He drew a folded sheet of cheap paper from his pocket and opened it. "This is all the proof I have of anything."

The writing on the paper was cramped and the words were queerly spelled:

> *To Whom It May Consern. This is to testifie that Wm. Green has worked for me six years and is a stedy reliabul man. He don't use lik-*

> *ker and he dont show temper. All the falt he has is being slow when hes thinkin and that aint mutch. Hes a good man. Sined J. Johnson. Sept.6, 1931.*

"You must have worked for him?" The girl was flushed with eagerness.

He nodded. "But I don't know where. There's thousands of J. Johnsons. Four years ago they told me I was Bill Green. I was struck by a car in a town out west and had concussion of the brain.

They told me at the hospital that a man had looked at me and said, "He's Bill Green. I know him. He's a war veteran. He's worked over in our State ever since the war.' Nobody thought of finding out who he was, and I hunted for six months after I got well but I couldn't find him. It was when I got well that I knew everything. I can't remember back of being hit by that car."

It seemed a long bit of talking, but he had to have some place to stay for the night and he had held her interest.

"Then how do you know you're not their Bill Green?" Her eyes were shining. "Wouldn't it be marvellous if you were? You'll have to go and see them."

"Where?"

"A little house up the lane on that street to the left. There's only Mr. Green and his niece from the east. She came to help when Mrs. Green was sick and she stayed. They say she has no people of her own."

He shook his head. "All I'm looking for is a job."

"They'd be awful glad to have a man," she went on. "It's a good farm, everybody says, but it's all run down as they can't afford to hire help. You ought to go and see them tonight." She was very eager.

"You don't get it," he said slowly, putting the folded paper in his pocket. "I said I wasn't him, and I know, see?"

"Look—oh!" The girl sprang up. "Here she is now. She brings us eggs." The girl was at the door before Green could interfere.

"See this man, Miss Green. He was in the war and he's red-headed and his name's Bill Green, and he can't remember anything."

Miss Green handed her basket to the girl. She was of the slender but capable type, he saw. The night chill had made her cheeks red and she was good-looking in profile, with grey serious eyes and the curved lips usual with impulsive persons.

For a moment she stood, gazing at him, the colour draining from her cheeks.

"Are—you—Bill?" Only her lips said it as she walked toward him. She could not articulate. He stood and faced her. "No, not the one you mean, Miss."

"Her name's Margery, Miss Margery Green," vouched the girl, watching them. "You sure?"

Her lips were trembling. She was scanning him with such intentness that she was unaware of it. Her colour returned, then ebbed again. She went on speaking.

"It doesn't seem possible—after all these years—but...."

She looked at his haversack, and sank to the seat that the waitress had occupied. He sat down opposite her.

"I wish she hadn't told you that." Green was tired again, achingly tired. "She's made all this fuss for nothing."

"But you look as if you could be. I mean, I never saw their Bill, but he had red hair and was..."

The door was swiftly opened and closed. Two men had entered and as Green saw them he guessed who they were. One man was hatless, with his black hair wet-plastered to his head. Their shoes were sodden and sounded queerly on the floor. Both men had been soaked above the knees, and their faces were yellow-pale, their eyes desperate.

"All right, sister." One of them pointed to the table next to where Green and the woman sat. "Rush it. Ham and eggs. Double order. And coffee. Get moving." He spoke jerkily in a sharp nasal fashion from the side of his mouth and he had an automatic pistol in his hand.

"You two," he nodded at Green, "just stay stuck where you are and say nothing."

The other man had raced on tiptoe to the kitchen. He called back through the order window. "Okay here, kid. Fix that phone."

The waitress brought a glass of water and a small plate of rolls and butter to the table. She was goggle-eyed with fright.

"Hell! I don't want water. Get the ham and eggs. Step on it." The man by the stove snarled his words. Then, watchful, he stepped backward until he was beside the telephone on the wall. He ran his fingers upward to the cord, gripped it, and wrenched it loose.

"All set," he called back to the kitchen. "I've fixed the phone."

Outside, a car drove by, not going very fast. The man stood where he was, watching the others. When the car had gone he stepped over to the stove, turned and stared outside, peering into the night. Then he glanced back to where he had been standing, and to the tables. Green saw his eyes quicken with a thought.

"You two move," the man snapped, "and sit here." He indicated the table, which the girl had made ready for him. It was in plain view from outside, while their seats were obscured by the stove. "Move!"

The waitress, cowering by the order window, motioned with her hands, pointing to the table. She was deathly afraid, and showed it.

Green's face darkened with a rush of blood. Inwardly, he refused the order. He had been indifferent at first, content to take the easiest way out of the situation, but a glance the woman had given him had knotted his muscles. She was pale and tense, watching him, and he understood the questioning in her eyes.

He held out his hand to her. "Come on," he said. "He wants us to move."

For a heartbeat she seemed unable to summon strength, then her fingers gripped his and she got up. He hesitated, burning with a desire to answer her queries, and as they stood another car went past.

"Scram over!" The man cursed them. He crowded behind Green. "You want me to move yuh?"

Then he tripped and almost fell into the seat. Sarge had ducked between his legs in an attempt to follow Green. "What in hell!" he gritted. "You—" He kicked savagely at the dog, his way blocked, ducked under the table again.

"Get from here or by—"

The big greasy bone Sarge had been gnawing was kicked out on the floor in front of the stove and Sarge gave a yelp of fear.

Green had turned back to get the dog, and Sarge's yelp fused all his impulses. He launched himself recklessly in headlong football style, diving straight over the table at the man.

His attack was so unexpected that it almost won. The man yelled for help and his cry was cut off as Green's head butted into his face. But the report of the automatic crashed in Green's ears and he felt a terrific blow on the shoulder. Then he had gripped the fellow's gun wrist.

They pitched from the seat in a fury of action, and as they writhed Green heard the automatic drop to the floor. The sound spurred him. He swung the man off his feet, twisting him over, and they crashed down, the man under. The back of the man's head struck the floor with a sickening thud and he lay without fight, inert.

"Watch out!" It was the waitress, huddled by the wall, who screamed.

Green tried to scramble quickly but his head was swimming. The sound seemed to come from a great distance. His shoulder had numbed and he didn't want to move.

He saw the second man come running from the kitchen, kicking the swinging door open, crouching as he ran, his gun arm half raised. "What happened, kid? What happened, kid?" The fellow kept shouting it crazily.

The stove was between him and the men on the floor. He swerved to avoid it, raising his arm to shoot. Then, in a stride, his legs shot backward. They swept from under him so violently that his body was whipped over. He had stepped on the greasy bone.

He crashed headfirst, his body arched. His legs flung high and flailed over. The impact was heavy. Green, partly raised and getting the gun near him, tried to hurry. An enormous tiredness was sagging him, pulling him down.

He saw the second man moving feebly, saw him sitting up, face and eyes vacant, as a woman's hand snatched up the gun that had been knocked from the fellow's hand.

A quick thrust of admiration throbbed through Green: the woman had nerve. "Goo' stuff," he applauded thickly.

He saw the man scrambling to his feet as a rush of cold air came from the door. He saw men plunging into the restaurant. Their presence made him realize that the waitress had reached outside by way of the kitchen. Then he was conscious only of the taste of blood, salty in his mouth, where the man had struck him, and of a warm, firm arm that was holding him from dropping back to the floor.

"Bill—oh, Bill!" a voice was sobbing in his ear.

Green knew he was in bed. He was aware of it for some time before he opened his eyes, but he did not hurry about anything. It was warm between the sheets, and restful. His shoulder ached but no one had bothered him with questions. He wouldn't have to travel for some time. Then he looked up. A nurse had stopped beside his bed.

"How do you feel, Mr. Green?" she asked.

"Where's Sarge?" he said weakly. "Where's my dog?"

"Miss Green is looking after him. He's perfectly all right," she said. "She has your haversack and the dog is guarding it."

Green relaxed. That is a fine idea, having Sarge watch his haversack. It would keep him contented.

Then he twitched. "My shoulder?"

"It'll be all right now. They've got you fixed up grand. All you need is quiet and rest. Just rest and rest and rest."

Green shut his eyes again. Very well, he would rest. He didn't want to talk. As long as Sarge was all right, nothing else mattered. He was glad Miss Green—Margery, was looking after him. He liked the name, Margery. She had pluck, he remembered. She had grabbed up that gun from the floor in the nick of time.

When he roused again they brought him something to eat. The nurse waited on him as if it were a privilege. She was nice, he reflected, but not as intelligent looking as Margery.

A doctor came and examined his shoulder. He was a kind-faced man and he hummed a little tune as he worked. "Feeling better?" he asked.

Green nodded.

There was no further conversation. The doctor appeared satisfied and he asked no questions. The nurse did not ask him anything about his past. No one came near to ask how much he remembered. He was much better when the nurse came and said, "Miss Green wants to see you."

"Oh!" He looked away. Had she come to question him? Then he thought of Sarge. "Tell her to come in," he said.

She came in quietly but he felt that a freshness like country air had entered the room. Her cheeks had their colour and she smiled with her eyes; they had lost their questions.

"I don't want to bother you," she said softly, "but I knew you wanted to know how Sarge was getting on. He's appropriated a big chair in the kitchen and he's resting that sore hip. He's made friends with uncle, and he eats plenty, but he keeps watch over your haversack."

She told him every little detail about Sarge going to her house. Then, as she was ready to leave, Green saw her look at him with a different manner. "Those two men were bandits," she said. "The doctor said I could tell you. You're to get the reward for their capture. It's two thousand dollars."

"Me!" The bed seemed to revolve and to sway. "I can't take it. It was you got that gun from the floor and—"

"That was nothing. It was risking your life when you dived over the table." Her cheeks flushed with emotion.

"But you made me. Don't you see that if you hadn't looked at me that way, wondering if I were really a soldier, I wouldn't have thought of tackling him?"

"You're excited." She tried to check him but he saw her lip quiver. "I won't ever wonder again. I didn't know a man would be that brave, for no real need, I mean."

His gaze met hers frankly. "I thought that to make you understand, was a need," he said. Then her eyes filled.

"Would you mind," she almost whispered, "if I called you Bill?"

"I'd be glad." Her whisper thrilled him.

"And you call me Margery?" He nodded, and she was gone.

The next time she came Margery told him about the fruit trees on her uncle's farm, and each day they discussed them further. She told him of every footpath in the fields, of a brook where there were trout, and of the work that needed doing. He enjoyed hearing her voice, and her descriptions, but at last he grew suspicious.

"I hope you're not trying to make me believe I'm your uncle's Bill," he said. "It worries me to have people think wrong things. Will you tell him I'm not?"

She shook her head. "I can't. Everyone in Lappan thinks that you are. That waitress told the reporters all she knew and people have accepted it as fact. Uncle's been so much better, too. He seems to have built so much on your coming to the house."

"I'll go," he relented, "but I'll tell him the truth as soon as I see him. Then there's another thing. I hate all this stuff about me being a hero, and I told that nurse so. She doesn't let anyone come to see me. I don't want to meet flocks of people asking questions." His bitterness was creeping into his voice.

"You won't have to meet them," she promised. "Everyone here in Lappan knows how you feel, and they'll be kind. You're taken for granted and they're proud to have you here. You won't have the war mentioned to you a dozen times."

"But I'm not staying," he broke in hastily. "As soon as I'm fit to travel I've got to be looking for a job. And listen. You're taking half that reward."

She shook her head. "I couldn't, Bill. There's no use in your trying to make me. It's all yours."

"Is this Bill?"

Green heard the voice as he waited in the sitting room of the little house up the lane. He had had a great half hour with Sarge, a Sarge so pleased that he had indulged in a frenzy of ridiculous antics, and now he was facing the climax he had visualized so many times while at the hospital.

The shuffling steps were nearer and he heard Margery speaking. Her voice made him tingle. After Sarge had stopped his wild romping Margery had joined them and, before he had realized what was happening, he had her in his arms.

"Bill!" she had murmured.

"Margery," he had choked on his words, "if I were different, knew who I was, I'd want you...."

Then her arms tightened about his neck. "I wouldn't want you if you were different," she had breathed, tears on her cheek.

Someone stood in the doorway. "Are you Bill?" An old man's voice.

"My name is Green, Bill Green," he answered.

The old man who came in and closed the door was shrunken and frail, with white hair and blue veins prominent on his temples.

"You don't think that you're my son?" His voice quavered but the old man made no demonstration. He came and sat beside Green.

"I know I'm not." Green put all his decisions into his voice. "And I'll tell you how I know. When I was hurt four years ago and was getting better we used to make up our beds because it was a military hospital. But instead of doing my covers in three folds I always did them in fours. They used to show me differently but every time I forgot I'd do them in four folds. So they investigated."

"Yes—yes." The old man was nodding all the time, a little dipping motion like a mechanical toy.

"They found that most of the western orphanages have their boys make up the beds that way. They said that only long practice, several years, could have made me to my bed that way without thinking."

"Ah, I see. You must have been one of those boys."

For a time they sat without speaking. The old man still nodded. Green looked away. He had been shown the room they had waiting for him. It was a nice room, freshly-aired. There were many pictures in it, pictures of a boy with a dog, a boy with a kite, a boy on sands near the sea, a boy with a gentle-faced lady—always a boy. He kept thinking of that boy, his expression in the pictures, his apparent enjoyment of life.

"You've heard about my son?" The old man gripped the arms of his chair. He had stopped nodding.

"Yes, sir. They told me about him."

"No one has told you that they doubted it?"

"Doubted it?" Green had a strange feeling. "Why, no. Why should they?"

"Because," the old man said slowly, "not a word of it is true."

There seemed to be no sound within or without the house as they gazed at each other.

"Our son was as fine a son as you could wish." Green knew instinctively that the old man had been making ready for his confession. "His mother almost worshipped him. He was clever at school, very clever, and tall and good-looking. Then he went wrong. We never realized what was happening until he was arrested. There was a trial but I couldn't help him. There'd been a killing by some of the gang, and he was sentenced to thirty years. I can hear the judge saying 'thirty years' every time I think of my boy."

His voice did not break but the old man rested to gain strength, then went on.

"His mother nearly lost her reason. She had built her life around her boy. He was all she cared about. It seemed incredible to her, some ghastly mistake. Then he tried to escape, and they shot him."

Again the old man paused. Green could see a tiny pulse hammering at his temples.

"His mother was in bed six months. She would not talk or see anyone. Then America declared war and something in the general excitement saved her. We moved east and it was while we were moving east that she had the idea of a 'missing' son. She did it so she could have all his pictures about the house, and the prizes he won at school. I didn't mind. Anything that would hold her reason was a godsend. Then the idea grew in her mind and at the last I think she really believed that Bill was missing overseas and that he might come back some day. The last thing she asked me was to keep his room ready."

Green found it difficult to speak. "I'm very sorry," he said. "It must have been hard on you."

"It doesn't matter about me." The old man shook his head. "Don't you see it's her, his mother, I'm thinking of? I'd like to be able to tell her that Bill came, that he's here."

Then Green knew what he meant.

"You want me to stay as if I were him?"

The old man nodded. "You see you're really a soldier, and you understand. I've never told anyone else. Margery doesn't know."

Green thought of her outside, waiting. He seemed to feel her in his arms. There'd be no more question of sharing the reward. He thought of the people of Lappan, the questions they might ask. Then he sat erect and put out his hand.

"Very well, Sir," he said, and he felt as if he were enlisting again. "You can tell her Bill came home."

The old man couldn't speak but happiness shone on his face as if sudden sunlight had reached it. He leaned back in his chair and his thoughts seemed far away. Green rose quietly, without disturbing him, and went to find Margery.

Acknowledgments

First and foremost, my profound thanks to Betty Murray, daughter of Will R. Bird, and to Steve and Heather Murray, for their permission to reprint Bird's stories, as well as their enthusiasm for this project.

Thanks also to Professor David Williams for his encouragement and help in connecting me with Bird's family. For help with tracking down copies of Will Bird's stories: Dianne Landry and the archivists at Dalhousie University; James Calhoun; Raymond Gallant at uMoncton; and Lara Andrews at the Canadian War Museum. For fruitful discussions about Bird and Canadian war literature, Zac Abrams and Jon Weier. For helpful suggestions on early drafts of the introduction, my colleague Laurie Cooper at uMoncton.

Thanks also to the team at Nimbus Publishing, especially editors Emily MacKinnon, Whitney Moran, and Elaine McCluskey, and production manager and designer Heather Bryan.

And to my family: thank you for all your patience and support.

Glossary

Art Currie: General Sir Arthur Currie, the first Canadian commander of the Canadian Corps during the First World War

bally: usually a euphemism for the British term *bloody*

balmoral: a kind of cap or men's bonnet usually worn by Scottish regiments

bandolier: a cartridge belt for ammunition

batman: an officer's servant

bayonet periscope: a mirror that could be mounted onto rifles in order to scout enemy activity

be in Dutch: to be in trouble

bivouacked: to be posted to an open-air area without tents or cover

Blighty: Britain

Boche: German soldier

box barrage: artillery shells that are dropped on three sides of an area, the front as well as the flanks

breeches: a type of pant that only goes to just below the knee

bully and lumps of soggy plum duff: canned corn beef and plum pudding

CO: Commanding Officer

crown and anchor: a dice game

CT: Communications Trench

dickey: of inferior quality or poor condition

dowager: a wealthy, elderly widow

duck walk: a slatted wooden walk in soft ground

Elinor Glyn: a British romance novelist and short-story writer (1864–1943)

estaminet: from the French, meaning "drinking house" or saloon

fire step: a step built a few feet off the trench floor, which allowed soldiers to peer over the top at enemy trenches or to fire at the enemy

fishtails: a type of small bomb

four flusher: a person who makes empty boasts or tries to deceive others

frowsy: having an untidy or neglected appearance

gink: an odd or unworldly person

Gott Mit Uns: from the German, "God is with us"

grenade cup: attachment that enables soldiers to launch grenades from a rifle

had a bead on you: take aim at something with a gun

Haig: Sir Douglas Haig (1861–1928), commanded the British Expeditionary Force from 1915 to 1919

Heinie: German soldier

HEs: high explosives

Hindenburg: Paul von Hindenburg (1847–1934), a German field marshal during the First World War

hoodooed: bewitched

Hoyle: Edmond Hoyle (1672–1769), who wrote books about the rules of card games

Hun: German soldier

jake: anything you are very satisfied with

Kaiser: Wilhelm II (1859–1941), German Emperor and King of Prussia from 1888–1918

last post: bugle call that signals it is time to retire for the night

Lee Enfield: standard-issue infantry rifle for soldiers of the British Empire

Lewis gun: a type of machine gun

limber: the detachable fore part of a gun-carriage, consisting of two wheels and an axle, a pole for the horses, and a frame which holds one or two ammunition-chests

long-range crumps: German artillery

Looey: Lieutenant

lorry: a large motor vehicle for transporting goods

"Mademoiselle from Armentières": a famous bawdy song from the First World War

maxims: a type of machine gun

minnie: a German trench mortar high-explosive shell

NCO: Non-commissioned officer, also known as "non-com"

parados: opposite the parapet, whose purpose is to stop the backward effect of shrapnel bursting behind the parados

parapet: the protective wall that runs along the top of a trench

Pershing: John Joseph Pershing (1860–1948), a US Army general

picture palace: a large, elaborately decorated movie theatre

pill-box: a round or square-shaped structure, made of iron and concrete, to protect soldiers from artillery and also used as a firing position

pontoon bridge: a temporary floating bridge

potato masher bomb: German hand grenade with a long stick handle

pound your ear: to lie down to sleep or rest

put their wind up: to annoy or provoke deliberately

puttee: a long strip of cloth or leather wound spirally around the leg from the ankle to the knee; worn by soldiers for protection and support in rough terrain

RAP: Regimental Aid Post

RSM: Regimental Sergeant Major

Ruby Ayres: a British romance novelist (1881–1955)

rum issue: soldiers were given a small amount of rum just before going into battle because it was believed to help with nerves; it was also used to treat shell shock

SAA box: Small Arms Ammunition

salient: a battlefield feature in which part of the forward line projects or bulges outward into enemy territory, meaning there is enemy on three sides

Sam Browne: a wide leather belt, that passes diagonally over the right shoulder, worn by officers

sap: a narrow trench that runs along at an angle from a main trench

scuttled: to run quickly, with hurried steps

shell shock: a disorder attributed to exposure to shellfire and characterized by severe anxiety and other psychological disturbances

skulker: someone who hides or acts in a sly or secret manner

square-head: German soldier

stand-to: at every sunset and dawn, front-line soldiers are ordered to stand alert, weapons ready, facing the enemy in anticipation of a possible attack

stiff-issue: a rum ration

togs: shorts

Very lights: signal flares, used to light up the battlefield. Named after their inventor, Edward Very

vin blink: anglicized term for white wine, from the French "vin blanc"

wag: a troublemaker or joker

whizz bangs: German artillery shells

zero [hour]: the time set for an attack

Bibliography

For readers interested in Will Bird's other war writings, it is recommended they consult Brian Douglas Tennyson's bibliographical entries on Bird in *The Canadian Experience of the Great War* (2013) as well as Arthur Smith's useful Will R. Bird Bibliography, housed on the Mount Allison University website: www.mta.ca/library/will_bird_bibliography/about.html.

"His Deputy."[1] *The Legionary*. Vol II, No 2 (July 1927): 11–14, 30.

"The Creeping Phantom."[2] *The Legionary*. Vol V, No 4 (September 1930): 5–7, 14–15, 20–21.

"Wire Overhead." *The Legionary*. Vol IV, No 4 (September 1929): 16–17, 34.

"Ghost Bayonets." *War Stories*. Vol 29, Issue 84 (August 1930): 128–138.

"The Three Dead Germans." *The Legionary*. Vol IV, No 1 (June 1929): 12–14, 34.

"Priscilla's Private." *The Busy East of Canada*. Vol 21, Issue 2 (September 1930): 7–12, 22.

"Sunshine." *The Legionary*. Vol III, No 3 (July, 1929): 18–24, 34.

"Sunrise for Peter."[3] *Sunrise for Peter and Other Stories*. Ryerson Press, 1946. 1–17.

"White Collars." *The Legionary*. Vol VI, No 9 (February 1932): 12–15, Vol VI, No 10 (March 1932): 18–21.

"Eyes! Eyes! Eyes!" *The Legionary*. Vol V, No 1 (June 1930): 14–16, 34.

"The Laughing Jackass: a Tale of the RAF" *The Legionary*. Vol VI, No 6 (November 1931): 16–19.

"The Russian Coat" *Maritime Advocate and Busy East*, 34 (May 1944): 15–19.

"The Finer Instincts." *The Legionary*. Vol VI, No 7 (December 1931): 6–11.

"If You Were Me." *The Legionary*. Vol IV, No 5 (October 1929): 5–8, 32–33. Vol IV, No 6 (November 1929): 16–17, 33.

"A Soldier's Place" *Maritime Advocate and Busy East*, 29 (October 1938): 15–20.

1: Originally appeared in *The Busy East of Canada*, 17:9 (April 1927): 12–18.

2: Originally appeared in *War Stories*, Vol 27, Issue 79 (March 27, 1930): 36–45.

3: Originally appeared in *MacLean's*, Vol 44, Issue 11 (June 1, 1931): 16–17, 50, 53–54.

More from Nimbus Publishing

In Their Own Words
978-1-77108-670-7

Letters Home
978-1-77108-203-7

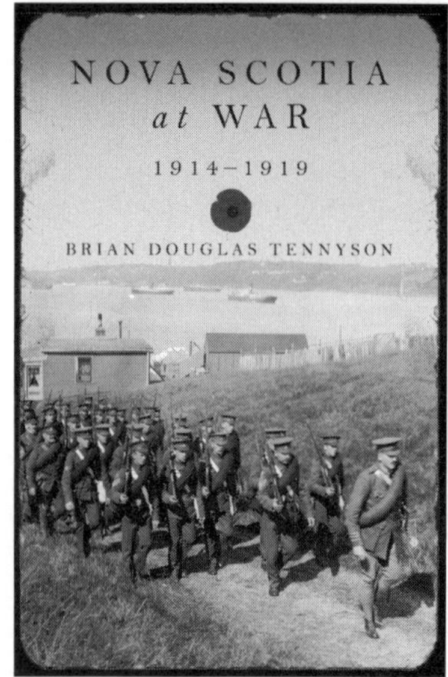

Nova Scotia at War, 1914–1919
978-1-77108-523-6

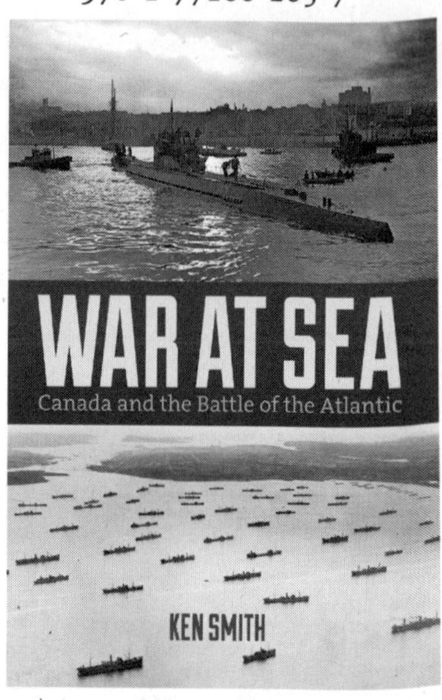

War at Sea
978-1-77108-265-5